Asian/Pacific American Literature I
Fiction

Masami Usui

GENDAITOSHO

All rights reserved. No part of this publication may be reproduced or transmitted in any from or by any means, electronic or mechanical, including photocopying, recording, or by any information storage or retrieval system, without prior permission in writing from the copyright holder.

The characters on the cover, 物語(*monogatari*), means "fiction." Calligraphy by Masami Usui

MASAMI USUI
Asian / Pacific American Literature I: Fiction

Copyright © 2018 by Masami Usui
ISBN 978-4-434-24245-8

First published in February, 2018 by GENDAITOSHO
2-21-4, Higashionuma, Minami-ku Sagamihara-shi,
Kanagawa, 252-0333, Japan

Table of Contents

Acknowledgements v
Preface vii

Chapter 1
Regaining Lost Privacy: Yoshiko Uchida's Story Telling As a *Nisei* Woman Writer ································1

Chapter 2
An *Issei* Woman's Suffering, Silence, and Suicide in John Okada's *No-No Boy* ················ 31

Chapter 3
Prison, Psyche, and Poetry in Hisaye Yamamoto's Three Short Stories ············ 67
—"Seventeen Syllables,"
"The Legend of Miss Sasagawara," and
"The Eskimo Connection"—

Chapter 4
"This is also an American Experience"
in Cynthia Kadohata's *The Floating World* ········ 105

Chapter 5
Sexual Colonialism in a Postcolonial Era
in Lois-Ann Yamanaka's Novels ···················· 133
— *Wild Meat and the Bully Burgers*,
Blu's Hanging, *Name Me Nobody*,
Heads by Harry, and
Father of the Four Passages —

Chapter 6
Holding Trauma in Lois-Ann Yamanaka's
Behold the Many ···································· 165

Chapter 7
Sexual Colonialism in Korea / Japan / America
Spheres in Nora Okja Keller's *Comfort Woman*
and *Fox Girl* ·· 191

About the Author ···································· 229

Acknowledgements

I would like to thank Japan Society for the Promotion of Science which enabled me to do researches and writings on Asian American literature: I received the 1994 Grant-in-Aid for Scientific Research (A) for "The Wartime Concentration Camp Experience and Postwar Quest for Peace in the Works by Japanese American Women Writers" (JSPS KAKEN Grant Number: JP06710288) and the 1990-2001 Grant-in-Aid for Scientific Research (C)(2) for "The Passage of the Japanese American Literature in Hawai'i: The Reconstruction with a Post-Colonial Perspective" (JSPS KAKEN Grant Number: JP09610482). As for my Asian American literature studies, I am very glad to thank Professor King-Kok Cheung, Professor Elaine Kim, Professor Gary Okihiro, Professor Stephen Sumida, and Professor Sau-Ling Wong.

Preface

It was at Bread Loaf Writers' Conference in 1988 when I happened to encounter a Japanese American poet from Hawai'i, Garry Kaoru Hongo. While I was writing my Ph.D. dissertation on Virginia Woolf, I just wanted to take a rest in summer and decided to attend Bread Loaf Writers' Conference in Middlebury, Vermont. I had taken creative writing classes by Professor Diane Wakoski, a Poet-in-Residence at Michigan State University, and she introduced us that prestigious writers' conference. During her poetry writing class, I was the only one Asian student so that I got a special attention from Dian as well as the other students. When I happened to write a short poem entitled "A Woman Warrior," Diane and one of my classmates told me about Maxine Hong Kingston's best-selling book, *The Woman Warrior*, which was published in 1976. It was a coincidence, yet I remember I felt so familiar. In 1989, when I returned to the Bread Loaf, a writer from Iowa told me about her friend, a Japanese woman writer from Kobe, soon after she knew about my background. It was Kyoko Mori. It was again a coincidence since Kyoko Mori went to Kobe College, from which I graduated. What I got those years turned to be the very beginning of my primary acknowledgement of Asian American literature.

My curiosity about those Asian American writers and poets began to be satisfied as soon as I found some anthologies and works by and about Asian American authors. After I returned to Michigan from Middlebury, I bought copies of *The Forbidden Stich: An Asian American Women's Anthology* and *Making Waves: By and About Asian American Women*. Both of them were published in 1989 and later I found out that that year was a landmark year for Asian American women writers. Co-edited by Shirley Geok-lin Lim, *The Forbidden Stich* includes quite a large number of works by Asian American women writers whether they are well known or not. In this anthology, Kyoko Mori's "Heat in October" is included and I reaffirmed her Japanese background. Even though I found those anthologies, I was till then quite ignorant of the prior works and studies. Rather than being involved in this newly-discovered sphere, I was deeply inclined in completing my dissertation and Virginia Woolf was in the center of my life.

The next time when I encountered a chance to make a further examination, I was quite ready to launch into a new study area. At the MLA Convention in New Orleans in 1989, I presented my paper on Woolf that sprung from my dissertation. During that convention, I attended some sessions, one of which was on Asian American literature. At that session, I got to know that there will be a session on new literary works by Asian Americans in the following year and they intended to be Cynthia Kadohata's *The Floating World* and Amy Tan's *Joy Luck Club*, both of which were accidentally published in 1989. Though *Joy Luck Club* became a best seller and was made into a film, *The Floating World* did not receive an equal attention. Compared to Chinese American writers such as Kingston and Tan, Japanese American writers and poets were not so popular then. As soon as I finished reading *The Floating World*, I affirmed that I should evaluate this work. Therefore, *The Floating World* became the threshold of my serious involvement in Asian American literature.

After I returned to Japan and began to teach at Hiroshima University in 1990, I started my researches on Asian American literature. I traced back to the origin of Asian American studies and literature, and at the same I needed to keep up with the ongoing presentations and publications on those subjects. I found out that Elaine Kim's *Asian American Literature: An Introduction to the Writings and Their Social Context* had been published in 1982. In history studies, Ronald Takaki played a leading part by publishing *Pau Hana* (1984) and *Strangers from a Different Shore* (1989). Later, I happened to meet him at Hiroshima University during his lecture trip in Japan. Those books by Takaki were followed by Gary Okihiro's *Cane Fires: The Anti-Japanese Movement in Hawaii, 1865–1945* (1992). Interestingly enough, both Takaki and Okihiro had to start their professional careers as scholars of African American studies rather than those of Asian American studies because

Asian American studies was not recognized or even accepted in academia. Asian American activism between the late 1970's and the beginning of the 1980's made it possible to found Ethnic Studies Department especially on the West Coast. However, this wave did not reach to the other part of the United States until the late 1980's and the 1990's.

After these forerunners, there appeared such works as King-Kok Cheung's *An Interethnic Companion to Asian American Literature* (1988) and Sau-Ling Wong's *Reading Asian American Literature: From Necessity to Extravagance* (1993). Moreover, there appeared Stephen Sumida's *And the View from the Shore: Literary Traditions of Hawaii* (1991). While I discovered that such an anthology as *Aiiieeeee* (1974) edited by Frank Chin et al., I needed to check newly published books such as *Making More Waves: New Writing by Asian American Women* (1997) and new writers' books. The MELUS: The Society for the Study of the Multi-Ethnic Literature of African, Native, Latino had been founded in 1973, and the society was blooming with the new area of Asian Americans in the 1980's and 1990's. In addition to the expanding area in American Studies Association, Asian American Studies Association was founded in 1979. In Japan, for example, the AALA: the Asian American Literature Association was born in 1989. In Europe, moreover, the MESEA: the Society for Multi-Ethnic Studies: Europe and the Americas was established in 1998.

In my research and reading, I began to be particularly interested in Japanese American wartime concentration camp

Preface

experiences in their literary works. As for the *nisei* poets whose works reflect their harsh experiences during World War II, I presented my paper on Japanese American poets for the first time, at Poetry Fair in 1992, and the paper entitled "Truth behind Myth and Reality in *Poets behind Barbed Wire*," later published in *Poetry Nippon* in 1993. In the same year, I presented my paper on Kadohata's *The Floating World* at the International Popular Culture Convention, York, UK, and in 1994, I presented my paper on *sansei* poets at session organized by the MELUS in the MLA Convention, Toronto, Canada. At the MLA in Toronto, I went to listen to a keynote speech by Stephen Sumida. Currently Professor Emeritus, Sumida served as President of American Studies Association between 2002 and 2003. It was quite an honor that I was a panelist in the same session with Sumida at the Bamboo Ridge Institute in Hawai'i in 2004 and also at the Academia Sinica in Taiwan in 2008.

For my research on Japanese American literature in the 1990's and the 2000's, I received several grants especially from the Japan Society for the Promotion of Science. My research area expanded from Japanese *nisei* writers to *sansei* and younger generations, from their wartime concentration camp experiences to the contemporary traumatic experiences, from the historical context to the personal sphere, from fiction to poetry and playwriting, and from the mainland to Hawai'i. I really appreciate my expanding connections with the scholars, writers, and researchers; Sau-Ling Wong arranged my research at the Ethnic Studies Library, where

I met Janice Otani who became my life-long friend; Gary Okihiro introduced me to Denis Ogawa and his *nisei* mother for my first research in Hawai'i with my daughter at age two then; Juliet Kono introduced me to Cathy Song and Lois-Ann Yamanaka and the Bamboo Ridge Institute; Elaine Kim invited me to attend the International Conference on Asian American Expressive held in Beijing in 2012, etc. This Chinese connection was succeeded in 2014 at the "Expanding the Parameters of Asian American Literature: An International Conference" at Xiamen University, China, where I met both Sau-Ling Wong and Shirley Geok-lin Lim, both retired. My Korean connection started in my attendance at the Annual International Conference of American Studies in 2003, led to the 2009 Conference of Korean Association of Feminist Studies in English Literature, where I got to know about the MESEA and I attended the 7th Biennial MESEA Conference in Hungary in 2010. After I was invited by Academia Sinica's International Conference on Asian American and Asian British Literature in Taiwan in 2008, I was involved in such conferences as The East Asian Popular Culture Association Inaugural Conference in 2011, the Twentieth Conference of English and American Literature Association in 2012, the 2014 International Symposium on Cross-Cultural Studies at Fu Jen Catholic University in Taipei, etc.

Without those connections, I could not have continued my studies on Asian American literature. After more than two decades, it is the right time for me to compile my works

Preface

on Asian / Pacific American literature.

All the papers included in this book were previously published in such journals as *Chu-Shikoku Studies in American Literature* (Chu-Shikoku Association of American Literature), *Journal of American Studies* (The American Studies Association of Korea), *Studies in Culture and the Humanities: Bulletin of the Faculty of Integrated Arts and Sciences, Hiroshima University, III*, and *Doshisha Literature* (English Literary Society of Doshisha University). I deeply appreciate the editors of these journals and also my colleagues of English Department at Doshisha University and the Faculty of Integrated Arts and Sciences at Hiroshima University. Since these papers were originally published between the late 1990's and the beginning of 2000's, I decided to maintain the 6th and 7th editions of *MLA Handbook*. To publish them in a form of book, I revised the papers only minor changes of especially updated references and cut all pictures and illustrations.

Chapter 1

Regaining Lost Privacy: Yoshiko Uchida's Story Telling As a *Nisei* Woman Writer

"The budding plum
Holds my own joy
At the melting ice
And the long winter's end" — Yukari[1]

Well known as a children's literature author and translator, Yoshiko Uchida underwent what all *nisei* (second-generation Japanese Americans) experienced during their lives, and regretfully passed away at age seventy in Berkeley, in June, 1992. The generation is going to be crucially changed from *issei* (first-generation Japanese Americans) *nisei* to younger generations. No matter what changes occur to Japanese Americans, Uchida's spirits will be inherited through her books both about Japanese traditional culture and folk tales, and about Japanese Americans' concentration camp experiences during World War II. It is actually presented in Uchida's special exhibition including her books,

1

manuscripts, and even letters from her young readers, at the Doe Library of the University of California at Berkeley.[2]

Recognized as "the only writer to have created a body of Japanese American literature for young people," Uchida was selected as one of ten women featured on the 1990 National Women's History Month poster, whose title is, "Courageous Voices Echoing in Our Lives" ("Uchida Featured on Commemorative Poster" 8684B).

Among Uchida's books of "courageous voices," *Journey to Topaz* (1972), *Journey Home* (1978), *Desert Exile* (1982), *Picture Bride* (1987), and *The Bracelet* (1993) are all focused on Japanese Americans' concentration camp experiences. Uchida had started her writing career much earlier after her camp year was over in 1943. She eventually moved to New York City after her graduate study at Smith College, and started her teaching career in Philadelphia. In 1949, her first book of Japanese folk tales, *The Dancing Kettle*, was published. In spite of this good start as a writer, Uchida had to wait until the late 1960's to write about the Japanese Americans' concentration camp experiences (Catherine E. Studier Chang 192); whereas Mine Okubo's autobiography with sketches and drawings, *Citizen 13660*, was published much earlier, in 1946, as the first book on Japanese Americans' concentration camp experiences.

According to Uchida, there are two reasons for its delay: first "the emphasis on ethnic awareness which emerged during the late 1960's created a desire among the *sansei* (third-generation Japanese Americans) to seek more information

Chapter 1 : Regaining Lost Privacy: Yoshiko Uchida's Story Telling As a *Nisei* Woman Writer

about their Japanese heritage" (Studier Chang 192); and the second, "before the late 1960's, the public wasn't ready to listen to the story of the Japanese Americans" because there was "still a lot of hostility about the war" (Studier Chang 193). In *Desert Exile*, Uchida remarks:

> In 1942 the word 'ethnic' was yet unknown and ethnic consciousness not yet awakened. There had been no freedom marches, and the voice of Martin Luther King had not been heard. . . . (148)

From a *sansei*'s standpoint with an intense awareness of ethnicity, David Mura, a poet and writer, insists that his *nisei* aunt's story telling should be valued in contrast to his *nisei* parents' silence in order to find the "missing mirrors" of identity as Japanese Americans (249-51). As for the importance and necessity of ethnic writings and writers, Uchida stated in 1975:

> "More writers from within the various ethnic groups must be encouraged to write for and about themselves; to describe from their own viewpoints their feelings and goals and values." ("Hope and No Monsters" 19)

Uchida's awareness of her role as a story teller was incorporated with the needs to be listened to both by *sansei* and American citizens, because "the ideal of the great melting pot has been replaced by the realization that enrichment comes from diversity" ("Hope and No Monsters" 21).

In addition to those two reasons in Uchida's statement, there must be a third reason in Uchida's psychology. Uchida had been convinced that she was different from the other *nisei* because of her parents' well-educated and established background.[3] Whether consciously or unconsciously, Uchida frequently refers to her ancestor's background as samurai, that is, the ruling class of the Japanese feudal times. It must have taken time to realize that her wartime experience not as a Japanese but as a Japanese American was the same as those of the other Japanese Americans who were originally blue-colored poor peasants or fishermen. As Uchida grew up in a Caucasian neighborhood and her family had many Caucasian and well-established Japanese friends (Ann Rayson 53), it was the first time for her to be deeply indulged in Japanese Americans when she was sent to camp. Uchida was one of those who had Japanese American peers for the first time in camp because they had lived being isolated from other Japanese Americans (James K. Morishima 16). It was in camp where those Japanese Americans "had to learn a new set of values, norms, roles, etc., to interact successfully with their Nikkei peers" (Morishima 16).

More than an embodiment of "a new set of values, norms, roles," Uchida considers the camp itself as what Yi-Fu Tuan calls "landscapes of fear" which "refers both to psychological states and to tangible environments" (6). Tuan explains that "the simplest answer to the threat of unruly people is to confine them in space, that is, in prisons

Chapter 1 : Regaining Lost Privacy: Yoshiko Uchida's Story Telling As a *Nisei* Woman Writer

and asylums" (189). Japanese Americans represent one race or people to be confined in an isolated massive space because they should be ruled and supervised. This practice is apparently accompanied by American original principles concerning confinement. In the nineteenth century, especially between the 1820's and the Civil War, "the philosophy and construction of places of confinement underwent changes that were revolutionary, idealistic, and rich in irony" (197). The tactics was to remove "deviants" from "the society that had corrupted them and put them in a corruption-free environment, namely, a prison" which needed "almost total isolation and the strictest discipline" (198). This seemingly virtuous principle was carefully employed in the case of Japanese Americans. Uchida challenges this well-constructed ideal of confinement under the name of democracy as the core of shared Japanese American experiences and intends to deconstruct "landscapes of fear."

Awakening as a *nisei* who experienced "landscapes of fear," Uchida finally projects her own and her family's experiences upon her books on Japanese Americans' concentration camp experiences published after the 1970's.[4] The strong sense of homogeneity due to camp experiences occured to Uchida's inward self, and "she got angrier and angrier about the (internment) experience" as she grew older (J. Yentsun Tseng 7). Uchida's hope to convey her anger to her readers is, however, concealed within her quiet and less-aggressive voice because she believes that "bitterness is destructive" (Studier Chang 193). Tuan interprets that fury, "whether perceived in another being or felt in himself, is personified as a monster, the shape of which probably depends on accidental daylight encounters of a disturbing sort" (18). Instead of forming a monster in her stories, Uchida devotes herself into creating a myth of human relationship in her "straightforward and simply written" books (Rayson 53). Uchida manipulates the strategies of Japanese story telling for the purpose of implying her negative emotions of anger and fury.

Uchida's inward self, or anger, begins to explore lost privacy. The most crucial and common trauma from which Japanese Americans suffered during the camp years is literally the lack of privacy. They lost their houses and homes as family gathering space, and were forced to inhabit what was ironically called "an apartment" in horse stalls and barracks with communal toilets and showers without doors.[5] In her splendid book entitled *Reading Asian American Literature*, Sau-Ling Cynthia Wong considers "Japanese American and Canadian narratives on internment" as "the undoing of home-founding" (136). Toyo Suyemoto Kawakami, who was also sent to Topaz, expresses this "undoing of home-founding" in a form of sonnet:

Barracks Home

    This is our barracks, squatting on the ground,
    Tar-papered shack, partitioned into rooms
    By sheetrock walls, transmitting every sound
    Of neighbors' gossip or the sweep of brooms

Chapter 1 : Regaining Lost Privacy: Yoshiko Uchida's Story Telling As a *Nisei* Woman Writer

> The open door welcomes the refugees,
> And now at last there is no need to roam
> Afar: here space enlarges memories
> Beyond the bounds of camp and this new home.
>
> The floor is carpeted with dust, wind-borne
> Dry alkali, patterned by insect feet.
> What peace can such a place as this impart ?
> We can but sense, bewildered and forlorn,
> That time, disrupted by the war from neat
> Routines, must now adjust within the heart. (28)

This sonnet represents the unfortunately transformed and deformed space named "home" with an ironical understatement that its significance and values are entirely destroyed.

In camp, privacy, "a sacrosanct ingredient to the Nikkei, disappeared," and all became "public," and ultimately the "Nikkei were in a glass menagerie — a small (20' x 20') room with cots and a potbelly stove" (Morishima 15). In addition to insufficient food and facilities, the lack of privacy was most intolerable for Uchida as well as for most Japanese Americans.

> After three months of communal living, the lack of privacy began to grate on my nerves. There was no place I could go to be completely alone — not in the washroom, the latrine, and shower, or my stall. I couldn't walk down the track without seeing someone I knew. I couldn't avoid the people

> I didn't like or choose whose I wished to be near. There was no place to cry and no place to hide. It was impossible to escape from the constant noise and human presence. I felt stifled and suffocated and sometimes wanted to scream. But in my family we didn't scream or cry or fight or even have a major argument, because we knew the neighbors were always only inches away. (*Desert Exile* 96)

Like Tanforan as one of what was called "Assembly Centers" which Uchida describes above in her autobiography, Topaz as one of eleven concentration camps turns to be nothing more than another "menagerie."[6] Both purely individual space and shared family gathering space were almost entirely lost in camp.

This physical loss of privacy in camp causes the change of family and community structure in daily life. Because of a small one-room home in camp and of a huge dining room gathering during meals, the pure family gathering became almost impossible. The camp life especially affected the young *nisei* people who "had grown up with love and respect for the ideals of American democracy which were somewhat shattered by these sweeping changes brought about by the international problems" (Edith W. Derrick 356). *Nisei*'s Americanization is different both from *issei*'s Japaneseness and *sansei*'s Japanization.[7] Due to a difference between *nisei* and *issei* regarding their involvement in and assimilation to the United States, another tension arises in a concept of family. As described in *Farewell to Manzanar*, "the family

Chapter 1 : Regaining Lost Privacy: Yoshiko Uchida's Story Telling As a *Nisei* Woman Writer

structure collapsed" (Rayson 51) in a camp whose "life led to a breakdown of traditional family roles" (Rayson 46). Uchida repeatedly mentions this family collapse in *Journey to Topaz*, *Desert Exile*, and *Picture Bride*. The traditional family roles of gender — between women and men — in the Japanese household '*ie*' system, were no longer necessary and the family members were scattered in a different scope of activities in camp.

In such a shift, *nisei* young people were neglected by and separated from their *issei* parents in camp; instead, they assembled and founded the body of their own community. According to Sylvia Junko Yanagisako, "the constant referent of 'family'" for *nisei*, "is a normative domain that, in different contexts, applies to different sets of people" (241). Being incapable of inhabiting a small "apartment" with the other family members and also encouraged to participate in school and leisure activities, *nisei* young people's concern about their future and life outside camp becomes intense enough to reveal their self-confidence and self-esteem. Concerning space as "a value," Gaston Bachelard remarks — by taking an example from Rilke — that space "has magnifying properties" because it connotes "the subject of the verbs 'to open up,' or 'to grow'" (202). The camp space provides *nisei* with "magnifying properties" as positive effects. The birth of *nisei*'s self-esteem accounts for that of their self expression of hope. *Nisei*'s departure from camp because of joining the U. S. Army, attending college, or having a job is equivalent to their departure from an exclusive and tightly-interwoven microcosm of Japanese American family and community. *Nisei*, in this sense, converts their rebellious energy to regaining lost privacy.

Privacy which was lost in the 1940's is virtually regained in Uchida's autobiographical voices. Uchida's story telling, however, is ultimately a mixture of history and autobiography. On history, Uchida states in her interview:

> "History is always more meaningful when it's told in human terms, in terms of one family, so I felt that was a good way to have each new generation learn what happened.... It was such a terrible travesty and betrayal by the government of American citizens." ("Children's Author Yoshiko Uchida Dies at 70" 2)

History comprised by accumulated factual incidents intends to be embedded in Uchida's story-telling.

The most remarkable example that actually happened at Topaz and whose modified versions repeatedly occur in Uchida's stories is the fact that a sixty-three-year-old *issei* bachelor chef, James Hatsuki Wakasa, was shot to death near the fence by a guard, Gerald B. Philpott, on April 11, 1943. It became known as "the Wakasa Incident."[8] In *Journey to Topaz*, Yumi's friend's grandfather was shot to death near the fence by a guard while looking for arrow heads and stones. The similar story appears in *Picture Bride* where Hana Takeda's husband, Taro Takeda, was shot to death in similar circumstances. In *Desert Exile*, Uchida mentions this

Chapter 1 : Regaining Lost Privacy: Yoshiko Uchida's Story Telling As a *Nisei* Woman Writer

incident that a sixty-three-year old man was shot to death by a guard, who insisted that he shouted four times for warning. As proved in those stories, Wakasa became "the most famous of the handful of Japanese Americans killed by guards during their wartime incarceration" (Brian Niiya, *Japanese American History* 346). It is because Philpott was proven "not guilty" even though Wakasa who in a report "had been shot while trying to escape" was, according to evidence, "facing the guard when shot" (Brian Niiya, *Japanese American History* 346). Uchida in *Desert Exile* explains that Wakasa was found dead within three feet from the fence, so that he could not have listened to the guard's voice, and also that the guard did not shoot for warning before shooting Wakasa. Wakasa's story was brought in as an untold story during the wartime experience by Senator Spark Matsunaga at the confessional debate (Brian Niiya, *Japanese American History* 346). Wakasa as a victim of injustice is transformed into a myth in Japanese American concentration camp history, and Uchida was definitely aware of this myth.

Uchida's strategy is to bring history into a personal account of one family, as Michael Weiner also points out (198). Lost privacy is told in a process of discovering what was neglected under the mainstream of history, and autobiography is the tool for achieving this purpose. Autobiography is "a self-representational practice that is complexly situated within cultures," and "autobiography studies, as an increasingly transdisciplinary critical practice, have incorporated postmodernist techniques and critiques with a variety of results" (Leigh Gilmore 3). Applying autobiography, therefore, results in accepting ideology in a mythological and private space where there is less conflict in understanding history. This tactic is, as Rayson points out, invoked especially by ethnic American women because they "are dealing with society and history on certain levels, as well as their place in this culture, autobiography becomes the proper form for the transmission of cultural reality and myth"(43).

Through this process, Uchida, moreover, creates a hidden sign of identity of one family which is transformed into a symbol of their concentration camp experiences as history. Yuki Sakane and her family in *Journey to Topaz*, Hana and her family in *Picture Bride*, and Emi and her family in *The Bracelet* all have the same number "13453" as family identification number when they are sent to camp. What is more, all those families were assigned to live in "Barrack 16, Apartment #40," at the Tanforan Racetrack, which was nothing but a temporal concentration camp for Japanese Americans before they were eventually sent to eleven camps. In different stories, Uchida emphasizes the common experience by applying the same family number and apartment number which Uchida and her family actually had as it is described in *Desert Exile*.

As a *nisei* writer, however, Uchida has been ignored partly because she was considered a children's book author rather than a writer, and partly because she was excluded from a majority of Japanese Americans who immigrated to

Chapter 1 : Regaining Lost Privacy: Yoshiko Uchida's Story Telling As a *Nisei* Woman Writer

the States as cheap laborers. Uchida was definitely proud of her *issei* parents' background as pointed out before, and her attitude toward Japan was supportive enough only to evaluate *issei* in terms of patriarchal virtues they had.[9] Elaine H. Kim, in her landmark book, *Asian American Literature: An Introduction to the Writings and Their Social Context* (1982), does not even mention Uchida though she discusses the other *nisei* writers such as Milton Murayama, John Okada, Hisaye Yamamoto, and Toshio Mori. Especially, Yamamoto who — as a short story writer — is quite compatible with Uchida, has been recognized more widely and her works have been included in major anthologies such as *Best American Short Stories* (Dorothy Ritsuko McDonald and Katharine Newman 25).[10]

Adapted to what Kim insists, however, Uchida is one of *nisei* writers "whose writing provides us with insights into the *issei* through their children's eyes as well as into *nisei* thoughts and feelings about what it has meant to be an American-born Japanese" (140). In persisting in the "children's eyes," in one sense, Uchida had more opportunities to create her world of literature outside what Frank Chin calls the "ghetto" of Japanese American newsprints and publications (Kim 141). Successful outside this ghetto, Uchida's creative activities were recognized in the children's literature world after the war by introducing Japanese traditional culture and literature; whereas they are ignored even now within the ethnic literature world. Unfortunately, Uchida is blinded between those two worlds. Uchida's stories, however, should be reevaluated at present when most of Japanese Americans, both *sansei* and *yonsei* (fourth-generation Japanese Amwricans), have no command of Japanese language and no direct experience with traditional Japanese society.

To her readers of different age groups ranging from the lower elementary level to adults, moreover, Uchida consequently attempts to overcome the limited boundary of nationality and ethnicity. In her 1986 interview, Uchida makes a comment:

> "I hope to give young Asians a sense of their own history. At the same time, I want to dispel the stereotypic image still held by many non-Asians about the Japanese Americans and write about them as real people.
>
> "I hope to convey as well the strength of spirit and the sense of hope and purpose I have seen in many of the first-generation Japanese Americans. Beyond that, I write to celebrate our common humanity, for I feel the basic elements of humanity are present in all our strivings." ("Children's Author Yoshiko Uchida Dies at 70" 2)

To deny and destroy the stereotype of Japanese Americans is one aim which is connected with another. Beyond the boundaies of history and ethnicity, Uchida believes that she should reach to the profound understanding of humanity.

Published as a Christmas gift book after her death, *The Bracelet* (primarily written as a short story in 1976), which targets young children of elementary school level, illustrates the hidden conflict and regained hope between two countries and two peoples. The bracelet which seven-year-old Emi was presented by her best friend Laurie Madison just before Emi and her family were forced to leave for the concentration camp is a symbol of friendship and promise as well as that of farewell. Whereas the house becomes empty like "a gift box with no gift inside — filled with a lot of nothing" (*The Bracelet* n.pag.), Emi's empty heart is comforted by the bracelet as a gift from her best friend. The bracelet provides Emi with the sense of security and bravery in the midst of her departure from her home to camp. The loss of the house as a settled and secured place for living is apparently compensated for by the gain of the bracelet as a token of a stable and everlasting friendship combined with the sense of spiritual security.

This gold chain bracelet "with a heart dangling on it," however, turns to be nothing but what is glittering on the surface yet what is unstable in its root. This irony reflects the destiny of Japanese Americans in respect of their unstable relationship with the United States. This irony is, however, lost as soon as the bracelet is lost on the first day of camp. In spite of Emi's agony and despair, she regains her strength and self-confidence by convincing herself that what is carried in her heart is more important than the bracelet as a visible and concrete object.

The first thing Mama put on the shelf was a photo of Papa.

> But Emi knew she didn't need a photo of Papa to remember him.
>
> It was as though Mama had the same thought. "You know, Emi," she said. "You don't need a bracelet to remember Laurie any more than we need a photo to remember Papa or our home or all the friends and things we loved and left behind. Those are things we carry in our hearts and take with us no matter where we are sent." (*The Bracelet* n. pag.)

The spirituality is emphasized in terms of possessing strength. The physical and settled place is neither secured nor trusted; on the other hand, the psychological and apparently unsettled space is evaluated and examined. The possibility is left as a future hope even though the story is ended in the beginning of Emi's camp life. The hope is what Uchida usually brings in as she states:

> "Today, so much of the world is dehumanizing. And a child is aware of a lot of ugliness in this life. I think a child needs hope. That's the main difference between adult and children's books . . . you always leave children with a sense of hope." (Nakao S-1)

This hope or possibility is prolonged to the departure from the camp at the end of *Journey to Topaz*, Uchida's novel for the intermediate-level readers, her autobiography *Desert Exile*, and *Picture Bride* for adults.[11] In *Journey to Topaz*, eleven-year-old Yuki and her family are also residents of Berkeley like Yuki and her family in *The Bracelet*. Yuki's story is more autobiographical as Uchida admits that *Journey to Topaz* is her story (Studier Chang 190) and the Uchida family were also sent to Topaz, Utah, where Uchida was devoted into teaching elementary school children within the barbed wire as it is precisely depicted in *Desert Exile* as "detached, impersonal recordings of a large-scale historical upheaval" (Sau-Ling Cynthia Wong 137). *Journey to Topaz* and *Desert Exile* are, in this respect, paired, and those tales are "made all the more horrifying by the compassionate and often humorous ways" (Weiner 199).

Desert Exile, which was published before *Journey to Topaz*, should not be merely considered as an autobiography, but presents to us "an archetypal pattern" that "emerged from the many accounts" (Houston 5). This is an archetypal pattern of journey, journey to concentration camps:

> The pattern reads like this: In the midst of their struggle to make a life in America, a family is forced to abandon their home. Though they have broken no laws, they are evacuated under military guard, carried by bus or train to a holding area or directly to one of the permanent camps, where they endure the kind of treatment ordinarily reserved for unwanted refugees or prisoners of war. (Houston 5).

This pattern underlines their journey of agony as Uchida defines it as "an exile in her own homeland" (Houston 5). As its destination, Topaz, "Jewelry of Desert," is an ironical name because there is no such beautiful jewelry in Topaz but it is in the middle of desert, "a treeless compound of fenced barracks, about 100 miles south of Salt Lake City" (Houston 5). According to Niiya in *Japanese American History*, temperatures in Topaz "ranged from 106 degrees in summer to — 30 degrees in winter" and it was located "at an elevation of 4,600 feet, the region was subject to a constant wind that resulted in frequent dust storms" (331). The exile in Topaz reinforces Japanese Americans to the most crucial environment, their trial pilgrimage.

Throughout an exile in *Journey to Topaz*, Yuki's psychological growth both through hardships of separation from her father and confrontation with tragic incidents of disease and death is determined by Uchida's attitude toward creating a blended literature of history and autobiography. Yuki's relationship with her family members and friends becomes intensified and deepened within the limited space of privacy. Yuki's conflict with her elder brother, Ken, leads her to understanding him as a young man with energy and abilities who first attempts to apply for the university from camp, yet who ultimately decides to volunteer for the U. S. infantry as a *nisei* man. Like Ken who was once obsessed with a strong desire to study at college, Uchida and her sister attempted to apply for as many places as possible as stated in *Desert Exile*. Regarding Ken as a character, however, Uchida states that one of "some adjustments for the sake of the story" is a change from her sister to an elder brother (Studier Chang 192). Yoshida explains its reason, saying: "I

Chapter 1 : Regaining Lost Privacy: Yoshiko Uchida's Story Telling As a *Nisei* Woman Writer

changed my sister to a brother because I wanted to bring in the story of the 422nd Division" as a historical incident (Studier Chang 192). Ken's involvement with the 422nd Division which challenges Japanese Americans' loyalty to the United States creates another myth.

As Uchida emphasizes the importance of continuity in history, *Journey to Topaz* is succeeded by *Journey Home*, whose focus is on the postwar hardships in the Sakane family. The hope is, however, diminished in the aftermath where Japanese Americans had to be confronted with another difficulty living and working in unchanged white dominant society. Whereas Uchida herself settled in East Coast for a while after her camp year, she deals with the Sakane's journey "home," which is their return to California. "Home" is, however, no longer their home. Ken's return from the Army is the core of this story depicting the hopeless reality of life in the postwar society. As the more complicated feelings of despair and anger were born outside the barbed wire, however, Yuki's scope becomes more widened and deepened along with her keen insights "to recognize the hypocrisy and prejudices of some individuals as well as to see the fears and seeming hopelessness of certain situations" (Elsie Wong 44). Hopelessness is, however, not the ultimate goal but a process to reach in remaining "optimistic for the future" (Elsie Wong 44).

Though the closure of *Picture Bride* is also the departure from camp, this is the only story that traces back to the *issei*'s immigration to the United States, though it contains

Uchida's own vivid memories which she recalls in *Desert Exile*. *Picture Bride* begins with a hope which most of picture brides possessed in leaving Japan for a new land to encounter and join their *issei* bridegrooms. The main character and survivor is such a picture bride, Hana, who ventures to arrive in the States at age twenty-one. In his book review, Niiya indirectly states that *Picture Bride* is not the "'great Asian American novel'" by pointing out the fact that it "has been practically ignored by both the Asian American and the mainstream presses" (Rev. of *Picture Bride* 153). This statement, paradoxically enough, delineates Uchida's attitude as a *nisei* writer who regains a strong sense of respect to Japanese traditional culture and customs after staying for two years in Japan as a Ford Foundation Fellow in the 1950's. Uchida's endeavor to reconfirm and reestablish what *issei* women named "picture brides" have embraced and strived for is accomplished in completing *Picture Bride*.

By contrast to Chinese American women writers such as Maxine Hong Kingston and Amy Tan, Uchida had to manipulate "the interpersonal communication" (Niiya, Rev. of *Picture Bride* 153) as a Japanese speech pattern. Between in Chinese and in Japanese, the way of placing silence in communication is different even though both possess silence as a cultural norm. In Japanese, verbal communication between women and men — Hana and Taro in *Picture Bride* — as controlled and suppressed embodiment sounds flat, unattractive, and unmoving. As Niiya interprets this quietness as "the inability of either character to verbalize

Chapter 1 : Regaining Lost Privacy: Yoshiko Uchida's Story Telling As a *Nisei* Woman Writer

what they really feel even to each other and the failure of the other to pick up on the nonverbal cues put out by their partner" (Rev. of *Picture Bride* 153). Uchida's retrospective narrative of *issei* experience is attained so that her story telling becomes much quieter and simpler on the surface. Moreover, an *issei* woman's view which is frequently overshadowed by an *issei* man's dominant perspective is enlarged and appreciated. The lack of verbal communication does not mean that of emotional vibrations, but connotes the existence of psychological and inward struggle and anguish which *issei* women were compelled to endure and overcome.

The conflict between *issei* and *nisei* diminishes in the middle of the story where Takeda's only child, Mary, elopes with a white man in her college days. Mary's disappearance also means the absence of *nisei* in one family who experiences the camp life. Mary's reappearance in the latter part of the novel, furthermore, does not influence Takeda's destiny. By contrast to Kingston's *The Woman Warrior* and Tan's *The Joy Luck Club* and *The Kitchen God's Wife*, all of which deal with the dynamic conflict and reconciliation between mother and daughter, Uchida's *Picture Bride* does not interest feminists, nor other ethnic writers and critics. Uchida's attention is rather devoted to evaluating the obedient yet courageous and enduring picture brides and *issei* women as survivors in the white male dominant society even after husbands died and their children left them.

The space in *Picture Bride*, however, leaves more possibilities than Uchida's other works. Like *Journey to*

Topaz and *Desert Exile*, *Picture Bride* is closed with the camp story. This ending is, however, not the departure from camp, but the decision to remain in camp, because the heroine is an *issei* woman. Hana's survival means her regaining privacy which she once lost as a picture bride, wife, mother, housekeeper, and 'prisoner' by suppressing her passions, desires, and wishes. Kiku Tokuda, another picture bride and *issei* woman, also faces her husband's unfortunate death and her sons' enlisting in the Army. *Issei* women — both Hana and Kiku who are left alone — are united in order to overcome "landscapes of fear" by themselves. Uchida as a *nisei* woman who left her *issei* parents in camp for the sake of her own freedom reconsiders another value which *issei* women preserved throughout their lives.

Uchida's story telling as an act of regaining lost privacy is awakened by her consciousness as a *nisei* writer and accomplished when the enclosed space is open to a hope. Uchida's story telling colors Japanese American history and Uchida engraves American literature with Japanese American woman's autobiographical voices which have been echoing in search for identity.

Notes

This paper is accomplished as part of my project of studies on Japanese American Women Writers with financial support of Japanese Ministry of Education. I especially thank both Professor Margarita Melville,

Chapter 1 : Regaining Lost Privacy: Yoshiko Uchida's Story Telling As a *Nisei* Woman Writer

Chair of the Department of Ethnic Studies of the University of California, Berkeley and Professor Sau-Ling Cynthia Wong, Director of Asian American Studies of UC, Berkeley who enabled me to use the Asian American Studies Library. I am also very grateful to Ms. Wei Chi Poon and Ms. Janice Otani of the Asian American Studies Library for making my research much easier and faster. And I was encouraged by Professor Ronald Takaki, who had a brief yet friendly chat with me during his busy schedule. This paper was originally published in *Studies in Culture and the Humanities: Bulletin of the Faculty of Integrated Arts and Sciences, Hiroshima University*, III 3 (1994): 1-22. After that, such excellent papers (Chen and Yu; Matthew, and Shimaburuko) were published.

1. Yukari is a pen-name of Yoshiko Uchida's mother, Ikuko Uchida, as a tanka poet. After her mother's death, Yoshiko Uchida published her mother's book of poetry which was written in Japanese, in Japan. The title of the book is *Yukari Shō* (1967). This book was translated into English by Yoshiko Uchida.
2. This exhibition was still held at the beginning of 1994 at the third floor of Doe Library, just in front of the main entrance and information center, when I was doing research at Asian American Studies Library at the University of California at Berkeley. In addition to this, Uchida's books and manuscripts have been stored at Berkeley's Bancroft Library, a rare book library.
3. Both James D. Houston and Annie Nakao emphasize the fact that Uchida's parents are both graduates of Doshisha Christian Academy, Kyoto, Japan, as a great difference from the other *nisei* whose parents "eked out a living as a truck farmers, gardeners or housekeepers for white families" (Nakao S-6). Uchida's father, Dwight Takashi Uchida, was working for the San Francisco Branch of Mitsui and Co., and her mother was leading a sophisticated life as an armature but quite accomplished poet of tanka. Due to her parents' background, there were

"many Caucasians connected with Doshisha" among Uchida's family friends (Nakao S-6). In addition to their Christian background, Uchida moreover has a strong sense of identity as a Japanese with "the samurai code of loyalty, honor, self-discipline and filial piety" (Houston 5).

4. Born in Alameda, California in 1921 and raised in Berkeley, Uchida entered the University of California at Berkeley at age sixteen. Just before graduation, at nineteen, Uchida and her family were forced to leave for a concentration camp. Uchida, her elder sister Keiko, and their *issei* parents were sent to the Tanforan Assembly Center in San Bruno, California, where Uchida received her college diploma by mail. They were later sent to Topaz camp in Utah and both Uchida and her sister stayed there about one year.

5. In Yukari's poem, the same feelings of regret and sorrow for having lost a home is expressed:

> "Four months have passed,
> And at last I learn
> To call this horse stall
> My family's home"   (*Yukari Sho*)

6. According to Roger Daniels' *Prisoners Without Trial: Japanese Americans in World War II*, at Topaz, "which was representative, the uninsulated barracks were twenty feet wide. Thus, all 'apartments' were twenty feet in one dimension: and as little as eight feet or as much as twenty-four feet in the other. The largest 'apartment' was an unpartitioned area of twenty by twenty-four feet; that 480 square-foot space would be 'home' for a family of six. Partitions between 'apartments' did not reach the roof, so that privacy within or between family living spaces was impossible" (67).

7. I would like to use a term, "Japaneseness," in order to characterize *issei*'s sense of identity as Japanese who were born in Japan and grew up in their home land until they immigrated to the States. To the

Chapter 1 : Regaining Lost Privacy: Yoshiko Uchida's Story Telling As a *Nisei* Woman Writer

contrary, *nisei* is more Americanized in terms of language and behavior, so that "Americanization" is suitable for expressing their identity. In accounting for *nisei*'s characteristics in camp, Morishima remarks that the "impact of 'Japanization' of the more assimilated Nikkei cannot be treated here. Suffice it to say that many of the interviewees felt their 'Americanization' retarded and many never recouped" (15). "Americanization" which Rayson uses is another tendency toward American identity "pushed by the war and internment allowed Japanese-American women to move away from the traditional family system which demanded specific behavior, obligation, duty, loyalty, and respect with observance of rank order between husband and wife" (46). Compared with *sansei*, however, *nisei* should be the first Americanized generation with an intention to be free from *issei*'s Japaneseness. Yet, *sansei* who are the second Americanized generation tend to return to the roots in search for identity, yet cannot return to the same place where their *issei* grandparents once lived. *Sansei*'s identity is, therefore, named "Japanization" in a different way from *nisei*'s "Japanization." In describing *sansei*'s sense of ethnic identity, Uchida remarks that "the Sansei are proud of their Japaneseness" ("Hope and No Monsters" 21).

8. According to Roger Daniels in "The Conference Keynote Address: Relocation, Redress, and the Report — A Historical Appraisal," "Mr. Wakasa was killed 'while attempting to crawl through the fence'" (6-7) according to the report released to the press by the army; however, it is now "clear that the story was fabricated and, based on an internal WRA report of the following month, this seems to be what really happened: The shooting took place in a relatively isolated corner of the camp, and apparently no one inside knew about it until about forty-five minutes later when 1st Lt. Henry H. Miller, commander of the Military Police company, informed a WRA staff member that 'a Japanese resident had been shot and killed . . . and that his body had been removed'" (7). Later, however, another evidence appeared by the WRA "indicated that the victim had been inside the fence when shot — the center of

a large bloodstain was five feet inside the fence — and a postmortem examination of the body found that there was 'a perforating wound point of entry made probably by a bullet which entered the thoracic cage [anterior to posterior at the] 3rd rib 2 1 / 2 cm left of mid-thoracic line. No powder burn. There is an exit wound measuring 1 cm by 3 cm jagged posteriorly at 6th thoracic vertebra 3 cm right of mid thoracic line.' In other words, Wakasa was facing the soldier who shot him, which is, of course, incompatible with the story that the army put out. In the meantime the M. P. commander armed his troops with riot weapons, high-powered rifles, and tear gas" (7). Mine Okubo, from a well-educated and established family like Uchida, expresses this Wakasa's funeral in her book, *Citizen 13660* (180-81).

9. Uchida is excluded from almost all the anthologies of Asian American literature such as *Aiiieeeee!: An Anthology of Asian America Writers* (1974), *Big Aiiieeeee!* (1991), *Making Waves: An Anthology of Writings By and About Asian American Women* (1989), *Home to Stay: Asian American Women's Fiction* (1990), and *Sister Stew: Fiction and Poetry by Women* (1991). Uchida's short story, "Something to Be Remembered By" is, however, included in *The Hawk's Well: A Collection of Japanese American Art and Literature* (1986), and "Tears of Autumn" in *The Forbidden Stich* (1989).

10. In her highly-accomplished book, *Articulate Silences* published in 1993, King-Kok Cheung places Hisaye Yamamoto with the other two Asian American women writers, Maxine Hong Kingston and Joy Kogawa. Cheung discusses Uchida only in a foot note and refers to Uchida's *Desert Exile*.

11. *Journey to Topaz* "was nominated for the Dorothy Canfield Fish Children's Book Award in 1972, the Sequoyah Children's Book Award in Oklahoma in 1973, and the William Allen White Award in 1974," and it was "also an American Library Association Notable Book" ("Hope and No Monsters" 44). It is the first Uchida's book that was translated into Japanese and published by Hyoron Sha in 1975. Regarding this

Chapter 1 : Regaining Lost Privacy: Yoshiko Uchida's Story Telling As a *Nisei* Woman Writer

translation project, Uchida said, "I'm really excited about it" and "I can see why they wouldn't want to do the others — books about Japanese in Japan written by a Japanese in American. But this one is about a Japanese-American experience. It's something they don't know much about" ("Hope and No Monsters" 44). Later on, both *Desert Exile* and *Picture Bride* were translated into Japanese and published in Japan. Regarding how Uchida is valued in Japan, there have been no literary criticism on Uchida's works. I found one introductory essay entitled "Message to Children: from Yoshiko Uchida's Works" by Itoko Kaneoka (*Jido Bungaku Hyoron* 22 (1986): 59-71).

Works Cited

Bachelard, Gaston. *The Poetics of Space*. 1958. Trans. Maria Jolas. Boston: Beacon, 1992.

Chen, Fu-Jen, and Su-Lin Yu. "Reclaiming the Southwest: A Traumatic Space in the JapaneseAmerican Internment Narrative." *Journal of the Southwest* 47.4 (Winter 2005): 551-70.

Cheung, King-Kok. *Articulate Silences: Hisaye Yamamoto, Maxine Hong Kingston, Joy Kogawa*. Ithaca & London: Cornell UP, 1993.

"Children's Author Yoshiko Uchida Dies at 70." *Hokubei Mainichi* 24 June 1992: 2.

Daniels, Roger. "The Conference Keynote Address: Relocation, Redress, and the Report — A Historical Appraisal." Roger Daniels et al. 3-9.

——. *Prisoners Without Trial: Japanese Americans in World War II*. New York: Hill and Wang, 1993.

Daniels, Roger, Sandra C. Taylor, and Harry H. L. Kitano, eds. *Japanese Americans from Relocation to Redress*. 1986. Seattle & London: U of Washington P, 1991.

Derrick, Edith W. "Effects of Evacuation on Japanese-American Youth." *School Reviews* 55.6 (1947): 356-62.

Gilmore, Leigh. "Introduction." Ashley, Kathleen, Leigh Gilmore, and Gerald Peters, eds. *Autobiography & Postmodernism*. Amherst: U of Massachusetts P, 1994. 3-18.

"Hope and No Monsters." *Jade* 1.4 (1975): 18-21.

Houston, James D. "A Review in Two Voices." Rev. of *Desert Exile*: *The Uprooting of a Japanese American Family*," by Yoshiko Uchida. *San Francisco Examiner* 2 May 1982: 5

Kim, Elaine H. *Asian American Literature: An Introduction to the Writings and Their Social Context*. Philadelphia: Temple UP, 1982.

Matthew, Theorey. "Untangling Barbed Wire Attitudes: Internment Literature for Young Adults." *Children's Literature Association Quarterly* 33.3 (Fall 2008): 227-45.

McDonald, Dorothy Ritsuko, and Katharine Newman. "Relocation and Dislocation: The Writings of Hisaye Yamamoto and Wakako Yamauchi." *MELUS* 7.3 (1980): 21-38.

Morishima, James K. "The Evacuation: Impact on the Family." Eds. Sue Stanley and Nattaniel Wagner. *Asian Americans: Psychological Perspectives*. Ben Lomond, CA: Science & Behavior, 1973. 13-19

Mura, David. "Mirrors of the Self: Autobiography and the Japanese American Writer." Eds. Shirley Hune et al. *Asian Americans: Comparative and Global Perspective*. Pullman, WA: Washington State UP, 1991. 249-63.

Nakao, Annie. "Nisei Author's Gift to Children." *San Francisco Examiner* 29 Sep. 1985: S1 & S6

Niiya, Brian. *Japanese American History: An A-to-Z Reference from 1868 to the Present*. New York: Facts On File, 1993.

——. Rev. of *Picture Bride*, Yoshiko Uchida. *Amerasia Journal* 14.2 (1988): 152-54.

Okubo, Mine. *Citizen 13660*. 1946. Seattle & London: U of Washington P, 1991.

Rayson, Ann. "Beneath the Mask: Autobiographies of Japanese-American Women." *MELUS* 14.1 (1987): 43-57.

Shimabukuro, Mira. "'Me Inwardly, Before I Dared': Japanese Americans

Writing-to-Gaman." *College English* 73.6 (July 2011): 148-71.

Studier Chang, Catherine E. "Profile: Yoshiko Uchida." *Language Arts* 61.2 (1984): 189-93.

Suyemoto Kawakami, Toyo. "Camp Memories: Rough and Broken Shards." Roger Daniels et al. 27-32.

Tseng, J. Yentsun. "Exhibit Highlights Japanese American Author's Life." *The Daily Californian* 2 Sep. 1993: 1 & 7.

Tuan, Yi-Fu. *Landscapes of Fear*. Minneapolis: U of Minnesota P, 1979.

"Uchida Featured on Commemorative Poster." *Rafu Shimpo* 23 Sep. 1989: 8684B.

Uchida, Yoshiko. *The Bracelet*. Illus. Joanna Yardley. New York: Philomel, 1993.

——. *Desert Exile: The Uprooting of a Japanese American Family*. Seattle & London: U of Washington P, 1982.

——. *Journey Home*. New York: Atheneum, 1987.

——. *Journey to Topaz*. New York: Charles Scribner's, 1971.

——. *Picture Bride*. Flagstaff, AR: Northland, 1987.

Weiner, Michael. Rev. of *Desert Exile: The Uprooting of a Japanese American Family*, by Yoshiko Uchida. *Immigrants & Minoritie*s 2.2 (1983) : 198-99.

Wong, Elsie. Rev. of *Journey Home*, by Yoshiko Uchida. *Bridge* 1979 (Summer): 44.

Wong, Sau-Ling Cynthia. *Reading Asian American Literature from Necessity to Extravagance*. Princeton: Princeton UP, 1993.

Yanagisako, Sylvia Junko. *Transforming the Past: Tradition and Kinship Among Japanese Americans*. Stanford: Stanford UP, 1985.

Chapter 2

An *Issei* Woman's Suffering, Silence, and Suicide in John Okada's *No-No Boy*

Being always read as Ichiro Yamada's story, *No-No Boy* connotes another story — a story of No-No boy's mother and *issei* woman.[1] Ichiro's suffering after he returns home from prison during the Second World War almost drives him mad and he is possessed with the desire to commit suicide, as he confesses: "Sometimes I think about killing myself"(61).[2] Though usually labelled as a powerful and stoic woman, Ichiro's mother is the one who actually becomes insane and kills herself after her twenty-eight years of suffering and silence following her arranged marriage and the subsequent immigration to the States.[3] Through Ichiro's story, his mother's story is told, illustrated, and ultimately acknowledged as a 'herstory' of an *issei* woman.

> Dead, he thought to himself, all dead. For me, you have been dead a long time, as long as I can remember. You, who gave

life to me and to Taro and tried to make us conform to a mold which never existed for us because we never knew of it, were never alive to us in the way that other sons and daughters know and feel and see their parents. But you made so many mistakes. It was a mistake to have ever left Japan. It was a mistake to leave Japan and to come to America and to have two sons and it was a mistake to think that you could keep us completely Japanese in a country such as America. (186)

What Ichiro acknowledges in the face of his mother's suicide is not so much her physical death as her psychological death. He defines her "life" in the States as a "death" in the sense that she is overwhelmed by her strong sense of identity as a Japanese. As a Japanese, she has neither been assimilated into nor even stimulated by the States.[4]

The psychologically "lifeless" or numbed *issei* mother is described, discussed, and remembered by Ichiro. On the other hand, Ichiro's father and an *issei* man illuminates the living and lively woman during her young days just before her suicide. Also, the sweet mother is seen in retrospect in Ichiro's elegy for her. The distance between those two opposite characteristics in one woman originates from that between two conflicting societies, cultures, and values, as well as the enormous hardship both inside and outside the Japanese American family and its community. This distance has been underestimated, whereas the distance between the *issei* and the *nisei* or the division within the family has been repeatedly validated by some critics.[5] Ichiro's mother's

Chapter 2 : An *Issei* Woman's Suffering, Silence, and Suicide in John Okada's *No-No Boy*

silence has prevented this distance from being remedied as Ichiro demands a trial inside himself in his last meeting with his mother, two days before her suicide.

> How is one to talk to a woman, a mother who is also a stranger because the son does not know who or what she is? Tell me, Mother, who are you? What is it to be a Japanese ? There must have been a time when you were a little girl. You never told me about those things. Tell me now so that I can begin to understand. Tell me about the house in which you lived and of your father and mother, who were my grandparents, whom I have never seen or known because I do not remember your ever speaking of them except to say that they died a long time ago. Tell me everything and just a little bit and a little bit more until their lives and yours and mine are fitted together, for they surely must be. (104-05)

Ichiro's mother's silence absolves her of constructing a self-identity or a story of her own.[6] Her words are frozen and her story is purposely and persistently untold rather than sinking into oblivion.

Her stubbornness obstructs both the overall view and the deeply spiritual side of her life. Ichiro's private wish for his mother is neither revealed nor conveyed to her, because he is also obsessed with silence.[7] As for the silence of both *issei* and *nisei*, the most crucial experience is usually considered the wartime concentration camp experience.[8] Though not precisely described in the text of *No-No Boy*, the camp experience has divided Ichiro's mother, just as the prison life during the war divides Ichiro. The aftermath to the war is not only their difficulty in finding jobs and houses, but also their psychological recovery from their camp experience and their unavoidable dilemma between the States' victory and Japan's defeat. However crucial the camp experience may be, there are many incidents that are summed up solely through the *issei* woman's life. Ichiro eventually realizes that "events had ruined the plans which she cherished and turned the once very possible dreams into a madness which was madness only in view of the changed status of the Japanese in America" (104). Ichiro's mother is a victim of these "events" and divisions which have never been cured inside herself.

The absence of the mother in Ichiro's home-coming delineates her life as a life-long laborer. It is difficult enough for Ichiro's *issei* parents to undertake the resettlement in the society after the war. The *issei* parents return to Seattle where they settled before the war, and they begin operating the grocery store, which was once owned by another Japanese American family, the Ozakis.[9] Ichiro cannot understand what his father means by "good business" when his mother goes to the bakery to buy bread for their store.

> Twenty-five cents for bus fare to get ten loaves of bread which turned a profit of thirty-five cents. It would take easily an hour to make the trip up and back. He didn't mean to shout, but he shouted: "Christ, Pa, what else do you give away?"

Chapter 2 : An *Issei* Woman's Suffering, Silence, and Suicide in John Okada's *No-No Boy*

> His father peered over the teacup with a look of innocent surprise.
>
> It made him madder. "Figure it out. Just figure it out. Say you make thirty-five cents on ten loaves. You take a bus up and back and there's twenty-five cents shot. That leaves ten cents. On top of that, there's an hour wasted. What are you running a business for? Your health?"
>
> Slup went the tea through his teeth, slup, slup, slup. "Mama walks." He sat there looking at his son like a benevolent Buddha.
>
> Ichiro lifted the cup to his lips and let the liquid burn down his throat. His father had said "Mama walks" and that made things right with the world. The overwhelming simplicity of the explanation threatened to evoke silly giggles which, if permitted to escape, might lead to hysterics. He clenched his fists and subdued them. (8-9)

Instead of asking for a delivery and even taking a bus to the bakery, Ichiro's mother walks "thirteen and a half blocks" uphill and walks back home with ten or twelve loaves of bread. She sacrifices herself in order to survive in the postwar society.[10] Ichiro's shock in learning about her real hardships makes him angry, and almost drives him to "hysterics."

Ichiro's mother's "hysterics," however, occur after she has been silenced long enough to hide her natural streams of emotions throughout her hardships. Her silence and her manner of communication is first observed in Ichiro's return.

"Mama. Ichiro. Ichiro is here."

The sharp, lifeless tone of his mother's words flipped through the silence and he knew that she hadn't changed.

"The bread must be put out."

In other homes mothers and fathers and sons and daughters rushed into hungry arms after week-end separations to find assurance in crushing embraces and loving kisses. The last time he saw his mother was over two years ago. He waited, seeing in the sounds of the rustling waxed paper the stiff, angular figure of the woman stacking the bread on the rack in neat, precise piles.

His father came back into the kitchen with a little less bounce and began to wash the cups. She came through the curtains a few minutes after, a small, flat-chested, shapeless woman who wore her hair pulled back into a tight bun. Hers was the awkward, skinny body of a thirteen-year-old which had dried and toughened through the many years following but which had developed no further. He wondered how the two of them had ever gotten together long enough to have two sons.

"I am proud that you are back," she said. "I am proud to call you my son." (10-11)

The *issei* mother is so suppressed that she cannot express her natural emotions of pleasure in her meeting with her son after his two-year absence. Silence gives her the ability to exist, so that her first "sharp, lifeless tone" symbolizes the subtle remark of her presence and her role as a laborer. Her

Chapter 2 : An *Issei* Woman's Suffering, Silence, and Suicide in John Okada's *No-No Boy*

next words define her role as a mother of a son who is loyal to Japan. Her manner of communication is deformed, along with her physical appearance.

Ichiro's first and over-all impression in his reencounter with his mother is, therefore, framed within a portrait of a consistent and long-silenced woman whose body and soul reflect her everlasting hardships. The *issei* woman's physical unattractiveness stems from her abject and life-long devotion to her husband and her children. All the labors — both inside and outside a domestic sphere — tear her apart, and imprisons her in a cage.

In such a cage, Ichiro's mother has already been suffering from depression and beginning to lose her balance. It is repeatedly mentioned that she is labelled as either "crazy" or "sick" so that the *issei* father tells both sons — Ichiro and Taro, to try to "understand" her (30&65). Her insanity has invaded the household, yet she is neither understood nor rescued by Ichiro or her husband. As a loyal Japanese, she is obsessed with a strong belief that Japan has not been defeated. Inflicted with two letters, one from South America and the other from Japan, she misplaces falsehood with truth in interpreting those two letters.

As for the letter from San Paulo, Brazil, Ichiro's mother assures herself of its truth and expects that the "boat is coming."

> She did not bother to pick up the letter. "To you who are a loyal and honorable Japanese, it is with humble and

heartfelt joy that I relay this momentous message. Word has been brought to us that the victorious Japanese government is presently making preparations to send ships which will return to Japan those residents in foreign countries who have steadfastly maintained their faith and loyalty to our Emperor. The Japanese government regrets that the responsibilities arising from the victory compels them to delay in the sending of the vessels. To be among the few who remain to receive this honor is a gratifying tribute. Heed not the propaganda of the radio and newspapers which endeavor to convince the people with lies about the allied victory. Especially, heed not the lies of your traitorous countrymen who have turned their backs on the country of their birth and who will suffer for their treasonous acts. The day of glory is close at hand. The rewards will be beyond our greatest expectations. What we have done, we have done only as Japanese, but the government is grateful. Hold your heads high and make ready for the journey, for the ships are coming."

"Who wrote that?" he asked incredulously. It was like a weird nightmare. It was like finding out that an incurable strain of insanity pervaded the family, an intangible horror that swayed and taunted beyond the grasp of reaching fingers. (14)

This letter from South America is from Japanese *issei* terrorists who were then called "*Kachigumi*" ("Victory Group" n.pag.). In South America, the Japanese *issei* were still obsessed with nationalism, even when Japan began to recover from the loss of the war. "*Kachigumi*" regarded Japan's loss as a conspiracy by the United States and delivered false information of Japan's victory over the States. To the Japanese who believed and even mentioned Japan's loss, "*Kachigumi*" lynched or even killed them (Susumu Miyao 131-34). Ichiro's mother is convinced of the statement by "*Kachigumi*" and entirely believes that she will be able to return to Japan.

This kind of "insanity" spread throughout the Japanese American community, as shown in another episode of a debate over the pictures which were taken and brought back by Watanabe's son who was stationed in Japan after the war. Ichiro's mother insists that those pictures, especially those of Hiroshima and Nagasaki where the atomic bombs were dropped, are propaganda. Her "madness" comes forth outside the household. As a mother whose son was loyal to Japan, she even feels superior to another *issei* mother, Mrs. Kumasaka, whose son joined the American army and was killed in the front.[11] Ichiro's mother is unconsciously addicted to terrorism which misguides her to extreme blindness.[12]

In addition to a letter from South America, Ichiro's mother receives a bundle of letters from her relatives in Japan who beg her to send them whatever she can, such as food, clothing, and money because of the enormous difficulty of living after the war. Among those letters, one from her sister makes her furious, yet consequently causes her to be confronted with her misunderstanding and ultimately drives her into insanity.

"Many, many pardons, dear Kin-chan," the father read, "for not having written to you long before this, but I have found it difficult to write of unpleasant things and all has been unpleasant since the disastrous outcome of the war which proved too vast an undertaking even for Japan. You were always such a proud one that I am sure you have suffered more than we who still live at home. I, too, have tried to be proud but it is not an easy thing to do when one's children are always cold and hungry. Perhaps it is punishment for the war. How much better things might have been had there been no war. For myself, I ask nothing, but for the children, if it is possible, a little sugar, perhaps, or the meat which you have in cans or the white powder which can be made into milk with water. And, while I know that I am already asking too much, it would be such a comfort to me and a joy to the children if you could somehow manage to include a few pieces of candy. It has been so long since they have had any. I am begging and feel no shame, for that is the way things are. And I am writing after many long years and immediately asking you to give assistance, which is something that one should not do in a letter until all the niceties have been covered, but, again, that is the way things are. Forgive me, Kin-chan, but the suffering of my children is the reason I must write in this shameless manner. Please, if you can, and I know not that you can, for there have been no answers to the many letters which brother and uncle and cousin have written, but, if you can, just a little will be of such great comfort to us —"

"Not true. I won't listen." She did not, however, move.

Chapter 2 : An *Issei* Woman's Suffering, Silence, and Suicide in John Okada's *No-No Boy*

Nervously, she rubbed her palms against her lap.

"One more place I will read," said the father and, casting aside the first sheet, searched along the second until he found the place he wanted. "Here she writes: 'Remember the river and the secret it holds? You almost drowned that day for the water was deeper and swifter than it looked because of the heavy rains. We were frightened, weren't we? Still, they were wonderful, happy times and, children that we were, we vowed never to tell anyone how close to dying you came. Had it not been for the log on the bank, I could only have watched you being swallowed up by the river. It is still your secret and mine for I have never told anyone about it. It no longer seems important, but I do think about such things if only to tell myself that there were other and better times.'" (108-09)

This letter is addressed to "Kin-chan" — Ichiro's mother's nickname from her first name — who possesses a shared secret with her sister. In this letter, her first name is mentioned. The tie between Ichiro's mother and her sister is strong enough to move a suspicious *issei* mother. No matter how humble her sister's letter may sound, its statement is consistent and demanding. In order to avoid a rejection, her sister reminds Ichiro's mother of their intimate relationship because she does not know the reason why Ichiro's mother rejected those letters from Japan. The distance between the sisters is like that between the two countries, Japan and the States. Ichiro's mother, who is convinced that the letters from Japan are propaganda, gradually launches into becoming awakened to the fact and being forced to stand at the threshold. [13]

A contradiction between the blindness and the awakening cannot be recovered because she is "only a rock of hate and fanatic stubbornness" (21). Ichiro's mother's cry was a "single, muffled cry which was the forgotten spark in a dark and vicious canyon and, the spark having escaped, there was only darkness, but a darkness which was now darker still" (68). The distance between Ichiro's mother and father is enlarged as she digs into the dark side of self as he becomes deeply addicted to drinking.[14] Ichiro's mother's struggle against her mental contradictions becomes rapidly more apparent after she receives her sister's letter:

> She sat stonily with hands in lap, her mouth slightly ajar in the dumb confusion that raged through her mind fighting off the truth which threatened no longer to be untrue. Taking the letter in her hands finally, she perused it with sad eyes which still occasionally sparked with suspicious contempt. (110)

In other words, she strongly insists that the letter is a fake. Inside herself, however, she has begun to doubt her assumption. The sense of fear prevents her from admitting Japan's loss of the war and Japanese relatives' starvation. To accept Japan's loss represents acceptance of the meaning of her self. Only saying that "she will be all right," neither Ichiro nor his *issei* father recognizes her dangerous conditions:

Chapter 2 : An *Issei* Woman's Suffering, Silence, and Suicide in John Okada's *No-No Boy*

> His disgust mounting rapidly, Ichiro peeked into the bedroom doorway. In the semi-darkness of the room, the mother sat on the edge of the bed, staring blankly at the sheets of paper in her hand. Her expression was neither that of sadness nor anger. It was a look which meant nothing, for the meaning was gone. (111)

There is a sign of mental breakdown as shown in her blank expression and her meaningless look in a dark isolated space. Her inner struggle — a mental breakdown symptom — is proven by her rejection of food and her strange behaviors. These symptoms begin just after she imprisons herself in the bedroom in face of a her sister's letter and it continues for two days.

> "Mama," he said more quietly and hopelessly, "one has to eat. It gives strength."
> And still he stood and watched, knowing that no amount of urging would move the beaten lump on the edge of the bed and vainly searching for the words to bring her alive. He brushed an arm to his eye and pressed his lips into a near pout. "The letter," he continued, "the letter, Mama. It could be nothing." Hope and encouragement caused his voice to rise in volume: "Your own sister would never write such a letter. You have said so yourself. It is not to be believed. Eat now and forget this foolishness." (114)

Ichiro's father's "encouragement" does not give her any hope because she has already begun to believe the letter from her sister. Her agony exists in her unforgettable "foolishness." His repeated persuasions to make her eat are not successful enough for her even to answer his words.

Another symptom is witnessed in her strange behavior, exhibiting conduct problems, by Kenji, Ichiro's friend.

> He was immediately impressed with the neatness of the shelves and the cleanness of the paint on the walls and woodwork. Inevitably, he saw Ichiro's mother and it gave him an odd sensation as he watched her methodically empty a case of evaporated milk and line the cans with painful precision on the shelf. He tried the door and found it locked and decided not to disturb her until she finished the case. It was a long wait, for she grasped only a single can with both hands each time she stooped to reach into the box. Finally, she finished and stood as if examining her handiwork.
>
> Kenji rapped briskly on the door but she took no notice. Instead, she reached out suddenly with her arms and swept the cans to the floor. Then she just stood with arms hanging limply at her sides, a small girl of a woman who might have been pouting from the way her head drooped and her back humped. (136-37)

A gap of two opposite actions illustrates that of her divided self. To arrange the cans neatly in order represents her personality who cannot accept laziness, irresponsibility, ingratitude, and disorder. To knock the cans down, therefore,

Chapter 2 : An *Issei* Woman's Suffering, Silence, and Suicide in John Okada's *No-No Boy*

means the destruction of her beliefs in herself. Ichiro's mother's internal anguish transforms "a woman" into "a small girl" whose seeming innocence is a reversed version of insanity. Her childish behavior is the evidence of her psyche which cannot heal the division in her personality.

In spite of those apparent symptoms of her mental breakdown, neither the *issei* father nor two sons — Ichiro and Taro — ventures to keep company with her and support her. All of them leave her alone for two days because they cannot be confronted with her insanity. In order to escape from her, Ichiro goes to Portland with Kenji and his father becomes deeply addicted to drinking.[15] Their irresponsible reaction to Ichiro's mother results in her suicide during their absence. Her last struggle and suicidal action occur after eight o'clock when Ichiro's father returns home from the liquor store with three bottles of whisky. Ichiro discovers her dead body in the tub after he has returned from Portland and dropped in at Kenji's house at "only a few minutes after nine" (180).

> "Mama," and he said it plaintively, "Mama, eat a little bit."
> She was lying on the bed, silent and unmoving, and it made him afraid. It was not the thought of death, but the thought of madness which reduced him to a frightened child in the darkness. When she was not lying or sitting almost as if dead in her open-eyed immobility, she was doing crazy things. It had started with the cans, the lining of them on the shelves, hurling them on the floor, brooding, fussing, repacking them

in the boxes, and then the whole thing over and over again until hours after Ichiro had gone. Then silence, and he forgot now whether the silence was of her lying or sitting on the bed, the silence which was of the water quietly heating to boil. Following that silence had come the rain, the soft rain as always, drizzling and miserable and deceivingly cold. And he had not heard a sound, but when he had gone to the bedroom to see about throwing another blanket on her, she was out in back hanging things on the line. How long she had been out in the rain, he couldn't say. Her hair was drenched and hanging straight down, reaching almost to the tiny hump of her buttocks against which the wet cotton dress had adhered so that he could see the crease. He called her from the doorway and was not disappointed when she hadn't heeded him, for that was how he knew it would be. So he had watched until he could stand it no longer and this time he had run right up to her and shouted for her to stop the foolishness and come in out of the rain, and it still had done no good. He had come in then and waited and drunk some whisky, and the bottle which had been half-full was almost gone when the back door slammed. And then, once again, the awful silence. She was sitting that time. He remembered because when he went out to take the rain-soaked things off the line, he had to turn sideways to get past her. (174-75)

Ichiro's father's only repeated suggestion is "eat," that is a human natural desire and necessary biological activity which provides her physical strength as well as nutrition.

Chapter 2 : An *Issei* Woman's Suffering, Silence, and Suicide in John Okada's *No-No Boy*

Her psychological strength, however, is not regained by eating food. Her rejection of eating is accompanied by her dual alternative conditions. One is a complete silence and self-enclosure in her bedroom as an absolute private space; the other is a wild and pointless conduct and disclosure which is guided by her pursuit of social and domestic labors. As arranging the cans in a store connotes her social labor, laundry and hanging is part of her domestic labors. As destroying the lined-up cans implies her self-destruction, hanging laundry in the rain is based upon her aggressive and rebellious attitude toward life itself. Those "crazy" behaviors externalize her inner struggle and her belief in life's meaninglessness.

In the last chapter of Ichiro's parents' suicidal pursuit, water is a metaphor of their longing for life.[16] Hanging laundry in the rain and getting drenched to the skin just before her suicide is Ichiro's mother's last attempt to gain water for her dried-up body and soul as well as her self-abandonment and self-punishment. Ichiro's father's alcoholism is another attempt to water his dried-up psyche. Even though water suggests their desperate search for life, both of them are literally and symbolically drowned in water. Inspired by her sister's letter and obsessed with the past secret of her getting nearly drowned, especially, Ichiro's mother chooses suicide by drowning. The water gradually invades Ichiro's parents' lives and finally overflows into their divided lives and selves.

Stopping short of the kitchen, she stood undecidedly for a

moment, shaking her head slowly as though to reshuffle her senses. Resolutely then she leaped onto the foot of the bed and began to pull down the several suitcases which had been piled atop the cardboard wardrobe.

"Mama!" It was an utterance filled with despair. He watched wretchedly as she pulled open drawers and proceeded to cram the cases full of whatever came into her grasping hands. How long this time, he thought gently rubbing the ache in his shoulder with an unsteady hand, let himself drop heavily into a chair. He gripped the bottle with both hands and his body shook tremulously. Biting his lip to imprison the swollen sob which would release a torrent of anguish, he crumpled forward until he felt the coolness of the table spreading across his forehead. It helped to relax him. Suddenly the scuffling and banging and scurrying in the bedroom stopped. Slowly, he looked up and, just as his gaze encompassed the door to the bedroom, he glimpsed her striding out and into the bathroom. She shut the door firmly behind her and, a moment later, he heard the bolt being slid into place. Then the water sounded its way into the tub, not splashing or gurgling heavily, but merely trickling, almost reluctantly so it seemed.

He gulped from the bottle and listened to the trickling of the water against the bottom of the white tub as it slowly changed into a gentle splashing of water against water as the tub began to fill. (176)

Another pattern depicting the opposition of violence to silence occurs just after the first one within two hours.

Chapter 2 : An *Issei* Woman's Suffering, Silence, and Suicide in John Okada's *No-No Boy*

As Ichiro's mother's urgent packing shows her unavoidable desire to return to Japan even though she is sure that it would be impossible, her unescapable agony drives her to be drenched into the water again. There is a shift from the rain in an open space to the water in a tub in an enclosed space of the locked bathroom. In this locked bathroom, Ichiro's mother attempts to convey her last sign to her husband.

Her sign, however, is not recognized by him. A parallel between Ichiro's father's addiction and Ichiro's mother's being drowned in the bath tub is proven as that of suicidal acts in their slow and deliberate embarkment. Neither Ichiro's father nor Ichiro's mother can help each other in their desperation; whereas, both of them expect the other to stop their suicidal actions. The sound of water falling into the tub is "reluctantly trickling" as though it symbolizes her hesitation and inner struggle. Ichiro's father realizes that this irritated way is different from her habitual way.

> Why doesn't she turn the faucets on full he thought impatiently. Turn it on like you always do. Be quick and efficient and impatient, which is the way you have always been. Start the water in the tub and scrub the kitchen floor while it is filling up. When the floor is done and the mop wrung out and hung in back to dry, the water is good, just the right depth. Like a clock you are. Not a second wasted.
>
> He gulped again and the progress of the water was so painfully slow that he could hardly discern any change in the pattern of its splashing.

> At length, irritated, he retreated into the store, holding the bottle in one hand and groping his way through the darkness almost to the front door, where the sounds from the bathroom couldn't reach him. (176-77)

Ichiro's mother's last sign is not transferred to Ichiro's father. It is her last revolt against her habitually "quick," "efficient," and "impatient" labors in which she has been engaged in since her marriage and immigration to the States. Her "clock"-like accuracy and diligence which has been acknowledged as her character has imprisoned her and consequently deprived her of both physical and psychological freedom.

Ichiro's father's insensitivity to his wife's cry for help and his refusal to rescue her results in his complete negligence. His blindness is repeated in his audible incapability. This dual ignorance results in part from his drug addiction which makes him half-unconscious and ultimately causes him to sleep. In his half-conscious condition, he fantasizes about the past when he first met "Kin-chan" as a young woman and decided to marry her. In his memory, "Kin-chan" is alive.

> Kin-chan, that is what your sister calls you now. Now that life has become too hard for her to bear, she once again calls you Kin-chan, for then she thinks of the days when we were all young and strong and brave and crazy. Not crazy like today or yesterday, but crazy in the nice, happy way of young people. No, not crazy like you, old woman. Once, I

Chapter 2 : An *Issei* Woman's Suffering, Silence, and Suicide in John Okada's *No-No Boy*

too called you Kin-chan. Kin-chan. Kin-chan. Kin-chan. You were good then. Small and proud and firm and maybe a little bit huffy, but good and soft inside. Ya, ya, I was smart too. I found out how good and soft before we married. Right under their eyes almost. Your papa was there and you beside him and your mama was already dead. Then there was myself and my mama and papa and the man who was the village mayor's brother, whose name I forget but who was making the match. How he could talk, that man, talk and drink and talk, talk, talk. But he was only talking then because it was time for business and he was talking about how fine a wife you would make for the son of my father and mother, and your head was down low but I could see you smiling. How sweet it was then. How wonderful! Then he was talking about me and I sat up straight and full and puffed my chest and I could see you stealing a look once or twice and you were pleased. I was pleased too. Everybody was pleased and the thing was settled quickly, for that time was only for making the matter final. And when one is feeling gay and full of joy, the saké must be brought out to lift the spirits higher. And they drank, your papa and mine and mayor's brother, and I only a little because I was even happier than they and needed no false joy. Then the moment was at hand when Mama was telling Papa not to drink so much and you were in the kitchen heating more saké and your papa and that man were singing songs not to be heard by such as you. It was to the toilet I was going when you saw me and I, you. There was nothing to be said. It was not a time for words but only deep feeling. And there, in the darkness of the narrow

> corridor between the house and the smelly toilet, I made you my wife, standing up. It was wonderful, more wonderful I think than even the night of the day when we really were married. Do you know it was never that good for me again? Ya, Kin-chan, that was the mistake. We should have waited and then everything would have been proper. We were not proper and so we suffer. Your papa, my papa, my mama, and that man did not know, but the gods knew. It was dark and we were standing, but they were watching and nodding their heads and saying: "Shame, black shame." (177-78)

The significant difference between a "sweet " and "smart" young woman, and a "crazy" and angry old woman is emphasized as the core of Ichiro's father's disappointment and despair, as well as Ichiro's mother's agony over her divided self. He stresses her charms and wisdom and appreciates the "good and soft" characteristics of their good old days. Their marriage is, however, based on a misconduct which is recognized as the first and most crucial mistake in her life.

Her mistake was her quick and inevitable decision to marry without any mutual communication, understanding, or true agreement. Ichiro's father's "deep feeling" can be interpreted as his sexual desire and passion. His confession about their secret sexual relationship is attributed to his sense of guilt of his terminating her to marry him. The lack of freedom to express her emotions, feelings, and opinions determine her fate to marry him, and, as a result, to leave

Chapter 2 : An *Issei* Woman's Suffering, Silence, and Suicide in John Okada's *No-No Boy*

Japan for the States. In a dreamlike consciousness, Ichiro's father discovers the reason for her insanity.

In reality, however, she is dying as shown by the "gurgling" which "continued for a while longer and ceased the moment he realized it was the bath water" (179). As the bath tub overflows, "his mouth was filled to overflowing" whisky (179). The overflowing water symbolizes the expression of their suffering, silence, and suicide.

> She was half out of the tub and half in, her hair of dirty gray and white floating up to the surface of the water like a tangled mass of seaweed and obscuring her neck and face. On one side, the hair had pulled away and lodged against the overflow drain, damming up the outlet and causing the flooding, just as her mind, long shut off from reality, had sought and found its erratic release. (185)

The water which comes forth into the tub is blocked by Ichiro's mother. Her hair that is prematurely "dirty gray and white" is a metaphor of her life-long silenced struggle. The outlet which is obstructed by her hair represents the locked existence of her struggle. The overflow symbolizes her tears which have never appeared yet have been swallowed. Ichiro's mother's suicide delineates her termination to her silenced struggle.

In her Buddhist funeral, Ichiro's mother's short biography is recited by their match-maker.[17] A part of her untold story is conveyed, yet for Ichiro it is about "a stranger."

As he shouted, Ichiro listened and, it was as if he were hearing about a stranger as the man spoke of the girl baby born in the thirty-first year of the Meiji era to a peasant family, of her growing and playing and going to school and receiving honors for scholastic excellence and of her becoming a pretty young thing who forsook a teaching career to marry a bright, ambitious young man of the same village. And as the large man transported the young couple across the vast ocean to the fortune awaiting them in America. Ichiro no longer listened, for he was seeing the face of his dead mother jutting out of the casket, and he could not believe that she had ever been any of the things the man was saying about her. (193-94)

There is a difference between Ichiro's mother as a young woman and as the psychologically paralyzed "old woman" whom Ichiro's father recognizes in his half-conscious condition. However different it may be, it shows us the fact that she is not really "an old woman," but only forty seven years old, since she was born "in the thirty-first year of the Meiji," that is, in 1898. At nineteen, she is married in Japan and at forty-seven, she is dead as the mother of a twenty-five-year old and an eighteen-year-old in the States. In Japan, she received a higher education and had a teaching career.[18] Because of her marriage and her move to the States, she was engaged in lower-class labor and accepted the lower status and worse living conditions.[19] As Ichiro observes, his mother in her working has "a power in the wiry, brown arms, a hard, blind, unreckoning force which coursed through veins of

Chapter 2 : An *Issei* Woman's Suffering, Silence, and Suicide in John Okada's *No-No Boy*

tough bamboo" (20). As a mother of two sons, she "had tried harder than most mothers to be a good mother" (104). Ichiro remembers how hard she attempted to educate both sons as Japanese, and finally how she broke his record player as an obstacle to his studies.

What Ichiro's mother left undone is accomplished by Ichiro's father. The real mourning for her is to send four packages to Japan and remodel the grocery store by what she "was saving for Japan."

> Ichiro watched his father, detecting an insuppressible air of enthusiasm and bubbling glee as he scratched in the names and addresses in both English and Japanese in several places on each package. There were four in all. The packages were the symbol of his freedom in a way. He no longer had just to think about sending them. It was his will to send them and nothing was any longer to prevent his so doing. He had no visions about Japan or about a victory that had never existed. While he might have been a weakling in the shadow of his wife, he was a reasonable man. He knew how things were and he was elated to be able finally to exercise his reasonable ways. Above all, he was a man of natural feelings and that, he felt, had always been the trouble with his wife. She tried to live her life and theirs according to manufactured feelings. It was not to be so. (212)

Ichiro's father surrenders himself to accepting reality; lower-class labor, camp life, Japan's defeat, difficulty in the postwar resettlement, and his wife's insanity and suicide. His "reasonable ways" and "natural feelings," however, could not save his wife. The packages alluded to as a symbol of his freedom are stored with his wife's as well as his own hardships. This freedom functions as his physical release from his insane wife, but it also signals his absolute loneliness. By packing, Ichiro's father undertakes to be forgiven. Ichiro's mother's life-long silence is also packed, tied, and sent back to Japan.

Ichiro, on the other hand, admits that he neglected having any direct communication with his mother and understanding her inner struggle while she was alive.

> Tragic, he said silently, so tragic to have struggled so against such insurmountable obstacles. For her, of course, the obstacles hadn't existed and it was like denying the existence of American. If only she had tried to understand, had attempted to reason out the futility of her ways. Surely she must have had an inkling during the years. He couldn't be sure and, much as he wished to know where and how the whole business had gone wrong, he could not, for he had never been close enough to his own mother. (205)

Ichiro realizes that he has taken a hint of the way of her recovery. He also assumes that she could be confronted with the war between Japan and the States while she was in the concentration camp. Though making an excuse, Ichiro admits that he was unable to lead his mother to the right

Chapter 2 : An *Issei* Woman's Suffering, Silence, and Suicide in John Okada's *No-No Boy*

direction.

To reread and reinterpret *No-No Boy*, which was published in 1975, demonstrates the margin of a forgotten part of Japanese Americans, that is, an *issei* woman's story of her own.[20] Ichiro's revival and his path to the future is accomplished by acknowledging this margin and attempting to evaluate the forgotten story.[21]

Notes

This paper was originally published in *Chu-Shikoku Studies in American Literature* 33 (1997): 43-60. After this publication of my paper, there appeared such excellent critical works by Apollo Amoko, Bryn Gribben, Daniel Y. Kim, Stan Yogi (1996), and Floyd Cheung and Bill Peterson (2006).

1. Okada himself had a desire to describe the *issei* in his fiction as he wrote in his letter to Charles Tuttle which published the first edition of *No-No Boy*: "I am now at work on a second [novel] which will have for its protagonist an immigrant Issei rather than a Nisei. When completed, I hope that it will to some degree faithfully describe the experiences of the immigrant Japanese in the United States. This is a story which has never been told in fiction and only in fiction can the hopes and fears and joys and sorrows of people be adequately recorded. I feel an urgency to write of the Japanese in the United States for the Issei are rapidly vanishing and I should regret if their chapter in American history should die with them" (Frank Chin, Afterward 256-57). The first draft of this second novel was almost completed in 1956, but it was burned by his wife, Dorothy Okada after his death in 1970 because *No-No Boy* was

rejected by the public, even by Japanese Americans (Chin, Afterward 257). Though it is considered a novel on the *nisei*, *No-No Boy* connotes Okada's strong intention to trace back to the *issei* Japanese immigrants.

2. Lawson Fusao Inada with a male-centered perspective remarks that Ichiro's "family and closed society is closed to him, leaving him with confusion, shame and guilt" ("The Vision of America in John Okada's *No-No Boy*" 281); and in spite of his compassion to Ichiro, he insists that the "most important event in the novel, however, is the death of Kenji," a war hero without a leg who dies during his operation (283). Though more compassionate to Ichiro's mother, Stephen H. Sumida conceives of Ichiro as "an alien" and "intruder" whom "we," the readers, "sympathize" upon his returning home (227).

3. In functioning "dual identity" of Japanese and Americans as the core problem in *No-No Boy*, Ichiro's mother's insanity and suicide has never been examined fairly. Compared with the forerunners who never counted Ichiro's mother as a person, Sumida and Junqi Ling have discussed Ichiro's mother. Sumida indicates that "Ma is herself a complex allegory of reaction against and yet imitation of her oppressors: her own logic tells her that if she has no choice but to be considered a 'Jap,' then she will be a 'Jap,' a desperate stand" (224). Corresponding to Sumida's "allegory," Ling emphasizes that Ma is "a caricature of the stubborn, unassimiable 'Japanese' of racial stereotyping. Beneath her uncompromising facade, Ma is perhaps the most vulnerable character in the novel; deprived of the ability to communicate and isolated from social realities, she draws her limited life force from an illusion that is inherently suicidal" (365). Though in an entirely negative tone, Gayle F. Fujita Sato analyses "the possibility of developing Mrs. Yamada's characterization" (251). It is, however, significant to do a more compassionate and thoughtful approach to interpret Ichiro's mother's personality as an *issei* woman's as historian Malve von Hassell examines the images of "both power and powerlessness" (549) as those of *issei* women. A psychological perspective,

Chapter 2 : An *Issei* Woman's Suffering, Silence, and Suicide in John Okada's *No-No Boy*

as well, is deserving especially on the ground that "Asian American women face the double jeopardy of being targets of oppression on the basis of both their sex and their race" or "in a sexist society and in the traditional Asian American family structure, men have more freedom and, therefore, fewer sources of psychosocial stress" (Laura Uba 177),

4. According to Uba, one of the main reasons of higher suicide rates of foreign-born Chinese and Japanese Americans than those of American-born counterparts is the stress resulting from the process of acculturation (184) and between 40% and 50% of the clients "were affected by problems with parent-child relationships, acculturation, somatic complaints, and isolation" (185).

5. Stan Yogi remarks that the "divisions within the family are rooted in binary oppositions resulting from racial distinctions exacerbated by wartime hostilities" and categorizes Ichiro's mother as a patriot and his father as alcoholic, "defeated and dominated by his stronger wife" ("The Collapse" 235).

6. As for the *issei* women, Hassell did remarkable research and study with a profound understanding of and insight into their lives and silenced selves. Hassell remarks that the *issei* women "generally did not talk about their fears, loneliness, doubts, sadness, or anger experienced in the years since leaving Japan, nor did they discuss their confusion and sense of shame as a result of the experience of being interned. Mrs Tasaki, for example, said there was 'not a single unpleasant experience'" (563).

7. Regarding a gap between the silenced *issei* and the *nisei*, Hassell concludes after pointing out the possible private secrets of the *issei* women, "To be open, to say what one feels, to tell of any bitter experiences one has had is to burden the other. This silence out of an attempt to shield and protect the other was an important element of *issei* and *nisei* relations. It is yet another factor that kept *issei* women from talking about their experiences. It prevented *nisei* children from asking direct questions, and it kept them from telling their parents about

many of their experiences" (563). Though Sumida observes that Ichiro as "an alien in a world gone mad in its social and moral reactions" never raises "his voice" in spite of his inner rages, he does not apply this interpretation to Ichiro's mother (233).

8. As for the concentration camps, Chin points out that "Very little of John's book is about the camps, but the camps are always in the atmosphere of his writings, just as they are in life ("Whites Can't Relate to John Okada's *No-No Boy*" 56). In *The Floating World*, a *sansei* writer Cynthia Kadohata employs the same strategy of avoiding describing the camp itself directly but rendering the role of the *issei* grandmother and the *nisei* parents as oppressed Japanese Americans who have been struggling during their lives and are still struggling after they are released from the camp.

9. Chan, et al., depict the postwar Seattle in *No-No Boy*: "Depression, despair, death, suicide, listless anger, and a general tone or low-key hysteria closed inside the gray of a constantly overcast and drizzling Seattle pervade the book (218). In his return, Ichiro "got off a bus at Second and Main in Seattle" and walked home on Jackson Street, whose area is called Nihonmachi or Japantown, "a large and lively ghetto in Seattle" where Japanese had become "an impressive economic force" before the war (David Takami 16-20). After the war, however, Nihonmachi in Seattle became "just a shell of its former self" especially for the *issei* people, though some of them "resumed their prewar professions in drugstores, apartment houses, groceries, hotels and dry cleaners, many were too broken in spirit and body to begin again" (Takami 50). As described in this novel, Nihonmachi is changed with the invasion of "growing black community" (Takami 51-52).

10. Though Elaine H. Kim makes an unfair judgement that most of Okada's characters "are not fully developed" (156), regretfully enough, she herself does not develop her theory even after she points out that Ichiro's mother — as well as Mrs. Ashida — work too hard and save "pennies" for her dream of returning to Japan (149).

Chapter 2 : An *Issei* Woman's Suffering, Silence, and Suicide in John Okada's *No-No Boy*

11. Yogi interprets that Ichiro's mother "celebrates" his home-coming "by using the very fact of his survival to hurt the Kumasakas" and its celebration "becomes a vehicle for Mrs. Yamada's cruelty" ("The Collapse" 238).
12. Yogi analyzes that actions "contradict convictions as cracks appear in the armor of patriotism that Mrs. Yamada and the Ashidas use to protect themselves from the painful truth or Japan's defeat and their own shattered identities as Japanese" ("The Collapse" 237).
13. In one of the two scenes which possess "the possibility of developing Mrs. Yamada's characterization," her reading a letter from her sister "divulges a secret in a desperate attempt to penetrate Mrs. Ymada's silence" (Sato 251).
14. Dorothy Ritsuko McDonald compares Ichiro's mother's "strength" and father's "weakness": "Her rock-hard, unloving, destructive dominance is intensified by the weakness of Ichiro's father who fearfully accedes to his wife's madness, takes to drink to escape its reality, and in a very untypical Japanese fashion, assumes the feminine role in the family" (21). Regarding the *issei* father's "weakness," Shirley Geok-lin Lim quotes from *Farewell to Manzanar* (1974) by Jenny Wakatsuki Houston and James Houston and explains that the concentration camp experience diminishes the patriarchal power within the Japanese American family and attributes to "the gradual emasculation of the powerful Papa figure" (580).
15. As for "escape," McDonald makes a positive conclusion that Ichiro's first escape from his mother by going to Portland is celebrated by his understanding of "her unhappiness" and his second escape from her funeral provide him with "love" and "peace" in mind (25).
16. Sato alludes to a negative "liquid imagery associated with" Ichiro's mother and all of "a near drowning laundry hung out in the rain," "evaporated milk," "excess alcohol," and "suicide by drowning" "play a crucial part in portraying her as insufficient mother dissociated from 'life-growing water'" (251)

17. A conflict between Ichiro's mother and Ichiro is considered that between Buddhism and Christianity in respect of their different attitude toward life and fate: "the Buddhist learns to accept fate (akirameru) with regards to earthly life, the Christian aggressively tries to make over destiny. Whereas the Buddhist tends to seek out the 'middle path,' the Christian tries to seek out an extreme. The Buddhist attempts to adjust to world, or tends to accept it as it is, while the Christian struggles to make over world. These distinctions serve to raise some very interesting problems when we inquire into the religious institutions of the Japanese in Seattle" (S. Frank Miyamoto 45).
18. In the *nisei* daughters' oral descriptions of their *issei* mother, Hassell uses the ones which ilustrate a gap between a teacher in Japan and a mere housewife and mother in the States.

> "Until then (1943) she had really had a soft life in town. . . . She was just an ordinary housewife and mother; all she did was to work at home. That is how we knew her when we were growing up. We never thought of what she was like when she was young or as a school teacher, or as a person with other interests."

> "My mother would be cooking all day for them. These would always be only my father's friends. I don't think they were friends, they were business associates. My mother came from a well-educated background. She was a schoolteacher in Japan. But she was one of the most hardworking women I have ever seen. I did so little work around the house, it was terrible. Whenever I came home she would by scrubbing the floor and doing all the housework. Every day my mother was on her hands and knees cleaning house. She did all the garden work, planted tomatoes and string beans and so on, even mowed the lawn. We took so much for granted. "Oh, Mom will do this, Mom will do that." (558)

Chapter 2 : An *Issei* Woman's Suffering, Silence, and Suicide in John Okada's *No-No Boy*

19. Hassell summarizes the *issei* woman's position where the "proper place of women was at home with their families; the only work approved of was that in the fields alongside their husbands, in the family business, and in all other work defined as supplementing the family income" (557). The chances and places for jobs are quite limited and even restricted; if there were chances, they could not take them. Even though most of *issei* women are better educated than their husbands, they have to follow their husbands' social and economic status rather than seeking for better opportunities. Teaching is, in such a condition, never allowed.

20. Chin, et all., criticize Roger Daniels for his comment on Inada's Introduction of *No-No Boy* as the 'ethnic ego-tripping' ("Asian American Literary Traditions: Real vs. Fake" 238). Inada, however, makes a significant comment on Okada's fate of being "'ahead of his time'" and being dead too young (Introduction v). Even with a male-centered perspective, especially Chan, Chin, and Inada influence such a woman writer as Jessica Hagedorn who "discovered John Okada's *No-No Boy* along with other neglected Asian-American writers" and expressed her sense of appreciation of *Aiiieeeee !* (xxv). In spite that Chin, et al, reevaluate *No-No Boy* in respect that it is "worth reading as a fairly accurate representation of the emotional and psychological climate of Japanese Americans at a certain period in history," they focus entirely on Ichiro as a hero ("An Introduction to Chinese- and Japanese-American Literature" 20). However, like most of Asian American women critics and writers, Kin-Kok Cheung accuses Chin and the other editors of *Aiiieeeee!* of their attempt "to advocate a 'masculine'language" and "valorize such novels as Louis Chu's *Eat a Bowl of Tea* and John Okada's *No-No Boy* (8-9), yet regretfully she herself did not attempt to deconstruct its valorization. Sau-Ling Cynthia Wong, also, does not make an endeavor to restore *No-No Boy*'s reputation by interpreting in a feminist perspective.

21. Inada concludes that "*No-No Boy* is a testament to the strength of a people, not a tribute to oppression" with an extreme male-centered

judgement on Ichiro as a hero, "a loving person" and "a positive person saying yes to life" ("Of Place and Displacement: The Range of Japanese American Literature" 264).

Works Cited

Amoko, Apollo O. "Resilent ImagiNations: *No-No Boy*, *Obasan*, and the Limits of Minority Discourse." *Mosaic* 33.3 (Sep. 2000): 35-55.

Baker, Houston A. Jr., ed. *Three American Literatures: Essays in Chicano, Native American, and Asian American Literature for Teachers of American Literature*. New York: MLA, 1982.

Chan, Jeffery Paul, Frank Chin, Lawson Fusao Inada, and Shawn H. Wong. "An Introduction to Chinese-American and Japanese-American Literatures." Baker 197-228.

Cheung, Floyd, and Bill E. Peterson. "Psychology and Asian American Literature: Application of the Life-Story Model of Identity to *No-No Boy*." *The New Centennial Review* 6.2 (Fall 2006): 191-214.

Cheung. King-Kok. *Articulate Silences: Hisaye Yamamoto, Maxine Hong Kingston, Joy Kogawa*. Ithaka: Cornell UP, 1993.

Chin, Frank. Afterward. *No-No Boy*. By John Okada. Seattle: U of Washington P, 1981. 253-60.

——. "Whites Can't Relate to John Okada's *No-No Boy*." *Pacific Citizen* 23-30 Dec. 1977: 55-56.

Chin Frank, Jeffery Chan, Lawson Inada, and Shawn Wong. "Asian American Literary Traditions: Real vs. Fake." *Transforming the Curriculum Ethnic Studies and Women's Studies*. Ed. Johnnella E. Butler and John C. Walter. Albany: State U of New York P, 1991. 227-42.

Chin, Frank, et al., eds. "An Introduction to Chinese and Japanese American Literature." *Aiiieeeee! An Anthology of Asian-American Writers*. 1974. New York: Mentor, 1991. 3-38.

Gribben, Bryn. "The Mother that Won't Reflect Back: Situating

Chapter 2 : An *Issei* Woman's Suffering, Silence, and Suicide in John Okada's *No-No Boy*

    Psychoanalysis and the Japanese Mother in *No-No Boy*." *MELUS* 28.2 (Summer 2003): 31-46.

Hagedorn, Jessica. Introduction. *Charlie Chan Is Dead: An Anthology of Contemporary Asian American Fiction*. Ed. Jessica Hagedorn. New York: Penguin, 1993. xxi-xxx.

Hassell, Malve von. "Issei Women: Silences and Fields of Power." *Feminist Studies* 19.3 (Fall 1993): 549-69.

Inada, Lawson Fusao. Introduction. *No-No Boy*. By John Okada. Seattle: U of Washington P, 1981. iii-vi.

——. "Of Place and Displacement: The Range of Japanese American literature." Baker 254-65.

——. "The Vision of America in John Okada's *No-No Boy*." *Ethnic Literatures since 1776: The Many Voices of America*. Vol. 9 of *Comparative Literature Symposium, Texas Tech Univ., 27-31 Jan. 1976*. 2 pts. Lubbock: Texas Tech P, 1978. 275-87.

Kim, Daniel Y. "Once More, with Feeling: Cold War Masculinity and the Sentiment of Patriotism In John Okada's *No-No Boy*." *Criticism* 47.1 (Winter 2005): 65-83.

Kim, Elaine H. *Asian American Literature: An Introduction to the Writings and Their Social Context*. Philadelphia: Temple UP, 1982.

Lim, Shirley Geok-lin. "Feminist and Ethnic Literary Theories in Asian American Literature." *Feminist Studies* 19.3 (Fall 1993): 571-95.

Ling, Jinqi. "Race, Power, and Cultural Politics in John Okada's *No-No Boy*." *American Literature* 67.2 (June 1995): 359-81.

McDonald, Dorothy Ritsuko. "After Imprisonment: Ichiro's Search for Redemption in *No-No Boy*." *MELUS* 6.3 (1979): 19-26.

Miyamoto, S. Frank. 1981. *Social Solidarity among the Japanese in Seattle*. Seattle: U of Washington P, 1984.

Miyao, Susumu. "Koritsu." *'Zaigai' Nihonjin*. Ed. Kazuko Yanagihara. Tokyo: Shobunsha, 1994. 131-34.

Okada, John. *No-No Boy*. 1957. Seattle: U of Washington P, 1981.

Sato, Gayle F. Fujita. "Momotaro's Exile: John Okada's *No-No Boy*."

Reading the Literatures of Asian America. Ed. Shirley Geok-lin Lim and Amy Ling. Philadelphia: Temple UP, 1992. 239-58.

Sumida, Stephen H. "Japanese American Moral Dilemmas in John Okada's *No-No Boy* and Milton Murayama's *All I Asking for Is My Body.*" *Frontiers of Asian American Studies: Writing, Research, and Commentary*. Ed. Gail M. Nomura, et al. Pullman: Washington State UP, 1989. 222-33.

Takami, David. *Executive Order 9066: 50 Years Before and 50 Years After: A History of Japanese Americans in Seattle*. Seattle: Wing Luke Asian Museum, 1992.

Uba, Laura. *Asian Americans: Personality Patterns, Identity, and Mental Health*. New York: Guilford, 1994.

Wong, Sau-Ling Cynthia. *Reading Asian American Literature: From Necessity to Extravagance*. Princeton: Princeton UP, 1993.

Yogi, Stan. "The Collapse of Difference: Dysfunctional and Inverted Celebrations in John Okada's *No-No Boy*." *RFEA* 53 (Aug. 1992): 133-44.

——. "'You had to be one or the other': Oppositions and Reconciliation in John Okada's *No No-Boy*." *MELUS* 21.2 (Summer 1996): 63-77.

Chapter 3

Prison, Psyche, and Poetry in Hisaye Yamamoto's Three Short Stories

— "Seventeen Syllables," "The Legend of Miss Sasagawara," and "The Eskimo Connection"—

In "The Eskimo Connection" (1983), Hisaye Yamamoto states that Emiko Toyama — the aging *nisei* narrator within the story — "had begun learning rather early to soft-pedal her critical instincts. As a young woman in camp, she had hung out sometimes with people who wrote and painted and she knew what vulnerable psyches resided in creative critters" (*Seventeen Syllables* 96). As a widow with several children and grandchildren, Emiko still writes and is asked for a "critique" by a twenty-three-year old Eskimo prisoner-patient-writer, Alden Ryan Walunga. Emiko's empathy with Alden originates from and even resonates her own internalized anguish over persecution in a concentration camp for Japanese Americans during the Second World War. In her 1986 article entitled "Yellow Leaves," Yamamoto, at 65, is confronted with aging; she so much resents that the *nisei* is "a vanishing generation" (36) that she needs to make a comment on the changed / changing lives and values from the prewar though the postwar ages. Yamamoto's three short stories — "Seventeen Syllables," "The Legend of Miss Sasagawara," and "The Eskimo Connection" — illustrate the imprisonment of human psyches which need to overcome imprisonment through creative activities in a sacred poetic space.

Those three stories are set in three different societies; prewar, wartime, and postwar societies, respectively. Emiko's maturity in the postwar society seems to have been nourished by and flourished from the other two young *nisei* women narrators' internal growth: Rosie Hayashi's prematurity before the Second World War in "Seventeen Syllables" (1949) and Kiku's awakening and growth during the war in camp in "The Legend of Miss Sasagawara" (1950). Rosie's internal rejection of her own *issei* mother's haiku and life in a prison-like household is reformed into Kiku's gradual understanding of another woman's mental breakdown. Her poetry sprung from her prison-camp experience, and is ultimately redeemed in Emiko's involvement with a young alcoholic murderer of another ethnic group who was transferred to a penitentiary four times. The actual / symbolic prison is the place which Yamamoto is opposed to,

Chapter 3 : Prison, Psyche, and Poetry in Hisaye Yamamoto's Three Short Stories

as she shows, according to Cheung, "remarkable compassion toward putative deviants and sinners, be they illicit lovers, gamblers, alcoholics, or prisoners" (Introduction, Ed. Cheung 8). The prison, however, represents the space where human psyches are oppressed, yet reborn, in creative activities as the remedy for their once-lost selves.

In "Seventeen Syllables," Tome Hayashi's true story was untold and unknown for seventeen years and it was even excluded from Ume Hanazono's traditional haiku poems for three months.[1] This story connotes the mother's past of having fallen in love with a man from the upper class, given "premature birth to" an illegitimate still-born baby, and consequently escaped from Japan.[2] This story is, however, revealed when a Hiroshige print — a token of the achievement of her creative activities — is ironically destroyed: "The story was told perfectly, with neither groping for words nor untoward passion. It was as though her mother had memorized it by heart, reciting it to herself so many times over that its nagging vileness had long since gone" ("SS," *SS* 19).[3] Tome's poetic space is established and its sharing with Rosie has been replaced by the disparity between Tome and Rosie at the very beginning of the story, whereas Rosie presents a question, "how to reach her mother, how to communicate the melancholy song?" ("SS," *SS* 8). As for Tome's haiku, Rosie "pretended to understand it thoroughly and appreciate it no end, partly because she hesitated to disillusion her mother about the quantity and quality of Japanese she had learned in all the years now that she had been going to Japanese school every Saturday" ("SS," *SS* 8). At the end, when Tome's haiku writing is finalized, Tome's true story, which was repeatedly recited inside her for seventeen years, is conveyed to Rosie, who seems to awaken to herself in her adolescence love experience.[4] Though not entirely accepting it, Rosie has no choice but to be confronted with her mother's psyche through her haiku.

From clues in the text we can work out that Tome is 35 and Rosie is 14. Rosie's prematurity corresponds to Tome's preadolescent ignorance and imprudence which caused the most tragic incident in her life. Rosie's parents' marriage is grounded upon the tragedy of an illegitimate baby's death.[5]

Rosie's initial view symbolizes the prewar Japanese immigrants' household whose psychological space was strictly ruled by Japanese patriarchy and whose land was virtually dominated by the Anglo-American laws.[6] In such a space, Rosie's father, an *issei* man, who was a farm laborer in a rented field, represents the Japanese former migrant workers who saved money and settled in rural California. He immigrated as "a young man of simple mind, it was said, but of kindly heart" ("SS," *SS* 19), and has never had any chance to improve himself except by growing tomatoes and hiring a Mexican migrant family during the harvest season. His spare time is used only to play flower cards and entertain "the non-literary members" ("SS," *SS* 9) of the family friends. Judging from these characteristics, Rosie's father is classified into a group of Japanese male immigrants whose endeavors are partly accomplished yet whose internal anguish is not

Chapter 3 : Prison, Psyche, and Poetry in Hisaye Yamamoto's Three Short Stories

resolved in their hard lives. Furthermore, Rosie's father's private space is entirely deprived and ignored.

On the other hand, Rosie's mother attempts to find more private space by writing haiku and exchanging the ideas of haiku with other family friends. Her creative activities ironically flourish during the tomato harvest season, the busiest period for farmers. Tome's private space is not only opposed to the farming job, but also to her household role; moreover, it conflicts with sharing space with her husband and daughter.[7]

> So Rosie and her father lived for awhile with two women, her mother and Ume Hanazono. Her mother (Tome Hayashi by name) kept house, cooked, washed, and along with her husband and the Carrascos, the Mexican family hired for the harvest, did her ample share of picking tomatoes out in the sweltering fields and boxing them in tidy strata in the cool packing shed. Ume Hanazono, who came to life after the dinner dishes were done, was an earnest, muttering stranger who often neglected speaking when spoken to and stayed busy at the parlor table as late as midnight scribbling with pencil on scratch paper or carefully copying characters on good paper with her fat, pale green Parker. ("SS," *SS* 9)

Tome' lack of her own room and time does not prevent her from writing haiku, but rather accelerates her coherency. By having her own pen name, as most critics agree, Tome dares to establish her new identity — the other self. Tome's new identity is inhabited "at the parlor table" at midnight, which neither Tome's husband nor Rosie can share with Tome. Tome's isolation, concentration, and appreciation is located in a physically-limited yet spiritually-enlarged space and time.

The names signify Tome's dual identity. Her real name, Tome Hayashi, implies her imprisonment in a male territory. In Japanese, the logograph "hayashi" means a forest, that is, a wild and uncultivated area surrounded by trees and bushes. Her parents chose the name "Tome" with a wish that she would be the last child in their poor family, because "tome" means closing and ending. Tome is different from "Tomi" which means fortune and property, as Mistri misinterprets Tomi as Tome. "Tome Hayashi" — her first name was given by her parents and her family name was given by her husband — connotes her fate as a woman. On the other hand, her pen name, Ume Hanazono, is an idealized self in a sacred space of the flower garden which men cannot invade. The word "ume" means plum flowers and "hanazono" means the flower garden. "Ume" has another meaning, "bearing," which is ironically opposed to "tome." These conflicting names imply the death of Tome's still-born baby. "Hanazono" is, moreover, not simply a flower garden, but the enclosed and meticulously-attended space for growing flowers. In summary, "hayashi" is an open space without any protection; on the contrary, "hanazono" is a closed space which is specially looked after and nourished. "Tome" symbolizes the barren ground; however, "ume" symbolizes

Chapter 3 : Prison, Psyche, and Poetry in Hisaye Yamamoto's Three Short Stories

fertility and fruitfulness. Its fertility is, however, different from the tomato harvest by which Tome and her husband make a living. Tome's creation of another self by having an idealized pen name elides her real life and her true self.

Tome's real life and true self is deeply rooted in a Japanese patriarchal society where her past secret is rejected, neglected, and completely buried.[8] Tome's psychology is also disguised and hidden under an invisible force which almost drives her to suicide, yet which ultimately leads her to the States. Tome's true "seventeen syllables" in her seventeen years are evaluated as a silent but repeatedly practiced story within her self. Cheung's analysis suggests that Tome's "creativity — poetry within 17 syllables is — also prematurely doomed" ("Double-Telling" 284). Tome's poetry writing is a disguise of her seventeen-year silence and her unresolved agony. During these seventeen years, in other words, internal family violence is concealed under the apparently well-settled and stable Japanese American family. This internal violence is exposed in Tome's words after it is affirmed by her husband's physical violence.

"Do you know why I married your father?" she said without turning.

"No," said Rosie. It was the most frightening question she had ever been called upon to answer. Don't tell me now, she wanted to say, tell me tomorrow, tell me next week, don't tell me today. But she knew she would be told now, that the telling would combine with the other violence of the hot afternoon

> to level her life, her world to the very ground. ("SS," *SS* 18)

Rosie's reaction to Tome's invention to tell her story is to "escape" and to want "to evade it" because Rosie intuitively senses "its darkness" (Yogi, "Rebels and Heroines" 145). Tome's story-telling, which brings another "violence" to Rosie, demonstrates Tome's self-redemption in her return from Ume Hanazono to her real name, Tome Hayashi. Rosie's future will be constructed by readers rather than being guided by Tome who "expects of her daughter" maturity (Yogi, "Legacies Revealed" 174).

As Tome's "seventeen syllables" are finally told in her words, the legend of Miss Sasagawara — which was created and illustrated in the gossip in the concentration camp in Arizona — is also finally recited in her own words. "Arguably a minor fault," according to Tajiri, "it does lessen the effectiveness of 'The Legend of Miss Sasagawara' where" Hisaye Yamamoto "provides no explanation for the World War II incarceration of Japanese Americans which is the key to the breakdown suffered by her title character" (256). This story was originally published in 1950 when there was still postwar hostility toward Japanese Americans. In addition, the "pain and trauma of the camp experience is not available to" many former evacuees "at a conscious level, and thus they are unaware of any effect it has on their current lives" (Mass 161). The legend is, moreover, what Yamamoto expects the reader to complete as Kageyama insists that the "story takes the reader there, back in history, into the camps, and he /

Chapter 3 : Prison, Psyche, and Poetry in Hisaye Yamamoto's Three Short Stories

she must piece together the fragments of images about the woman, to try to understand her condition" (32-33).

In "The Legend of Miss Sasagawara," a 39-year-old single woman who was a professional ballet dancer before the war is faced with a lack of space for her activities as well as a lack of privacy in her camp life. The distance in age and generation between Tome and Rosie corresponds to that between Miss Sasagawara and Kiku. Rosie, at fourteen before the war, is developed into Kiku in her late-teens in camp. Unlike Tome, however, Miss Sasagawara possessed her own creative and independent life before the war. Though Tome is a picture bride who immigrated to the States in order to get married to a farmer, Miss Sasagawara is neither an immigrant nor a picture bride but a well-educated and trained daughter of a Japanese minister who was transferred to the States for his missionary duty.

Miss Sasagawara is an outsider in the Japanese American society because her family is well-established and distinguished and she herself had an established professional life in white society. Her father, Reverend Sasagawara, is a Buddhist priest whose social status is higher than that of immigrants in general. Miss Sasagawara's pride, therefore, cannot allow her to mingle with other Japanese Americans and also to sacrifice her own personality and life-style for her father. Though Tome is usually calm and obedient, Miss Sasagawara is described as "temperamental" or "crazy" and called "Mad-woman" solely because she reveals her anger and irritation openly. In an interview, however, Yamamoto insists that she "didn't really consider her (Miss Sasagawara) insane," and Yamamoto rather "tried to say that if it weren't for being put in the camp, she (Miss Sasagawara) might have gone on" (Crow, "MELUS Interview" 81).[9] As Mass analyzes, the Japanese Americans, in general, "used psychological defense mechanisms such as repression, denial, rationalization, and identification with the aggressor to defend ourselves against the devastating reality of what was being done to us" (160). In ". . . I Still Carry It Around," Yamamoto herself indicates that the camp experience for the *nisei* was "a complex event whose ambiguities further muddled our identities" because the *nisei*, "in the years after the war, was preoccupied with survival" (70), yet the camp experience is at the same time "an episode in our collective life which wounded us more painfully than we realize" (69). Miss Sasagawara's existence in camp, therefore, reveals evidence of the severe torture and victimization caused by camp experience as well as the unseen structure of the layered and complicated Japanese American society. The Japanese American society was reconstructed and acknowledged owing to the war, and consequently retrieves a double-aloofness which causes Miss Sasagawara's nervous breakdown.

Miss Sasagawara's double aloofness is framed within such patriarchal institutions as the American laws, the wartime concentration camp, the Japanese American society, Buddhism, and the hospitals.[10] Kiku's imagination and keen sense is nourished in her college education outside

Chapter 3 : Prison, Psyche, and Poetry in Hisaye Yamamoto's Three Short Stories

the camp, but she does not entirely grasp Miss Sasagawara's psychology.

> Elsie puzzled aloud over the cause of Miss Sasagawara's derangement and I, who had so newly had some contact with the recorded explorations into the virgin territory of the human mind, sagely explained that Miss Sasagawara had no doubt looked upon Joe Yoshinaga as the image of either the lost lover or the lost son. But my words made me uneasy by their glibness, and I began to wonder seriously about Miss Sasagawara for the first time. ("LMS," *SS* 32)

Kiku's awakening occurs long after Miss Sasagawara was treated in the camp hospital, sent to a sanitarium in Phoenix, returned to the camp, and finally imprisoned in a state institution in California. Yamamoto's awakening by writing this story occurs in 1950, when she did not know that the woman, after whom Miss Sasagawara is modeled, actually had written poetry in camp, but Yamamoto invented it (Crow, "MELUS Interview" 80).

Miss Sasagawara's legend is filled in during the camp; whereas the Sasagawaras' legend is, however, already sketched before the war by Kiku's mother's generation.

> Well, if Miss Sasagawara was not one to speak to, she was certainly one to speak of, and she came up quite often as topic for the endless conversations which helped along the monotonous days. My mother said she had met the late

Mrs. Sasagawara once, many years before the war, and to hear her tell it, a sweeter, kindlier woman there never was. "I suppose," said my mother, "that I'll never meet anyone like her again; she was a lady in every sense of the word." Then she reminded me that I had seen the Rev. Sasagawara before. Didn't I remember him as one of the three bhikshus who had read the sutras at Grandfather's funeral? ("LMS," *SS* 22-23)

Both Mrs. Sasagawara and Rev. Sasagawara are different from the other *nikkei* (Japanese American) peers as Kiku's mother describes Mrs. Sasagawara as "a lady" and also mentions Rev. Sasagawara who Kiku did not usually see except at her grandfather's funeral.

The Sasagawaras themselves can be the target of observation in the *nikkei* community.[11] The war, moreover, changed their status because the leaders and authorized people in the *nikkei* communities such as representatives of the Japanese American Citizens Leagues, teachers of Japanese schools, priests and ministers of Japanese churches and Buddhist temples were considered dangerous, first arrested and evacuated, and finally interned in camps such as Tule Lake with a special watch. On the night of December 7, 1941, when Imperial Japan attacked Pearl Harbor, "the F.B.I. agents were busy arresting Japanese leaders all over the West Coast" and especially Buddhist priests, "were all taken into custody" (Suzuki 6). Both Rev. Sasagawara and Miss Sasagawara "had gotten permission to come to this Japanese evacuation camp in Arizona from one further north"

Chapter 3 : Prison, Psyche, and Poetry in Hisaye Yamamoto's Three Short Stories

after Mrs. Sasagawara had died there ("LMS," *SS* 20). It is possible to assume that Rev. Sasagawara already undertook a hard life in a prison, an assembly center, and some camps since the outbreak of the war. During Rev. Sasagawara's absence, both Mrs. Sasagawara and Miss Sasagawara had to manage everything by themselves. Mrs. Sasagawara's death in camp connotes the result of her enormous responsibilities and difficulties. When both Rev. Sasagawara and Miss Sasagawara are transferred to an Arizona camp — possibly Poston —, they are still mourning for Mrs. Sasagawara, which consequently makes both of them eccentric. The death in camp must be "a shattering experience to any family so hit" (Bailey 99) and a funeral in camp cannot be the same as outside the camp before the war.[12] The more public their life is, the more they are suspected even after such a family tragedy as their wife / mother's death, and the more privacy as well as dignity they lose. Tome's son's death is attributed to the core of her psychological agony and the tragedy behind her marriage. Mrs. Sasagawara's death manifests the source of psychological conflict which both Rev. Sasagawara and Miss Sasagawara share yet with which they never communicate.

In addition to the Sasagawaras' trapped destiny in the political context, Miss Sasagawara is a victim of sensationalism because of her unusual career as a ballet dancer. Because she is always seen, observed, and examined on a stage in her public life, she is more concerned about regaining privacy once she is interned. Her profession as well as her physical beauty make camp life less comfortable for her, so she becomes obsessed with a strong sense of isolation and loneliness. As Yamamoto remarks, the camp life deprives Miss Sasagawara of her "medium," that is, "the people she knew outside" the Japanese community and camp, "who were her friends and co-performers" (Crow, "MELUS Interview" 81). Her loneliness also results from the loss of her mother by her physical death and consequently that of her father by his spiritual death. In such a camp life, Miss Sasagawara is suffering from harassment by the same *nikkei* peers. The most serious harassment that she experienced is sexual harassment by male doctors in a camp hospital.[13]

> Miss Sasagawara came back to the hospital about a month later. Elsie was the one who rushed up to the desk where I was on day duty to whisper, "Miss Sasagawara just tried to escape from the hospital!"
> "Escape? What do you mean, escape?" I said.
> "Well, she came in last night, and they didn't know what was wrong with her, so they kept her for observation. And this morning, just now, she ran out of the ward in just a hospital nightgown and the orderlies chased after her and caught her and brought her back. Oh, she was just fighting them. But once they got her back to bed, she calmed down right away, and Miss Morris asked her what was the big idea, you know, and do you know what she said? She said she didn't want any more of those doctors pawing her. *Pawing* her, imagine!" ("LMS," *SS* 26)

Chapter 3 : Prison, Psyche, and Poetry in Hisaye Yamamoto's Three Short Stories

Miss Sasagawara's over-reaction to the doctors' "pawing" originates from her first visit to a hospital at night when she said she had "appendicitis" with symptoms such as "chills and a dull aching at the back of her head, as well as these excruciating flashes in her lower right abdomen" ("LMS," *SS* 24-25).[14] A young doctor, Dr. Moritomo, is on night duty so is called to take care of Miss Sasagawara:

> Dr. Moritomo (technically, the title was premature; evacuation had caught him with a few months to go on his degree), wearing a maroon bathrobe, shuffled in sleepily and asked her to come into the emergency room for an examination. A short while later, he guided her past my desk into the laboratory, saying he was going to take her blood count. ("LMS," *SS* 25)

Nobody knows what happens in such a closed space as the emergency room where a young intern in a bathrobe carries out some sort of "examination" in order to check some parts of Miss Sasagawara's body in addition to simply taking blood count. Though Miss Sasagawara does not express any reaction just after the examination but only going "over to the electric fountain for a drink of water" ("LMS," *SS* 25), she consistently and intensely refuses to take an ambulance home. George, a young ambulance driver, repeats that Miss Sasagawara "wouldn't even listen to" him even though it is Dr. Moritomo's "orders" ("LMS," *SS* 25). Her total refusal to be alone with a man again in such a closed space as a car represents her silent yet internally furious attitude toward her doctor's physical examination.

One month later, her manic depressive illness is observed in the middle of all the hospital staff's "concentrated gaze."

> I knew this by her smile, for as she continued to look at that same piece of the floor, she continued, unexpectedly, to seem wryly amused with the entire proceedings. I peered at her wonderingly through the triangular peephole created by someone's hand on hip, while Dr. Kawamoto, Miss Morris, and Miss Bowman tried to persuade her to lie down and relax. She was as smilingly immune to tactful suggestions as she was to tactless gawking.
>
> There was no future to watching such a war of nerves as this. ("LMS," *SS* 26-27)

Miss Sasagawara's blankness and ignorance is her strategy to avoid the hospital staff who treat her in a vulgar manner and regard her as more or less a sex object by covering her "only by a brief hospital apron" ("LMS," *SS* 26).

One more piece of evidence that Miss Sasagawara might receive sexual harassment is rooted in a conversation between two ambulance drivers, George and Bobo Kunitomi. The contents of their conversation are not explicitly revealed, yet their "murmuring" and George's shrugging, nodding, and "little ruddier" expression connote some sexual secret which they own as young men. Bobo might have suggested to George that he should go to "a good place" outside camp in Phoenix, that is, a place for men to solve their sexual

Chapter 3 : Prison, Psyche, and Poetry in Hisaye Yamamoto's Three Short Stories

desire. This is at the moment when George is about to take Miss Sasagawara to a Phoenix hospital outside camp. Miss Sasagawara is a victim of the young male hospital staff's concern and interest since she is a beautiful and sexy single woman.

Miss Sasagawara's transformation after returning from a sanitarium in Phoenix several months later is, however, not ultimate but still leaves a slight symptom of her sexual harassment experience. Kiku's ten-year-old sister, Michi, shows feelings of fear to Miss Sasagawara in a shower room; "She's scary. Us kids were in there and she came in and we finished, so we got out, and she said, 'Don't be afraid of me. won't hurt you.' Gee, we weren't even afraid of her, but when she aid that, gee!" ("LMS," *SS* 28). Miss Sasagawara's words sound unsual for those female children. Those words, 'Don't be afraid of me. won't hurt you,'' can be manipulated by men who try to seduce or sexually abuse women or children. Those words must have been whisperedly male doctors to Miss Sasagawara who was under medical treatment. Her unusual gaze at the young boys, Jeo and Frank Yoshinagas, and her right invasion into Joe's room symbolize her desire for an innocent young boy.[15] Miss Sasagawara's internal violence is finally exploded when she is accused by Mrs. Sakaki of gazing at the Yoshinaga boys "in the manner of a shy child confronted with a marvel" ("LMS," *SS* 31). This internal violence surges up in the form of physical violence, bangng on the wooden walls with some heavy thing, using all her strength for five minutes. Miss Sasagawara's changed manners and behaviors, which were once trained and formulated carefully in a sanitarium, cannot withhold but only cover her inner conflict.

Kiku's unsatisfactory interpretation of Miss Sasagawara's "human mind" is revised with new evidence from her poem. When Kiku accidentally discovers Miss Sasagawara's poem, Kiku encounters Miss Sasagawara's poetic space where she sacrificed herself under the enormous pressure and stress of her father's personality and sacred self.

> Was it not likely that the saint, blissfully bent on cleansing from his already radiant soul the last imperceptible blemishes (for, being perfect, would he not humbly suspect his own flawlessness?) would be deaf and blind to the human passions rising, subsiding, and again rising, perhaps in anguished silence, within the selfsame room? The poet could not speak for others, of course; she could only speak for herself. But she would describe this man's devotion as a sort of madness, the monstrous sort which, pure of itself, might possibly bring troublous, scented scenes to recur in the other's sleep. ("LMS," *SS* 33)

There is a conflict between Rev. Sasagawara and Miss Sasagawara in a household after Mrs. Sasagawara's death in camp. In such a limited and closed space, they cannot avoid being confronted with a series of gaps: one is obsessed with "moral purity and universal wisdom" ("LMS," *SS* 32) and "that serene, eight-fold path of highest understanding,

Chapter 3 : Prison, Psyche, and Poetry in Hisaye Yamamoto's Three Short Stories

highest mindedness, highest speech, highest action, highest livelihood, highest recollectedness, highest endeavor, and highest meditation" ("LMS," *SS* 33); and the other with "sensitive," "admiring," and "human passions rising, subsiding, and again rising, perhaps in anguished silence, within the selfsame room" ("LMS," *SS* 33). The gap is widened in "sheer imprisonment" where Rev. Sasagawara lost his wife and a good living as a priest owing to the war and obtained freedom for the first time in his life. Kiku remembers her grandfather's funeral at the well-established Buddhist temple in Los Angeles and guesses that one of the three men in black robes must have been Rev. Sasagawara. The Los Angeles Hompa Hongwanji Buddhist Temple was, according to Niiya, a major branch of the North American Buddhist Mission and later, the Buddhist Churches of America which was newly founded at Topaz in 1944 with the new *nisei* ministers (114-15). It is at such a turning point of leadership of Buddhist temples when Rev. Sasagawara is interned. When a Buddhist temple was later established along with an initially founded Christian services at Poston camp, Rev. Sasagawara must have been replaced by young English-speaking *nisei* priests. Though not actually "mad," Miss Sasagawara illustrates Rev. Sasagawara's religiously pure and "intense idealism as madness" as McDonald and Newman refer to it (137). Like her daughter, Rev. Sasagawara consequently suffers from a divided self in a divided life.

Miss Sasagawara also experiences losing her mother and her competitive life as a professional ballet dancer. In her case, however, she loses freedom and self-esteem entirely for the first time in her life. Moreover, Miss Sasagawara has no choice but to take care of the divided self of her father, who becomes her dependent, a burden for her, and ultimately an aging man who cannot save her from harassment which she receives outside the household. Crow makes an unfair judgement on Miss Sasagawara whose "identity has remained somehow unfocussed, as her ambiguous age and mother / lover roles indicate (as the narrator surmised): finally her father's madness has become her own, and she is bound forever in anguished silence" ("The Issei Father in the Fiction of Hisaye Yamamoto" 37). Miss Sasagawara's identity is too clear to be solely repressed in the unusual camp life. The *nisei* narrator, Kiku, as well as Rosie and Yoneko, cannot entirely understand Miss Sasagawara's manic depressive illness because they have not faced "the same realities that confront Mari Sasagawara" (Kim 115) and their understanding will not come at the end of the story, but long after the war is over and the camp is closed. The *nisei* narrator is expected to become aware of *nisei*'s own suppressed life which has been buried inside herself till the postwar period.

In "The Eskimo Connection," Yamamoto — as an aging *nisei* who is keenly aware of her oppressed wartime life — plunges into a more multicultural and mutiracial perspective, or what Cheung names "crosscultural bonding" (Introduction, Yamamoto xiv). Yamamoto, as Cheung insists in interpreting "A Fire in Fontaria," used to be involved in the other ethnic

Chapter 3 : Prison, Psyche, and Poetry in Hisaye Yamamoto's Three Short Stories

group and even attempted to examine "inter-group relationships" since they "remain invisible, and the big picture is missing" ("The Dream in Flames" 122). Yamamoto's experience as a reporter on the black newspaper, *Los Angeles Tribune*, and her interracial marriage to a Philipino American made her realize the importance and necessity to "foster a sense of accountability across racial lines" (Cheung, "The Dream in Flames" 128). Yamamoto remarks that the reason why she was hired by the *Tribune* is that her "perceptive employers, heir to all the ambiguities of the Negro intellectual in a white society, had sensed in me kinship" ("Writing" 64). Though Yamamoto modestly confesses that she could not play the role for which the *Tribune* "had in mind": "a collaboration between the returning Japanese and the African American community" in the postwar Little Tokyo, she definitely insists that her "education" on racial discrimination and prejudice "was furthered" with her own awareness of the camp experience while she was working for the *Tribune* (Cheung, "Interview" 78). In Yamamoto's narration, there is compassion rather than conflict between different races with a wish that racism disappear.[16]

In "The Eskimo Connection," the aging *nisei* writer plays an important role in transcending the racial boundaries and in trying to understand the true story of life behind fictional poems and stories. The Eskimo-Emiko connection is buried in that between the Yupik (or Yup'ik) and the Japanese. Like the "Indians," Eskimo is what the white invaders named the native people of Greenland, Canada, and Alaska; whereas the Bering Sea Eskimo call themselves "Yupik" which means "true human beings." More interestingly, they name the Japanese "yugngalnguq" which means those who are similar to the Yupik (Miyaoka 56). Beyond the physical similarities between the Yupik and the Japanese, Yamamoto is aware of her role in connecting her own experience with a Yupik man's life.

As well as the above Eskimo-Emiko connection and their creative activities, there is another connection of prison between them. Emiko connotes her strong sense of objection to imprisonment.

> Besides, Emiko was not sure that prisons were the answer to crime. It was a known fact, was it not, that prisons, as most of them were now constituted, rarely rehabilitated? Not only was she against capital punishment, she was also against prisons, even though, pinned down in an argument, she admitted that there must be some system to temporarily segregate those who persisted in preying on other. She agreed with the wise man who had called for a society 'in which it is easier to be good.' ("EC," *SS* 99)

Emiko's objection to prisons stems from her own experience of being interned in the wartime camp. Emiko intuitively senses "something like a cold hand touch her" when she receives the polite yet strongly-rejected official letter from the prison chaplain's office ("EC," *SS* 98). Beyond her personal experience and intuitive distaste, however, Emiko

Chapter 3 : Prison, Psyche, and Poetry in Hisaye Yamamoto's Three Short Stories

disagrees with the idea of a penitentiary system and with the idea of a death penalty. It was in 1989 when the United Nation General Meeting adopted "Second Optional Protocol To The International Covenant On Civil and Political Rights Aiming At The Abolition Of The Death Penalty" which must contribute to the "enhancement of human dignity" and the "progressive development" of human rights (Dandou 219-20). In the States, the death penalty had been revived in thirty six states after the Furman v. Georgia ruling in 1972 and the Gregg v. Georgia ruling in 1976 (*When The State Kills* . . . 129). Yamamoto set this story at the time when the death penalty was revived. Though Alaska abolished the death penalty, Washington still carries it out even now. Alden might have been sentenced to death because he committed "felony murder," the sentence for which is death (*When the State Kills* . . . 130).

Without knowing the reason for Alden's incarceration, Emiko simply "decided that he was in prison for forgery" ("EC," *SS* 99) until she happens to discover in his short story entitled "The Coffin of 1974" that he murdered his uncle and a female relative after he raped her. Alden is "a prisoner-patient at a federal penitentiary in the midwest" ("EC," *SS* 96) in 1975, transferred to McNeil Island Penitentiary "via Terminal Island and Lompoc" ("EC," *SS* 100) in Washington in Feb, 1976, moves to the Seattle City Jail in September, and is finally transferred to Alaska. McNeil Island Penitentiary is an isolated island prison of 4,400 acres for 250 men (*McNeil Pilot* 3). Yamamoto describes its strict discipline consisting of exclusive and complicated procedures to accept female visitors who "were 'requested to be careful of the attire they wear to the institution,' with 'skin-tight leotards and stretch pants, short miniskirts and lowcut dresses considered improper in the prison setting'" ("EC," *SS* 101).[17] Because Alden complains about the danger of "a homosexual rape" at McNeil, however, he is transferred to Seattle City Jail. In planning to reestablish coed prisons in the States, homosexual violence became a controversial issue in sex-separated prisons (Fujimoto 143-44). Then, Emiko's card is returned from an Alaska prison, stamped "Unclaimed." Because the magazine is not returned, Emiko "liked to think that Alden still kept it somewhere among his prison mementos even though paroled" ("EC," *SS* 104). It is interesting to notice that the Alaska Board of Parole had a special parole program with the McNeil hearing, 6 to 8 weeks after which the eligible inmate was notified of the decision (*McNeil Pilot* 17). It is not clearly described what happens to Alden in Alaska, but Emiko's positive way of thinking and imagination closes this story.

> Or, if not paroled, there would be frequent visits there in the Alaska prison from his mother, his sisters and brothers, from his beloved Ophelia, and Lord knows whom else. There would be piles of studying to do, lots of poems, stories and essays to write.
>
> Either way, Emiko — holding fast to the Lord Jesus Christ and refusing to consider any other alternatives — imagined

Chapter 3 : Prison, Psyche, and Poetry in Hisaye Yamamoto's Three Short Stories

he was probably much too busy back there on his home ground to continue to be the pen pal of some old woman way down there in California. ("EC," *SS* 104)

Eligible for parole, the story presents Alden as a model prisoner in the rehabilitation and possibly probation programs. Alden is affected by the Christian Program, Alcoholic Seminars — involving both Alcoholics Anonymous and "an American Indian Alcoholic Seminar and Transactional Analysis seminar given by the Pacific Institute" ("EC," *SS* 100). Thus, he is affected by psychotherapy. In particular, the McNeil chapter of Alcoholics Anonymous "provides an extremely useful form of group therapy, as do several nondemoninational religious discussion groups and a course in 'Effective Speaking and Public Relations' offered to inmates" (The Federal Bureau of Prisons, *United States Penitentiary* 21). Regarding minority groups, McNeil carried out three programs of "Black Culture, Indian Culture, Mexican Culture" in an attempt to enhance knowledge of their ethnic heritages, but there is no Eskimo Culture program (*McNeil Pilot* 18). In the process of his rehabilitation programs, Alden's intellectual pursuit reaches a high point.

First, Alden's educational background should be taken into consideration: he had studied "two semesters at the University of Alaska" ("EC," SS 97) and joined the Air Force. In prison, he keeps reading Robert Penn Warren, Victor Hugo, Fyodor Dostoevsky, N. Scott Momaday, Yukio Mishima, as well as the Bible and is expecting to take classes at Tacoma Community College in addition to participating in "a course in Greek New Testament Grammar from the Moody Bible Institute" ("EC," *SS* 102). According to *McNeil Pilot*, McNeil had the Study Release program for those who were determined by the Classification Committee (33), and the Education Department offered "courses ranging from remedial subjects all the way to the awarding of an Associates of Arts Degree from the Tacoma Community College" (16-17) which was established in the landmark year 1972 (*McNeil Pilot* 98).[18] Alden's academic pursuit was considered to be the highest among the inmates of McNeil.

Second, Alden is blessed with the freedom of letter writing, which was another second, prison life development at McNeil in 1972 with "the advent of open mailing (the privilege of writing to whomever a prisoner wants without prior approval or censorship)" (*McNeil Pilot* 98). Thanks to this new policy, Alden can write to Emiko freely. In creative activities, Alden publishes his essay in a prison weekly, his poem in "a New York Magazine called *A. D.*," and two additional works in a weekly inmate paper named *Newsbuoy* and "a quarterly for us American Indians" ("EC," *SS* 100) named *Smoke Talk*. As well as a McNeil's bimonthly magazine, *Island Lantern*, *Newsbuoy* consisted of contributions from and was printed by the inmates and McNeil personnel under the support of the Educational Department, and published on Fridays (*McNeil Pilot* 30). McNeil encouraged the inmates "to engage in creative activities" though they had to obtain special permission from the Education Department (*McNeil Pilot* 30). Alden takes advantage of these writing activities and enlarges his inward space in such a restricted environment.

Yet, Alden's language is English, which the Yupik had been practically forced to use since 1867 when Alaska became an American state with a strict assimilation and monolingual education program in English. In 1970, however, a bilingual program began in Alaska when President Lyndon Johnson and Congress founded the bilingual education system in 1968 (Miyaoka 199-206). In spite of this fact, English has been a very powerful and overwhelming influence with respect to the Yupik. Alden — at twenty three in 1975 — went to elementary and middle school before 1970 while there was a coherent English program which strictly prohibited the Yupik children from using their native tongue in the classroom. Many Yupik who went to school before 1970 believed that the experience was insulting (Miyaoka 200). Alden was admitted to the University of Alaska when the bilingual program was encouraged and there was a revival of Yupik culture. Alden is crushed between these two languages just as Emiko as a *nisei* is divided between English and Japanese. Emiko's "critique" targets Alden's language, which needs "'corrections, suggestions, and remarks'" ("EC," *SS* 103) which do not destroy his creative ambition to express their Yupik identity in English, because Emiko is convinced that "most egos were covered with the thinnest of eggshells" ("EC," *SS* 97).

Alden is now definitely conscious of his identity

search and awakening as a Yupik, as shown in the fact that he recommends to Emiko two books on Eskimo, Peter Freuchen's *Book of the Eskimo* and a Stanford University study of the Alaskan native. His strong consciousness of his identity is articulated in his poetic space. The first essay which he sends to Emiko, there is "a passionate cry against the despoiling of his native land which somehow turned into a sermon repeating the Biblical prophecy that such an evil was only part of the wholesale corruption to precede the return of Christ" ("EC," *SS* 96). Judging from these factors, Alden is also one of the Eskimos who underwent acculturation, such as a ban on their traditional religion and its ceremony by the Christian missionaries, and settlement by the establishment of fur exchange places and public schools, and the crisis of the traditional life styles by epidemics and alcohol brought from outside their community (Miyaoka 6). It is in his last story entitled "The Coffin of 1974" that he embraces his intense persistence in his native land as a space which ironically encloses both wild nature and cruel human nature which has been suppressed and deprived by the white people.

 In such an intellectual and moral pursuit, Alden suffers from "spiritual crisis involving 'deception,' implying a self-delusion" ("EC," *SS* 99). Emiko insists that he should write a stronger and clearer "voice" which "was needed to speak up on behalf of the Eskimo" ("EC," *SS* 97). Yet, the same kind of "crisis" is described in his first letter from McNeil.

Chapter 3 : Prison, Psyche, and Poetry in Hisaye Yamamoto's Three Short Stories

> "It is beauty that I am after in my writing. There is lots of beauty in McNeil. Today I was a little depressed as I had allowed my mind to stray away from Jesus Christ and that attitude chain-reacted to a sin that reinforced the negative feelings. After supper I isolate myself in the sloping green lawn and layed down, closed eyes. ("EC," *SS* 100)

Alden's "crisis" results from the uncertainty of his Christian faith. Alden's redemption should be, however, concluded with the recognition that God forgives him. A similar conclusion is reached at the end of Alden's bloody confessional story, "The Coffin of 1974," which is "disturbing" and "afflicted with the same dichotomous anguish" as his first essay ("EC," *SS* 102). At the end of Alden's last story, the oldest son who shot both his uncle and a female relative is dead, yet "reborn in Christ, a new man, washed clean of his sins!" ("EC," *SS* 103). The story also illustrates the approaching spring after a long frozen winter and the spring-time hunting of walruses. Alden's confession is made in order to call for the forgiveness of God, and at the same time in order to convey to Emiko the true story of himself as a Yupik who began to break the long winter of Eskimo identity covered with ice and snow. Spring is a short and busy season for the Yupik as its native word, "up'nerkaq," which means to prepare for summer (Miyaoka 95). Alden's wish is buried in the meaning of the spring season when he breaks his silence and is ready for the next season of production.

Yamamoto's three short stories depict the literal and

symbolical imprisonment of human psyche which needs to overcome imprisonment through creative activities in an internal poetic space. Their poetic space is a common ground to resolve both their private agony and their public difficulties. Yamamoto's coherent strong wish aims to demolish the racial and cultural boundaries and to reconstruct trans-racial and cultural space in her own creative activities.

Notes

I am very grateful to Mr. John W. Roberts, Chief of Communication and Archives, Federal Bureau of Prison of the United States, for assisting and supporting my research on McNeil Island. This paper was originally published in *Studies in Culture and the Humanities: Bulletin of the Faculty of Integrated Arts and Sciences, Hiroshima University,* III 6 (1997): 1-29.

1. Goellnicht, who did important research on the history and meaning of haiku in Japan, regards Tome's haiku as "artistic and linguistic conservatism" (185).
2. It is said that Japanese women or "picture brides" for *issei* immigrant men, had reasons to leave Japan and emmigrate to the States: "For women who found themselves in social predicaments, marriage with men abroad offered an avenue of escape" (Ichioka 346).
3. Wong interprets this Hiroshige print "which depicts an idyllic seascape: pink clouds, pale blue sea with sampans, distant pine trees and thatched huts" as representing the idealized Japan for "those tempted by Extravagance" (174). Yamamoto describes this Hiroshige print as follows:

Chapter 3 : Prison, Psyche, and Poetry in Hisaye Yamamoto's Three Short Stories

> There were pink clouds, containing some graceful calligraphy, and a sea that was a pale blue except at the edges, containing four sampans with indications of people in them. Pines edged the water and on the far-off beach there was a cluster of thatched huts towered over by pine-dotted mountains of grey and blue. The frame was scalloped and gilt. (17)

4. Cheung states:

   > Yamamoto's method of what I call 'double-telling' within Japanese American culture illustrates her artful deployment of thematic and rhetorical silences I hope also to stretch the bounds of prevailing feminist analysis by showing how Yamamoto uses muted plots and bicultural codes to reveal the repression of both women *and* men ("Double-Telling" 277-78).

5. Compared with Yamamoto's "Yoneko's Earthquake" where, as Crow indicates, the reader "sees behind those events of tragedy of the Hosoumes' marriage" which include the earthquake, the car accident, the dog's death, and an illegal abortion ("Home and Transcendence" 201), the tragedy of "Seventeenth Syllables" is buried in a more subtle way.

6. Cheng makes a close examination of Rosie's father who, "an ordinary man of simple means, is driven by a non-traditional wife's extravagance to commit an act of violence to regain a necessary measure of control, economic and social, within the limitations inherent in the struggle of first-generation immigrant life" (93).

7. In an interview, Yamamoto herself faces "a certain conflict between female creativity and domestic responsibility" which can be shared with Tome (Cheung, "Interview" 82).

8. Cheng remarks that Tome is "a woman with passions which consume, who ignores the limits imposed by societal mores and the norms of behavior indicated by traditional gender roles" and concludes that in "this interplay between necessity and extravagance, tradition clashes with the unyielding passions of a youthful Tome, superseding and

nearly destroying her" and "for the first time, her disregard of limits set forth by tradition and society leads to her downfall" (94).

9. Parentheses are mine. Yamamoto herself suffered from a nervous breakdown which her psychiatrist said was caused by "fear of responsibility" (Writing 67).

10. Cheung describes Miss Sasagawara as a *nisei* women "driven 'insane' by the combined pressures exerted upon her as an 'other' — but not only as a women — in her own family, ethnic community, and American society at large" ("Thrice Muted Tale" 109).

11. According to Schweik, who quotes from Ann Rosalind Jones, the "'of' and the 'to,' the context and the audience, must be the starting-points for any understanding," especially for understanding the *nisei* women writers (89).

12. According to Bailey, in California "the law required that ashes of the deceased must permanently repose in a mausoleum, cemetery, or church vault" and the "Buddhist temples of California, or the family burial grounds of Mother Japan, had received much of the human ashes prior to Pearl Harbor. Now, indeed, it was different" (99).

13. Cheung also assumes that Miss Sasagawara can be sexually abused by the doctors and remarks:

> Her allegation of being "pawed" by the doctors can be construed in two ways. If one assumes (as does everyone in the story) that Miss Sasagawara overreacts, then she is guilty of "misinterpretation" (Yogi 118). Her "misreading" of the doctor's gestures foreshadows several subsequent events in which her own behavior is possibly misread. Nevertheless, in view of her physical beauty, there is reason to suspect that excessive groping did occur during the medical examinations. But no one takes her allegation seriously; it is automatically dismissed as one of her hysterics. The dismissal is quite understandable. The predominantly male medical profession has traditionally been sanctified as an unquestionable authority. The female patient who dares to challenge and literally turns her

Chapter 3 : Prison, Psyche, and Poetry in Hisaye Yamamoto's Three Short Stories

back on such authority becomes the one conspicuously on trial ("Thrice Muted Tale" 112).

14. According to Bailey, the Poston camp hospital was fully occupied:
    The physical travail and mental suffering, always increasing rather than diminishing, kept Poston's makeshift hospital constantly full. The "Poston zephyrs," in which the savage, swirling desert winds laid their gritty filth into every shelf and corner of the tarpapered tenements were bad enough. But the coughings and the wheezings were indicative of the fact that emphysema, tuberculosis, and that dreaded form of desert silicosis, already endemic in the Army camps, were alarmingly present, and aggravated by the wind-blown dust. (108)

15. Rolf makes a male-centered yet interesting comment on Miss Sasagawara whose "problem" is largely "sexual," as described in "her innocent but abnormal voyeurism and interest in much younger men" and whose sexual desire is restricted because the only man in her life is her father (101).

16. In her interview, Yamamoto says that "only if a new human being evolves — and there's not much chance of that will — racism disappear. So I guess we're stuck with the knowledge that there will always be people who will find us different and menacing and subhuman. Or quaint, at best. But there will be some who will accept us as fellow human beings, right? Maybe eventually, if the planet survives, everybody will be a product of this blending of races" (Osborn and Watanabe 36).

17. According to the Federal Bureau of Prisons' "Visiting Regulations" which "would have been in effect during the mid-1970's, and which would have applied to all of the Bureau's facilities" (Roberts), there is no such regulation of female visitors though there is a similar description of physical contact policy: "Handshaking, embracing, and kissing by immediate members of the family may be permitted within the bounds of good taste at the beginning and end of the visit" (7).

18. The year 1972 was McNeil's year of growth and improvement under

its fifteenth warden, Loren E. Daggett, who determined "the three most important events from a prisoner's viewpoint" which includes the advent of open mailing, "the enlargement of visiting room facilities, and the increased number of visits from three to four a month," in addition to the education development program at college level, the hiring of first full-time psychiatrist, and the construction of cubicles (*McNeil Pilot* 98-99).

Works Cited

Bailey, Paul. *City In the Sun: The Japanese Concentration Camp at Poston, Arizona*. Los Angeles: Westernlore, 1971.

Cheng, Ming L. "The Unrepentant Fire: Tragic Limitations in Hisaye Yamamoto's 'Seventeen Syllables." *MELUS* 19.4 (Winter 1994) 91-107.

Cheung, King-Kok. *Articulate Silences: Hisaye Yamamoto, Maxine Hong Kingston, Joy Kogawa*. Ithaca: Cornell UP, 1993.

——. "Double-Telling: Intertexual Silence in Hisaye Yamamoto's Fiction." *American Literary History* 3.2 (Summer 1991); 277-93.

——. "The Dream in Flames: Hisaye Yamamoto, Multiculturalism, and the Los Angeles Uprising." *Bucknell Review* 39.1 (1995) 118-31.

——. Interview with Hisaye Yamamoto. Cheung, "*Seventeen Syllables*" 71-86.

——. Introduction. Cheung, "*Seventeen Syllables*" 3-16.

——. Introduction. Yamamoto, "*Seventeen Syllables*" xi-xxv.

——. "Thrice Muted Tale: An Interplay of Art and Politics in Hisaye Yamamoto's 'The Legend of Miss Sasagawara.'" *MELUS* 17.3 (Fall 1991-1992): 109-25.

——, ed. "*Seventeen Syllables*." New Brunswick: Rutgers UP, 1994.

Crow, Charles L. "Home and Transcendence in Los Angeles Fiction." *Los Angeles in Fiction*. Ed. David Find. Albuquerque: U of New Mexico P, 1984. 189-205.

Chapter 3 : Prison, Psyche, and Poetry in Hisaye Yamamoto's
Three Short Stories

——. "The Issei Father in the Fiction of Hisaye Yamamoto." *Opening Up Literary Criticism*. Ed. Leo Truchlar. Salzburg, Austria: Wofgang Neugebauer, 1986. 34-40.

——. "A *MELUS* Interview: Hisaye Yamamoto." *MELUS* 14.1 (Spring 1987) 73-84.

Dandou, Shigemitsu. *Shikeihaishiron*. 1991. Tokyo: Yuikaku, 1993.

The Federal Bureau of Prisons. "Visiting Regulations." Washington, DC: U.S. Department of Justice, 1972.

——. *United States Penitentiary. McNeil Island, Washington*. Washington, DC: U.S. Department of Justice, 1961.

Fujimoto, Tetsuya. *Gendai America Hanzaigaku Jiten*. Tokyo: Keisoushobou, 1991.

Goellnicht, Donald C. "Transplanted Discourse in Yamamoto's 'Seventeen Syllables.'" Cheung, "*Seventeen Syllables*" 181-93.

Ichioka, Yugi. "Amerika Nadeshiko: Japanese Immigrant Women in the United States, 1900-1924." *Pacific Historical Review* 52.9 (1980) 339-57.

Kageyama, Yuri. "Hisaye Yamamoto — Nisei Writer." *Sunbury* 10 (1981) 32-42.

Kim, Elaine H. "Hisaye Yamamoto: A Woman's View." Cheung, "*Seventeen Syllables*" 109-17.

Mass, Amy Iwasaki. "Psychological Effects of the Camps on Japanese Americans." *Japanese Americans From Relocation to Redress*. 1986. Ed. Roger Daniels, Sandra C. Taylor, and Harry H. L. Kitano. Seattle: U of Washington P, 1991. 159-62.

Matsumoto, Valerie. "Desperately Seeking 'Deirdre': Gender Roles, Multicultural Relations, and Nisei Women Writers of the 1930's." *Frontiers* 12.1 (1991): 19-32.

McDonald, Dorothy Ritsuko, and Katharine Newman. "Relocation and Dislocation: The Writings of Hisaye Yamamoto and Wakako Yamauchi." Cheung, "*Seventeen Syllables*" 129-42.

McNeil Pilot. A Guide For the Men of McNeil. McNiel Island: McNeil

Island Penitentiary, 1966.

Mistri, Zenobia Baxter. "'Seventeen Syllables': A Symbolic Haiku." *Studies in Short Fiction* 27.2 (Spring 1990): 197-202.

Miyao, Shizuo. *Meisho Edo Hiyakkei: Hiroshige Ga.* Tokyo: Shueisha, 1992.

Miyaoka, Osahito. *Eskimo.* Tokyo: Iwanami, 1987.

Niiya, Brian, ed. *Japanese American History: An A-to-Z Reference from 1868 to the Present.* New York: Facts On File, 1993.

Osborn, William P., and Sylvia A. Watanabe. "A Conversation with Hisaye Yamamoto." *Chicago Review* 39. 3-4 (1993): 34-43.

Price, Lester K., ed. *McNeil: History of a Federal Prison.* McNeil Island: Vocational Training Publication Department, 1970.

Roberts, John W, Chief of Communications and Archives, Federal Bureau of Prisons. Letter to the author. 15 Sep. 1997.

Rolf, Robert T. "The Short Stories of Hisaye Yamamoto, Japanese American Writer." Cheung, "*Seventeen Syllables*" 89-108.

Schweik, Susan. "The 'Pre-Poetics' of Interment: The Example of Toyo Suyemoto." *American Literary History* (Spring 1989) 89-109.

Suzuki, Lester E. *Ministry in the Assembly and Relocation Centers of World War II.* Berkeley: Yardbird, 1979.

Tajiri, Vince. Rev. of "*Seventeen Syllables*" *and Other Stories*, by Hisaye Yamamoto. *Amerasia Journal* 16.1 (Summer 1989-90): 255-57.

When The State Kills . . . The Death Penalty v. Human Rights. London: Amnesty International, 1989. (Japanese version).

Wong, Sau-Ling Cynthia. *Reading Asian American Literature: From Necessity to Extravagance.* Princeton: Princeton UP, 1993.

Yamamoto, Hisaye. ". . . I Still Carry It Around." Cheung, "*Seventeen Syllables*" 69-70.

——. "*Seventeen Syllables*" *and Other Stories.* Latham: Kitchen Table, 1988.

——. "Writing." Cheung, "*Seventeen Syllables*" 59-68.

——. "Yellow Leaves." *Rafu Shimpo* 20 Dec. 1986 36, 38-39.

Chapter 3 : Prison, Psyche, and Poetry in Hisaye Yamamoto's Three Short Stories

Yogi, Stan. "Legacies Revealed: Uncovering Buried Plots in the Stories of Hisaye Yamamoto." *Studies in American Fiction* 17.2: 169-81.

——. "Rebels and Heroines: Subversive Narratives in the Stories of Wakako Yamauchi and Hisaye Yamamoto." *Reading the Literatures of Asian America*. Ed. Shirley Geok-lin Lim and Amy Ling. Philadelphia: Temple UP, 1992. 131-50.

Chapter 4

"This is also an American Experience" in Cynthia Kadohata's *The Floating World*

> "We were told
> that silence was better
> golden like our skin,
>   useful like
> go quietly,
>   easier like
> don't make waves,
>   expedient like
> horsestalls and deserts."
> Janice Mirikitani, "Breaking Silence"[1]

In her first novel, *The Floating World*, Cynthia Kadohata describes one very important experience of Americans — Japanese Americans' long and silent suppression and struggle within the postwar socio-geographical and historical context.[2] As a *sansei* — the third generation of Japanese Americans — Kadohata, moreover, recreates their experiences within the context of the entire history of oppression of voiceless minority people in the white-dominant American society. Before Kadohata, *nisei* fiction writers such as Toshio Mori (*Yokohama, California*, 1949), John Okada (*No-No Boy*, 1957), and Yoshiko Uchida (*Picture Bride*, 1987) have apparently represented the autobiographical voices of Japanese Americans with the historical context of the wartime relocation and internment. Regretfully enough, those novels have been strictly considered autobiographical writings and excluded from the mainstream of American literature. Unlike those forerunners, Kadohata neither describes the concentration camp itself directly nor mentions it as a fact frequently, not solely because she belongs to the generation which has no wartime experience, but because she intends to overcome the potentiality of the restricted scope, so that she can achieve the universality of the unfolded and multiple angles of human stories. For this purpose, the concentration camp experience is concealed and connoted underneath Kadohata's voice.

Kadohata's honest, modest, and even gentle voice throughout the novel conveys the multiplied agony hidden under powerless Japanese immigrants since the *issei* — the first generation of Japanese Americans — immigrated into a new world with a dream. It is Olivia Ann Osaka — a twelve-year-old girl — who tells her family's story which covers three generations, especially through her grandmother and her mother. In her narration, Olivia undergoes adolescence while her family drives from one town to another encountering

Chapter 4: "This is also an American Experience" in Cynthia Kadohata's *The Floating World*

difficulties finding a job and a place to settle down in the 1950's and 1960's. Such a life is named "the floating world" or "ukiyo," by Hisae Fujiitano, an *issei* woman and Olivia's grandmother. The utopia which the *issei* pursued in their immigration is dissolved into a literally floating world during the postwar resettlement period for Japanese Americans.

> We were traveling then in what she called ukiyo, the floating world. The floating world was the gas station attendants, restaurants, and jobs we depended on, the motel towns floating in the middle of fields and mountains. In old Japan, ukiyo meant the districts full of brothels, teahouses, and public baths, but it also referred to change and the pleasures and loneliness change brings. For a long time, I never exactly thought of us as part of any of that, though. We were stable, traveling through an unstable world while my father looked for jobs. (3)

In Olivia's view, the floating world is nothing but the road on which she and her family travel and wander in quest for the means of their living. It was at this time that there was still discrimination and prejudice against both Japanese and Japanese Americans after World War II. As Michiko Kakutani points out in her book review, *The Floating World* portrays "the transient life on the road" which comprises the experiences of the three generations (27). But, how is this title related to the traditional Japanese term and world of the floating world?

The floating world has a more important meaning in its origin. *Ukiyo* — originally a Buddhist term whose meaning is "the dark, shifting world of existence" — was turned into the world of material and sexual desire and pleasure in the Edo Period (Smith 7). It became the isolated place where the licensed brothel district was rebuilt and Kabuki theaters were removed in order to establish a distinction between these districts and the decent residences of the feudal class. From a ruling class's view, *ukiyo* was "a symbol of the independence and pride of the ever-increasing urban classes" because it turned "frivolity into its own virtue" (Smith 7). From a subject's point of view, however, *ukiyo* is a cruelly insulated and restricted world that imprisons its inhabitants who are forced to be engaged in such business as prostitution and its related jobs. The human souls are entirely killed and their physical beauty and attraction are paid attention. In such imprisonment, human conditions are retarded and damaged because they are sacrificed in order to survive.

However, the floating world connotes, for Japanese Americans, the prewar exclusive acts, the wartime concentration camps, and the postwar hardships. This novel opens in the 1950's when Olivia as a child observes the hardships with which her family is actually confronted. It is, however, within a larger context of several decades that Olivia, as a Japanese American, responds to bitterness and exclusiveness through her grandparents' and parents' experiences. Olivia frequently perceives Hisae's furies which desperately occur to her without any specific reason, and Olivia does

Chapter 4 : "This is also an American Experience" in Cynthia Kadohata's *The Floating World*

not exactly know why, but strongly relied on Olivia's own instinct.

> With all the older people I knew, even my parents, I occasionally saw that fierce expression as they exclaimed over something that had happened years ago, losses in a time and place as far removed from my twelve-year-old mind as the dates in a school book. (28)

The long-untold and unexpressed furies have been deeply buried in the oppressed people's minds. Kadohata attempts to demythologize the hidden aspect of their long-silenced stories as well as histories, and presents us an American experience. The floating world is, therefore, a long and endless path of Japanese Americans filled with anger, agony, pain, and fear.

Olivia's grandmother, or "Obāsan," came to the States as a child with her parents who had a dream to live in "*ukiyo*." Hisae's fate as a Japanese woman determines her name and her life. The fact that Hisae's family were not allowed to have their family name in a Japanese village is intriguingly associated with their family origin, poverty, and misery which had been determined by the Tokugawa Federal Government in the Edo Period. This fate was once changed in 1875, when Hisae's family was given the same family name "Sato," as the other villagers. It was one of the policies of the Meiji Government that the official social classes were abandoned and the ex-peasants and farmers were given family names. Considering this historical remark, Olivia's grandmother's family acquired the equal opportunities that they had not had in the floating world of the Edo Period.

This fate, however, did not change the actual conditions of ex-farmers' lives, especially in some rural area of southern Japan. As the eighth child, Hisae was called "Shimeko" which in Japanese indicates a wish that she would be the last child in the family because her family was too poor to support a large number of children. Hisae's fate would be different in the floating world in Japan. As the eighth child — and, worse, as a daughter — Hisae could be sold as a prostitute to one of the brothels in the floating wrold. In those days, poor peasants would often sell their daughters to such brothels as Yoshiwara in Tokyo or even to brothels in the States, solely because they could not pay the land tax.[3] Hisae's crucial moment was once solved, whereas she is confronted with the second floating world in the States. The floating world implies the hidden yet possible fate for a poor peasant's daughter. Even during the Meiji Restoration, such rural districts as Hiroshima and Kumamoto suffered from overpopulation and poverty and, consequently, sent many farmers to the States (Melendy 90). The poverty and difficulty in living in a village in a rural area after tax reformation particularly motivated many peasants to immigrate to the States. Hisae's nickname represents the crucial alternative of immigration in the possibility of being sold as a prostitute or starving to death. Olivia's view can be, in this sense, enlarged into a wider one which corresponds to the profound

Chapter 4: "This is also an American Experience" in Cynthia Kadohata's *The Floating World*

and neglected aspect of human life in the floating world.

Immigration provides Hisae's family with an opportunity to change their family name. Their strong hope for the future in a new land is represented by their newly created name, "Fujiitano." "Fujiitano," which sounds unnatural as a Japanese name, originates from two family names, one rich family and one happy family whom they knew, with a wish that they would make a success in a new country. Their name change symbolizes their intention to be liberated from their deeply-rooted burden and fate in the newly established, yet predominantly unchanged, Japanese society.

Even though the *issei* indulged the hope of success in their new family names, they were ironically disillusioned when the *nisei* were forced to have new Anglo-American first names at the beginning of World War II. Olivia mentions her parents' case: "in Hawaii at the start of World War II, the local school made my grandparents change their children's first names before they could enroll" (2).[4] Under this circumstance, Olivia's mother's name was changed from Mariko to Laura, and the *nisei*'s original first names become only "shadows following them" (2). Their name changes against their will prove that the *issei*'s dream was broken, and the *sansei* as well as the *nisei* began to have Anglo-American first names instead of Japanese names without a complete assimilation into the American society. The name changes, both according to their will and against their will, connote their unescapable destiny in the new world.

The new world is, as their name changes suggest, not an

ideal place to dwell in because it is floating, unstable, and exclusive. Only the hardship has remained in the immigrant family since it changed Hisae from "a young woman of spirit" to "an old woman of fire" (1). Hisae's dual difficulties as an immigrant worker and as a woman represent the roots of Japanese American women's fear and anger. "The Japs Must Go" echoed during the entire period from the 1907 Gentlemen's Agreement of the Japanese Immigrants to the 1952 McCarran-Walter Immigration Act (Melendy 114). At the same time as the policy denying U. S. citizenship to Japanese residents as a symbol of discrimination and hostility ended, the vast majority of *issei* became American citizens by the 1960's (Ritter 70). Hisae's life-long oppression as a minority woman in the white-male dominant country is observed through Olivia's eyes and discovered in her memories.

> She always said her experience showed that if you hated white people, they would just hate you back, and nothing would change in the world; and if you didn't hate them after the way they treated you, you would end up hating yourself, and nothing would change that way, either. So it was no good to hate them, and it was no good not to hate them. So nothing changed. (9)

Hisae's strong fear over "hakujin," or white people, never alters in her life. Her complete silence and her "wildest smile" (11) at "hakujin" are nothing but strategies to

Chapter 4 : "This is also an American Experience" in Cynthia Kadohata's *The Floating World*

avoid problems. In spite of her strong hope in her young days, Hisae remains powerless and marginalized in a white-male-centered society in order to defeat her fear of and conceal her hatred toward them.

What Olivia as a child witnesses is a crucial accident where Hisae's sense of fear and anger is overwhelmed in her silence, but is reformed into her intense attitude toward defending her granddaughter. When a white madman speaks strangely to Olivia in the middle of the lonely fields, Hisae instinctively feels an immense danger and secretly becomes ready to protect her granddaughter from a possible attack by the white man. Hisae's hidden intention to kill him is later revealed, through Olivia's keen perception, in Hisae's "several deep indentations and a thin cut on her palm" because Hisae squeezes the stick so hard that it "cut into her hand" (12).

On another occasion, Hisae's fear of "hakujin" is indicated by the scene in which Hisae hides a burning cigar in her pocket immediately after she gets a warning from an old white man, owner of the fields where they are trespassing. Hisae's fear is again concealed inside herself as her smoking cigar is quickly hidden inside her pocket. Hisae's fear, in both cases, can be seen as being transformed into deeply-rooted feelings of anger which are never expressed openly to the white people but only enclosed inside herself. These enclosed emotions of anger are deformed into her "meanness," "insults," and "hatred" (11), over which Olivia cannot help possessing a negative and even devil-like image of Hisae. In spite of this devil image, Hisae is the only grandparent for Olivia because Hisae's husbands and lovers are only shadows of the past in Hisae's stories and Hisae's influence is enormous enough for Olivia to trace back her grandmother's life.

Hisae's hardship as a daughter of a Japanese fisherman, as a seasonal farmer, and as a boarding house keeper dispels the myth of the passive and obedient Japanese woman, and ultimately transforms her into "an old woman of fire."[5] Hisae's first and everlasting fear as an immigrant woman is caused by her father's and her first husband's fishing job.[6] Though small in number, some Japanese like Hisae's father turned to commercial fishing for salmon on the Sacramento and San Joaquin rivers, fishing in the Monterey Bay area, and working for the salmon canneries in Oregon and Washington (Wilson and Hosokawa 67).[7] By 1923, 50% of the fishing boats were crewed by Japanese; yet they were confronted with difficulties from the white fishermen as Hisae's father was. Though Caifiornia was quite liberal as to the game laws, the success of Japanese fishermen resulted in the introduction of an anti-Japanese fishing act at every legislative session around 1927, three years after the 1924 Act, though it was never passed (Mears 234). Hisae's father's unemployment in the fishing industry and her first husband's death by being "drowned off the Coast of Honolulu" outline the misfortunes in the early years of her life.

Along with these misfortunes in her family, Hisae herself cannot be relieved from financial anxiety as a

Chapter 4 : "This is also an American Experience" in Cynthia Kadohata's *The Floating World*

migrant labor. Her persistence in controlling her "magic purse" indicates the poverty through which she has gone while picking celery, maintaining a boarding house in San Francisco, and traveling without a home until she is dead and buried in Wilcox, California. Hisae's own engagement in laboring in the fields and in domestic service as a cheap immigrant hand determines her position in society. Rather than fishing, more Japanese, like Hisae who "had worked on a celery farm" (23), were needed as cheap hands in the railroad and farming industries in the 1900's. Especially in agriculture, the Japanese had success even though they had to work as seasonal workers and had no choice but settle in the wastelands of the Sacramento, Central Coachella, and Imperial Valleys.[8] When Olivia and her family visit Hisae's second husband, his latest wife and widow, another *issei* woman, confesses that she cannot stand the smell of marigolds because she used to pick tomatoes as a farmworker, and the tomato plants smell like marigolds (55). Olivia, not a tomato picker, responds to this, saying "I loved the scent of marigolds, and I couldn't imagine things happening in my life that would make me hate it. But I couldn't be sure" (55). This is a particularly symbolical episode, which was previously published as a short story entitled "Marigolds" in the *New Yorker*. The marigolds divide Japanese American women's experience into two generations, the *issei* and the *sansei*. It embodies a disparity in immigrant experience as well as in generation. At the same time, however, the marigolds are the flowers through whose smell Olivia comes to realize the unstable world of Japanese American women. The story is told, its spirit is inherited, and consequently the myth is transcended beyond the history.

In addition to the grandmother-to-granddaughter relationship, the mother-daughter relationship is also interwoven in three generations. Both Hisae and her daughters are engaged in housekeeping jobs in the boarding house which Hisae's father and brother originally bought after giving up their fishing jobs. The boarding house business is accompanied by the farming industry, and its importance is tightly associated with the immigrant women in two generations. The boarding houses for the Japanese workers are especially needed because the keepers were middlemen of the group laborers. These boarding houses are, however, largely supported and managed by women, both the *issei* and the *nisei*. From the mid-nineteenth century until World War II, domestic service was the most common employment for migrant women and their daughters because of their lack of language skills and industrial skills, and the necessity of helping with the family finances (Glenn 4). The Japanese women were especially valued as boarding housekeepers and private maids because they were hard workers. Even their young daughters, like Olivia's mother and aunts, were needed because of the still-unbalanced sex ratio between men and women and of women's roles. The boarding house represents the women's place, neither solid nor settled, and also symbolizes impermanence. This house had almost fallen apart before it was finally sold and Hisae's

Chapter 4 : "This is also an American Experience" in Cynthia Kadohata's *The Floating World*

family moved to Hawaii, as if symbolizing women's destiny in a foreign land. Hisae's house is not a permanent dwelling for her family members, but a temporary lodging where both family members and seasonal workers have their temporary jobs, their temporary friends, and a temporary relationship. The women from two generations are only burdened by domestic duties and roles within this place, and the house is, ironically enough, nothing but another floating world.

The most crucial floating world is found in the wartime concentration camps which altered the fate of the Japanese immigrants who had just begun to establish themselves in better circumstances.[9] It is, at the same time, the experience which exists between the *nisei* and the *sansei*. The *nisei* who spent their childhood and adolescent days in the camps were the direct victims of the wartime agitation because they were considered most dangerous, being those between two cultures, two languages, and two countries.[10] Unlike those in *No-No Boy* and *Picture Bride*, none of the *nisei* in *The Floating World* speaks about or even mentions his or her most horrifying experience during the war. Their deeply-rooted agony is, paradoxically, counterpointed by their silence. Their forty-year silence is proof of their unforgettable experience because many *nisei* were torn by mixed feelings of shame, frustration, and bitterness at the denial of their civil rights" (AWUC 119).[11] Instead, Olivia interprets the *nisei*'s wartime experience, saying that it was "the first big fear" for her parents (146), and can delineate the fact that on the West Coast all the Japanese were ordered to move "across the street" with all their things packed and "next year they were interned" (171). It is what Kadohata intends to bring out as an issue of unspoken, unwritten, and unlistened truth. The central theme is not the real description of the concentration camp, but the long-neglected truth that has haunted the *nisei* and that is now spoken by the *sansei* daughter.

Olivia as a *sansei* daughter and a story-teller of her parents is enlarged and implied in the myth of the concentration camp experience in the context of the postwar society. Even though they spread all over the States and some success stories of resettlement and reestablishment appeared after the concentration camps, most of the Japanese were still "homeless and jobless" (Kitano 47). As Olivia confesses, "it could be hard even into the fifties and sixties for Japanese to get good jobs" (4), and especially the *nisei* had a great difficulty in finding "decent jobs" (Strong 1). Even the *nisei* servicemen who fought for the States found themselves only "second-class citizens" upon their return home, and faced serious segregation both in housing and at work (AWUC 11).

One of the occupations which exemplifies this dimension is chicken-sexing. When Olivia's family finally settle down in Gibson, Arkansas, Olivia at sixteen is engaged in a job inoculating chickens at the hatchery among the Japanese chicken-sexers. In this hatchery, Olivia demythologizes her parents' wartime experience and ultimately the Japanese Americans' spiritual imprisonment. Ironically enough, Arkansas is one of the states to which Japanese Americans

Chapter 4 : "This is also an American Experience" in Cynthia Kadohata's *The Floating World*

were evacuated during the war. For Olivia, however, it is a new place:

> My family had lived many places, and traveled many places. I thought then that Arkansas was the most beautiful place I had ever been in, yet I wanted badly to leave, and I knew that unlike Toshi and Nori and Kazuo — and even my father, committed not to his garage — someday I would have that freedom. (133)

Olivia's instinct of longing to leave Arkansas and possess freedom is implied in her symbolic imprisonment in the chicken hatchery in Arkansas.[12]

Most of the Japanese that Olivia met while she was moving from place to place in Arkansas were chicken sexers: Olivia remarks that there were five hundred chicken sexers in Arkansas alone. Chicken-sexing is a technique of identifying male chicks soon after hatching. It developed in Japan and became a popular occupation for "a small but specialized segment in the Japanese community" (Kitano 54), eventually becoming monopolized by the Japanese and Japanese Americans in the late 1930's (Wilson and Hosokawa 66). The demand for this expertise was especially high during World War II and the postwar era (Kitano 54). In the novel, Mr. Tanizaki was working as a chicken-sexer for thirty years, and Collie Asano learned chicken sexing "at school" (95).[13] Chicken-sexing as a segregated and monopolized occupation encompasses a poetic space for

Japanese Americans in the ever-lasting floating world.

Olivia confesses chicken-sexing was "awful" (111), "so real" and "so close" to sex (112). Though it was well paid, it is neither pleasant nor ideal so that it was available almost solely to Japanese Americans. As Olivia describes it, the hatchery is a small Japanese community, and it definitely constitutes a prison during the war. Those who worked at the hatchery were both physically and psychologically imprisoned. Even two towns in Arkansas, Gibson and Lee, represent two divisions inside the Japanese community: one for families who owned small businesses, and the other for those who worked as chicken sexers (73). The chicken hatchery exists at the bottom of the two-layered Japanese community which is submerged in the Anglo-American society. Japanese Americans' marvelous success in chicken-sexing before and after the war outlines the dimensional aspect of their being faced with racial segregation at work in the American society as well as symbolizing the concentration camp itself.

In addition to racial segregation at work, Japanese Americans suffered from many problems due to their hardships caused by the concentration camp experience. Olivia's step-father Charlie-O's difficulty at work and in marriage drives him to being deeply addicted to drinking and gambling. Japanese Americans are usually considered members of a model minority group whose crime, mental illness, and broken family rates are the lowest among the minorities and low even compared to white Americans. As

Chapter 4 : "This is also an American Experience" in Cynthia Kadohata's *The Floating World*

not only the Japanese dwellers in Hisae's boarding house but also Charlie-O and his Japanese friends were badly addicted, alcoholism and gambling were the two most common offenses from 1940 to 1960 (Kitano 118)."[14] The wartime experience changed the *nisei* men from dreamers into failures. Olivia's observation of Charlie-O reflects a broken code which the *nisei* had to undergo, recondition, and vanquish in a process of recovering from their broken life caused by the concentration camp.

Olivia's observation of the *nisei* at the hatchery also explains the mental conditions of Japanese Americans whose core experience is the concentration camp, as shown in Mr. Tanizaki who is finally mentally damaged. Generally, Asian Americans have been regarded as a mentally healthy group and its positive statistical data created a positive stereotypical image. It is, on the contrary, important to notice that Asian American mental patients as victims of discrimination, prejudice, and social oppression were not sent to hospitals, nor properly treated, because their families considered it a shame on the family (Sue 27). In this novel, Mr. Tanizaki was immediately excluded from the Japanese American community and hatchery as soon as he proved mentally ill, and consequently moved to Indiana. Mr. Tanizaki's thirty-year life as a chicken sexer before, during, and after the war depicts his segregated and alienated life. His mental corruption is caused by his life-long struggle and agony which has been silenced and which is deeply hidden inside him even after the war. Similar to Mr. Tanizaki,

Olivia's foster father, Isamu, who is described as "a little crazy" (13), is suffering from loneliness because he is the only Japanese in a Nebraska town, and worse, his daughter almost abandons him. Mr. Tanizaki and Isamu are excluded both from the American society and the Japanese American community because they do not meet the ideal image of the mentally healthy Japanese American.

Unlike Charlie-O, Mr. Tanizaki, and even Isamu, Olivia's mother, Laura, cannot be addicted to drugs and gambling, cannot go mad, and cannot even abandon her husband and children, because she is a woman. Laura's role as Olivia's mother is definite, whereas her father's role is divided into three; her real father, her step-father, and her foster father. Laura's invisible and spiritual imprisonment results from her silent acceptance of the Japanese traditional women's roles and conventions. Laura's natural and strong emotions of love are intruded upon and abolished twice, by Hisae and by Charlie-O. Laura is a victim of patriarchal values of marriage and family inside the limited Japanese American community as well as of racism outside it.

Despite the fact that Laura's life is contradicted by Hisae's life, a mother-daughter relationship is tightly constructed upon their fate as women. Hisae, who was "unusual" as a Japanese woman because she married three times, had six lovers, and smoked cigars, ultimately forced Laura to marry Charlie-O when Laura was only seventeen yet seven months pregnant by another married Japanese man — Olivia's real father — in Fresno. Hisae rebels against the

Chapter 4 : "This is also an American Experience" in Cynthia Kadohata's *The Floating World*

Japanese convention in her own life, yet she is unwilling for her daughter to be an unmarried mother because it is highly disgraceful according to the Japanese convention.[15]

Though carefully and cunningly arranged by Hisae, Laura's marriage is broken yet cannot be finalized by divorce. The relationship between Laura and Charlie-O, which once seemed stable through Olivia's eyes, becomes worse and worse until they leave their children at foster homes. Their temporary separation is, however, ended with a reunion without satisfaction. Laura's betrayal by adultery and Charlie-O's addiction to drinking and gambling leave shadows upon their children, especially upon the eldest Olivia. In her former lover's sudden and unexpected visit, Laura remains silent but shows an unusual symptom of terror.

> My parents still didn't move, and I went to the window. On the walkway stood a man I'd seen around in Florence, Oregon — a friend of my mother's. At first I didn't know why he was out there, why he didn't come in. Charlie-O went outside to talk to him. While my mother waited, her hands started shaking. We stared at the hands. It seemed as if someone else, someone invisible, were shaking them. I thought about how my grandmother's soul was inside all of us. So for a second I didn't know whether it was my grandmother inside my mother, shaking the hands, or whether something was physically wrong with my mother. My own body also seemed to hold revelations more profound than I could grasp. My face

> flushed and my stomach grew tense, and then I understood who the man was: my mother's lover. (74)

Laura's oppression and extraordinary sense of terror conveys her inescapable fate as a woman. Her "shaking hands" which correspond to her internal vibration symbolize the haunted terror which is inherited from Hisae and passed on to Olivia as women's untold agony and pain.

Women of three generations are gradually yet tightly interconnected in the process of Olivia's self-discovery. As for Laura's marriage, Olivia discovers later in Hisae's diary that even Hisae regretted forcing Laura to marry, yet confessed that it was too late. Olivia's strong hatred toward Hisae as a wicked old woman rather than as her own grandmother in her childhood days is changed into her understanding of and even admiration for Hisae as a woman. Hisae's diary which had been kept secretly during her life conveys to Laura how a woman's voice sounds and what a woman's life tells.

Hisae's diary written in Japanese which Olivia, years after her death, attempts to translate into English with Laura's help, is proof of the good educational background of Japanese immigrants.[16] Though they had great difficuly in mastering English, most of the *issei* were literate in their native language. Unlike other immigrants, Japanese Americans had a solid educational background (Glenn 439) and had a literature of their own in a written form. Even compared with African Americans' and Native Americans'

Chapter 4 : "This is also an American Experience" in Cynthia Kadohata's *The Floating World*

oral tradition, Japanese Americans' literary tradition in a written form is unique because it contains the Japanese oral tradition. This tradition is inherited from Hisae to Olivia via Laura even though there is no stable educational opportunity both for Laura and Olivia in the States. It is the women's voices that have been learned, understood, and inherited by daughters and granddaughters in an informal form of self-education.

As for formal educational opportunities for Japanese American women, Laura could not even finish high school like the other *nisei* who were obliged to work in the rural and poor areas. The *nisei* parents, like both Laura and Charlie-O, have strong ideas about their children's formal education. While they were moving around, Laura always helped Olivia to improve her English reading skills. Though bilingual themselves, Olivia's parents are even prouder of Olivia who can speak English as fluently and naturally as the white Americans. Olivia as a child has a vague dream of becoming a white collar worker such as a typist. When Olivia decided not to go to college after she leaves home, She reads Charlie-O's mind: "I think he felt going to college would guarantee me my place in the world. Maybe he worried I might end up unhappy, the way he thought my mother was" (188). The novel, however, ends with Olivia's decision to apply to university, suggesting a different fate of the *sansei* woman.

Before her decision to receive a formal advanced education, Olivia has already educated herself by discovering minority women's voices and their stories in American society. What Olivia has learned in this process is how to collect those voices, construct a story from stories, and establish her own self. After working as a salesgirl and having a Chinese American boyfriend in Los Angeles, Olivia reaches a final point. Olivia meets her dead father's ghost in finishing his job of servicing vending machines along the route through California, Arizona, and Nevada, which again embodies another floating world and her father's life as *nisei*. Olivia, who has three fathers, her biological father, her step-father, and her foster father, has finally overcome her mixed and complicated sense of identity as a Japanese American *sansei* woman. Except in a form of ghost at a moment of this open closure, Olivia's real father is neither seen nor heard throughout her life, whereas her mother and her grandmother have always haunted her and their stories are reborn in Olivia's voice.

Olivia's travels are over when she leaves "another stop." Yet, her own life in the floating world has just begun when she has a strong sense of commitment for the future and experiences a turning point in the floating world: "it was high time I left" (196).

Notes

An abridged form of this paper was presented at the International Popular Culture Association Convention in York, England, on August

Chapter 4 : "This is also an American Experience" in Cynthia Kadohata's *The Floating World*

9, 1993. This paper was originally published in *Chu-Shikoku Studies in American Literature* 30 (1994): 93-105.

1. Mirikitani (33).
2. Diana O'Hehir in her book review is totally ignorant of this Japanese Americans' historical and socio-geographical aspect in the novel and fails to read the novel's profundity, except for Olivia's grandmother's role (16). However, such scholars as Frank Cha and You-me Park and Gayle Wald examine Kadohata's *The Floating World* with a new perspective.
3. In the Edo Period, three major cities such as Edo, Osaka, and Kyoto in addition to Nagasaki — the only official foreign trade harbor during the Edo Period — were allowed to have the official brothel districts. The Tokugawa Government prohibited human traffic officially, but most of the prostitutes in those floating worlds were actually sold and sent to the brothels (*Nihon Josei Shi* 128). Officially, the flesh traffic was again prohibited and prostitutes were liberated in 1872, at the beginning of the Meiji Period. It does not mean, however, that prostitution was extinguished because the Meiji Government admitted prostitution officially (*Nihon Josei Shi* 195).
4. In 1942, during World War II, almost 250 Japanese last names were also officially changed to Chinese, Hawaiian, Portuguese, or even Scottish names in Oahu (Ogawa 325).
5. The labors in which the Japanese Americans were engaged also indicate their everlasting conflict as new immigrants. After the wave of plantation laborers in Hawaii which started in the 1860's and was ended in 1924 by the Japanese Exclusion Act, there was a big migration to the mainland in the 1900's (Ritter 48-49) because of the need for laborers in the agricultural, railroad, mining, lumber, landscape gardening, and fishing industries from 1891 to 1907 (Ichioka 57).
6. Already in the 1880's, Japanese fishermen were at White Point, San Pedro (Ritter 49).

7. Especially when the tuna canneries were built in 1913 in Terminal Island, San Pedro, not only did the Japanese fishermen introduce the traditional Japanese technique of landing tuna with line and pole, but also their wives worked in the canneries (Wilson and Hosokawa 68).
8. By 1940, there were 1,575 farmers on a total of 71,000 acres in the three West Coast states; they produced 95 % of the spring and summer celery, 95 % of the snap beans, 67 % of the fresh tomatoes, and 44 % of the onions on the market (Ritter 51).
9. The bombing of Pearl Harbor on Dec. 7, 1941 caused hostility against the Japanese Americans as well as the Japanese. By Federal Executive Order 9066, approximately 120,000 Japanese Americans living on the West Coast were forced to leave their houses and abandon their property and to be literally imprisoned in the evacuation camps (AWUC 10).
10. In order to show their loyalty to America, about 26,000 *nisei* youths, like Collie Asano in this novel who was "paid for by the G.I.Bill" (95), both men and women, volunteered to the military forces of the United States.
11. The *nisei* kept silent about their life-long depression until the 1982 hearings investigating the World War II Internment of Japanese Americans (AWUC 21).
12. In her short story, "Devils," Kadohata sets an Arkansas chicken hatchery as a turning point of the heroine's *nisei* parents after a divorce, implying again that a hatchery is an enclosed space of conflict. In her interview in 2007 after she won the 2005 Newbery Medal for *Kira Kira* (2004), Kadohata remarks that she wrote about non-traditional families because she was herself brought up in a non-traditional family because her parents got a divorce (Lee 170) and also the communities built up during travelling especially in *The Floating World* are "substitutes for traditional families" (Lee 171).
13. S. John Nitta of Pennsylvania actually studied this technique in Japan and founded the American Chick Sexing School where hundreds of men were trained: "An expert can examine from 900 to 1,400 baby

Chapter 4 : "This is also an American Experience" in Cynthia Kadohata's *The Floating World*

chicks per hour and separate males from females with 99% accuracy" (Ichioka 485).

14. Though the crime rate peaked in 1940 and dropped after that, Japanese Americans were addicted to alcohol and gambling, which were inherited culturally because they were oppressed and suppressed in the white male dominant country. Gambling was, especially, "a major source of recreation, since it offered a hope, however illusory, of striking it rich instantly" (Ichioka 84). The early immigrants in the nineties patronized Chinese gambling houses, and continuously, Japanese gambling houses in such cities as Los Angeles and Seattle. As it became a problem in the Japanese community, the Labor League discouraged the Japanese from being involved in gambling, and community leaders issued warning notices (Ichioka 178). Actually, the Evacuation in 1943 resulted in closing the clubs, for the *issei* liked Chinese gambling. Yet after the war, the *nisei*, like Charlie-O, preferred such kinds of gambling as horse racing, dice, blackjack, and poker (Hosokawa 126).

15. Though not in Hisae's case, the *issei* women are known as "picture brides." Most of the *issei*'s marriage were arranged; especially the *issei* bachelors found their Japanese brides by exchanging pictures. During the years from 1911 to 1920, 10,000 picture brides arrived in the States to join their husbands (Ritter 48). Those brides, however, were usually disappointed with their unexpectedly older husbands, the wastelands, and hard labor in the new country. In spite of their unhappy married life, the *issei* remained married and even encouraged their children to marry by arrangement. Considering this fact, Hisae is excluded from those typical Japanese *issei* women.

16. In 1872, Meiji reforms were established; consequently, both males and females had to be enrolled in elementary school for four (later six) years, with the optional two- or three- year middle school.

Works Cited

Asian Women United of California, ed. *Making Waves: An Anthology of Writings By and About Asian American Women*. Boston: Beacon, 1989.

Cha, Frank. "Growing Up in the Margins: Asian American Children in the Literature of the New South." *Southern Quarterly* 46.3 (Spring 2009): 128-44.

Glenn, Evelyn Nakano. *Issei, Nisei, Warbride: Three Generations of Japanese American Women in Domestic Service*. Philadelphia: Temple UP, 1986.

Hosokawa, Bill. *Nisei: the Quiet Americans*. New York: Morrow, 1969.

Ichioka, Yuji. *The Issei: the World of the First Generation Japanese Immigrants, 1885-1924*. New York & London: Free Press, 1988.

Kadohata, Cynthia. *The Floating World*. New York: Viking, 1989.

———. "Devils." *How We Live Now: Contemporary Multicultural Literature*. Ed. John Repp. Boston: St. Martin's, 1992. 142-48. Originally published in the *New Yorker*, in 1989.

———. "Marigolds." *New Yorker* 9 Feb. 1987: 36-39.

Kakutani, Michiko. "Growing Up Rootless in an Immigrant Family." Rev. of *The Floating World*, by Cynthia Kadohata. *New York Times* 30 June 1989: C27.

Kitano, Harry H. L. *Japanese Americans: the Evolution of a Subculture*. Englewood Cliffs, NJ: Prentice-Hall, 1969.

Lee, Hsiu-chaun. "Interview with Cynthia Kadohata." *MELUS* 32.2 (Summer 2007): 165-86.

Lim, Shirley Geok-lin, Mayumi Tsutakawa, and Margarita Donnelly, eds. *The Forbidden Stitch: An Asian American Women's Anthology*. Corvallis, OR: Calyx, 1989.

Mears, E. G. *Resident Orientals*. New York: Arno, 1978.

Melendy, H. Brett. *The Oriental Americans*. New York: Hippocrene, 1972.

Mirikitani, Janice. *Shedding Silence*. Berkeley: Celestial Arts, 1987.

Nihon Josei Shi. Haruko Wakita, Reiko Hayashi, Kazoko Nagahara, et al.

Tokyo: Yoshikawa Kobun Kan, 1987.

Ogawa, Dennis M. *Kodomo no tame ni: For the Sake of the Children: the Japanese American Experience in Hawaii.* Honolulu: UP of Hawaii, 1978.

O'Hehir, Diana. "On the Road with Grandmother's Magic." Rev. of *The Floating World*, by Cynthia Kadohata. *New York Times Book Review* 23 July 1989: 16.

Park, You-me, and Gayle Wald. "Native Daughters in the Promised Land: Gender, Race, and the Question of Separate Spheres." *American Literature* 70.3 (Sep. 1998): 607-33.

Ritter, Ed, et al. *Our Oriental Americans.* St. Louis: McGraw-Hill, 1965.

Smith, Lawrence. *Ukiyo: Images of Unknown Japan.* London: British Museum, 1988.

Strong, Edward K. *The Second-Generation Japanese Problem.* 1934. New York: Arno, 1970.

Sue, Stanley, and James K. Morishita. *The Mental Health of Asian Americans.* San Francisco: Jossey-Bass, 1982.

Wilson, Robert Arden, and Bill Hosokawa. *East to America: A History of the Japanese in the United States.* New York: Morrow, 1980.

Chapter 5

Sexual Colonialism in a Postcolonial Era in Lois-Ann Yamanaka's Novels

—Wild Meat and the Bully Burgers,
Blu's Hanging,
Name Me Nobody, Heads by Harry,
and
Father of the Four Passages —

I. Introduction

Lois-Ann Yamanaka has been pursuing the theme of sexual colonialism in a postcolonial era by presenting her Pidgin-written works set primarily in local Hawaiʻi from the late 1960s to the late 1970s. Yamanaka's prolific career as a writer is proven in her successful production of novels after her collection of poetry, *Saturday Night at the Pahala Theatre*, was published in 1993. Though her first book was published by Bamboo Ridge Press, a small yet locally-celebrated press in Hawai'i, all of the other novels were published in the major publishing companies in New York: *Wild Meat and the Bully Burgers* by Harvest in 1996, *Blu's Hanging* by Farrar in 1997, *Heads by Harry* by Farrar in 1999, *Name Me Nobody* by Hyperion in 1999, *Father of the Four Passages* by Farrar in 2001, and *Behold the Many* in 2006. Throughout these productions, Yamanaka's challenge to retrieve and reveal the neglected voices of sexually and psychologically violated victims has been constructing the unique space in the postcolonial era.

Yamanaka's hard path, however, began when her first book, *Saturday Night*, was published, and reached the steepest cliff when she was nominated for the winner of the Association of Asian American Studies award for *Blu's Hanging* in 1997.[1] In both works, Yamanaka's portrayal of Filipino men as sexual abusers and rapists was criticized, especially by Asian American scholars including Japanese Americans such as Jonathan Okamura and Candace Fujikane of the University of Hawai'i, to say nothing of Filipino Americans. In spite of her strong shared sense with Yamanaka who, Fujikane herself believes, reminds the local people that "Pidgin is a language of great power, beauty, and pain, and in that language, she [Yamanaka] records the textures of our lives as locals," Fujikane makes her straightforward and consistent criticism on Yamanaka's stereotypical portrayal of Filipino man in *Blu's Hanging* ("'Blu's Hanging'" A-9). In addition to her critical comment on Yamanaka's perpetuation of "racist stereotypes of Filipinos and Hawaiians"

Chapter 5 : Sexual Colonialism in a Postcolonial Era in Lois-Ann Yamanaka's Novels

in *Saturday Night*, Fujikane repeatedly emphasizes in her argument on *Blu's Hanging* that it is read "in the historical context of the persistent stereotype of sexually predatory immigrant Filipino men, a stereotype that dates from the plantations in Hawai'i and the farms on the Mainland."[2] Fujikane further points out that "reinforcing stereotypes of Filipino sexual violence" leads to "the disempowerment of real Filipino communities" ("'Blu's Hanging'" A-10). Even though the novel's theme is the disempowerment of a Japanese family, the Ogatas, Fujikane insists that Uncle Paulo's anger over disempowerment caused by Japanese racism to Filipino and the Filipino characters' lack of escaping their disempowerment should be considered more carefully and compassionately ("'Blu's Hanging'" A10-A11).

Against those negative or even hostile comments, there are compassionate opinions to Yamanaka who is "the victim of her own success" because her book was published by a major publishing house in New York and she received quite favorable reviews nationwide.[3] As for the theme of *Blu's Hanging*, Yamanaka remarks that childhood is "such a scary and dangerous time" that it reveals "issues of hypocrisy in religion, blood relations and human intentions" (Kam, "So Many Stories" n.pag.). As for the controversy over her work, she was "pierced by the conflict" (Oi, "Novelist" n.pag.) and only "objects to the notion that because she has such a prominent voice in Hawaii literature that she should be a spokesperson for all" and insists that "the complainers should be convincing others to write their own stories"

(Kam, "Writer's Blu's" n.pag.). Instead of reacting to the critics' reaction to her work, Yamanaka decided "to act," that means, "to write" (Tanner n.pag.), and with her enormous yet painful efforts, she has been continuing to write and has the other three novels published successfully in 1999 and 2001. In other words, Yamanaka's hardships drove her to establish the solid and consistent view of her creative works.

Yamanaka's success and struggle as a local / national / transnational writer represents a passage from the literary colonialism to the canonbreaking postcolonialism. The theme of her works, moreover, embodies a colonial passage in a postcolonial era and it implies a sexual politics in the postcolonial Hawai'i: for example, the violated landscape filled with widespread brutal and cruel treatment of all the oppressed inhabitants, the absence of mother as the fortress, the children's hetero / homo sexual abuse in the lower-income and racially / ethnically diverse yet poor neighborhood, and the neglect of and discrimination against local children at the American-oriented educational institution. Yamanaka's sexual colonialism in the postcolonial era should be examined and evaluated as it represents not only Hawai'i but also other societies, whether local or national, in the contemporary era.

II. Hawai'i as the Violated Landscape

Hawai'i is a symbol of the violated islands against superficial and ideal image of the paradise from the

Chapter 5 : Sexual Colonialism in a Postcolonial Era in Lois-Ann Yamanaka's Novels

colonial to the postcolonial era. The sacred native land is invaded not only by the different races but also by their political, economical, social, and legal powers. The destiny of Hawai'i has been controlled and determined by the outside force during some transformation steps from the self-governed and self-contained islands to the kingdom and to the Christianization by the missionaries from Europe, the sugarcane and coffee plantations founded and run by the American capitalists and occupied by the immigrant laborers from European and mostly Asian countries, the decline of the Hawaii's Kingdom and Americanization, the 1959 statehood of the US, the rushing tourism by the American Big Five, the establishment of military base as the economic source, and the rise and fall in the globalization and Japanese economy's influence.[4] Hawai'i as the inviolated islands is the unknown and even hidden side of Hawai'i that should be explored and examined through a set of ideological embodiments.

Hawaii's natural environment that has been violated by the industrialization, air and water pollution, and the land development has a paradoxical element in its foundation and evolution in Hawai'i islands. In Yamanaka's works, there appear the scenes and episodes of killing wild and tamed animals. As its title, *Wild Meat and the Bully Burgers*, connotes, to kill and eat wild and tamed animals is regarded as the natural act for local people. In *Heads by Harry*, more interestingly, pig hunting in the rain forest in the Big Island is the central motif of Toni Yagyu's going through struggle, self-awareness, and resolution. Hunting and taxidermy, which is also described as an important means to earn money in *Wild Meat and the Bully Burgers*, seems the violent action to kill wild animals and destroy nature, and must be misinterpreted only as "a metaphor for the art of the novelist" who ignores Hawaii's native culture (Pennybacker n.pag.). There is, however, a paradox that the feral pig is the worst example of dozens of introduced animals and plants that destroy Hawaii's natural heritage so that hunting those destructive animals is "somehow part of Hawaiian cultural heritage" because Hawaiian heritage can be preserved by excluding them from the important and diminishing native ecosystems (Smith 262). Since Hawai'i is geographically isolated and never connected to any continent, Hawai'i was blessed with a rich ecosystem: "the few hundred animals and plants that arrive during the first 70 million years were free to evolve rapidly to fit into the extensive range of ecosystem niches available" in Hawai'i till the first Polynesians migrated in Hawai'i in A.D. 400 and foreign species were brought by humans over the past 1,600 years (Smith 261-62). Hunting wild pigs developed into a sport, and then its purpose became to slaughter them as they were quite destructive to forests (Crawford 108-109). It was in the middle of the nineteenth century when the better breeds for food were introduced by Europeans and Americans and hunting wild boars began to disappear by the mid-twentieth century (Crawford 108-109). Before the industrialization and land development, Hawaii's native land had been violated and threatened by the animals and plants introduced by humans.

Chapter 5 : Sexual Colonialism in a Postcolonial Era in Lois-Ann Yamanaka's Novels

Along with animals' invansion to the native soil, Europe and America are the second intruders to the self-governed Polynesian community, and their economic power transforms Hawai'i into the plantation-based society that is the core of Yamanaka's works. Hawai'i as well as Asia are placed in the same position of being the feminized victims by the masculine power of the West in the nineteenth century. Gary Okihiro, quoting from Ronald Takaki's statement in *Iron Cages: Race and Culture in 19th-Century America* that Orientalism "supports Europe's and America's masculine thrust toward a feminized Asia — their invasion, conquest, and colonization of Asia," concludes that America's westward march did not end "inward-bound," but continued to Hawai'i and Asia (Common 18). Throughout Hawaii's Westernization, Christianization, and Americanization, the introduction and establishment of the sugarcane plantation transforms Hawaii's landscape into the multi-racial and multi-cultural society as the foundation of contemporary Hawai'i. As Takaki remarks, modern and contemporary Hawai'i is founded upon the social changes that resulted from the newly-established communities in the plantation camps. The landscape in Yamanaka's works originates from this plantation heritage which is blessed with racial and cultural diversity, yet which is trapped in violations of human rights, equal opportunities, healthy living conditions, and privacy. The plantation laborers were confronted with dual conflicts, both a conflict among laborers of different racial backgrouds and a conflict between the planters and laborers. Due to the unbalanced sex ratio and the prejudice and discrimination among different races, the camp laborers would often face violent incidents. The racial and sexual harrasement and abuse or even kidnapping was common in the uncivilized camp, and the plantation rules and the prolonged customs to punish the strikers contained physical abuse (Okihiro, *Cane Fires* 32-35). As Yamanaka frequently remarks that Hawaii's local people, especially those in local islands such as the Big Island, lived in 'colonialism' even in the 1960's, the plantation heritage is deeply rooted in Hawaii's local people's lives that are always violated, wounded, silenced, and forgotten.

The hidden violating act of Hawaii's colonialism that affects Hawaiian native and immigrants' inhabitants is the wide spread of Hansen's disease as the outcome of Chinese immigrants' bringing the disease to Hawai'i in mid-nineteenth century and in 1865 inhuman life imprisonment was finally founded in colonies on the Kalaupapa Peninsula, Molokai.[5] Even after the sulfone therapy was introduced in the 1940's and the isolation in Kalaupapa was legally abolished by the Committee on Leprosy in 1969, the patients and former patients had to go through the most difficult transitional years in the 1970's and 1980's (Law npn). Never seriously discussed, this dark side of Hawaii's history is the backbone of Yamanaka's *Blu's Hanging*. In this novel, Poppy Ogata and his dead wife, Eleanor Ogata, as children before and after World War II, suffered both Hansen's disease and discrimination that result in their unforgettable agony

Chapter 5 : Sexual Colonialism in a Postcolonial Era in Lois-Ann Yamanaka's Novels

and consequently the family tragedy. Poppy's confession symbolizes the unfortunate family history: "Ivah, this hard for me say 'cause been one secret for so long from you — me and your madda, us had leprosy. I like your promise that you neva call us lepers" (*Blu's Hanging* 41). Eleanor's death from her obsession of taking the sulfone drug even after she was declared negative and damaging her kidneys proves that her childhood experience to be separated from her own parents and imprisoned at Kalihi Receiving Station in Honolulu, Oahu and eventually in Kalaupapa in Molokai, was intolerable and unforgettable. The family history of Hansen's disease is so deeply rooted in the Ogata family that Poppy cannot return to his hometown, cannot have any stable and respectable job, and cannot escape from the invisible discrimination and prejudice against his past.

The beautiful native island of Molokai is transformed into the dreadful land to imprison the Hansen's disease patients when the Act to Prevent the Spread of Leprosy was passed in 1865 and King Kamehameha V issued an order to remove indigenous people in 1865 and 1895, and the forced isolation of patients to Molokai was carried out from 1866 till 1969. Molokai as a land of Hansen's disease colony is already portrayed in *Molokai* by Hawaii's celebrated writer O. A. Bushnell, and Father Damien as the founder of the colony is not only studied by historians and biographers but also dramatized in *Damien* by Aldyth Morris. Yamanaka's *Blu's Handing* examines the former patients who were separated from their parents and sent to Molokai's

Kalaupapa colony in their infancy before World War II and left the colony to live an independent and married life in the 1960's. In 1930, however, an Advisory Committee on Leprosy in Hawai'i carried an innovative plan that there will "be no further involuntary transfer of patients to Kalaupapa, but that patients be hospitalized at an improved hospital in Kalihi" (Judd 329).[6] It was, however, still scary for worsened patients to be sent to Kalaupapa as the last destination; Poppy and Elenoar, the patients who were first hospitalized in Kalihi Receiving Station were actually sent to Kalaupapa during the war because Kalihi was close to Pearl Harbor and they had to avoid bombardment by Imperial Japan's Army (Morison). Both Poppy and Elenoar experience the dreadful imprisonment at Kalaupapa and cannot leave there even after they are cured because of the introduction of the sulfones in 1946. According to Dr. Edwin Chung-Hoon in his 1956 report, among 271 new cases treated with sulfoned during 1946 and 1956, 92.5 % improved and 60 % could be discharged home after the two-year treatment (Judd 333-34). Even after such an improvement, the settlement had physical barriers between patients and nonpatients and "the patients' mail was fumigated well into the 1960's" (Law and Wisniewski 63). It was not until 1969 that the isolation policy was completely abolished and the imprisoned patients were legally liberated. The prolonged strife after the liberation from imprisonment continued till 1988 when the patients can regain their home at the old Hale Mohalu site by the Coalition for Specialized Housing Project (Law n.pag.).

The former colonies of Kalaupapa and Kalawao had been transfigured into Kalaupapa National Historical Park in 1980 and even there is the mule tour to the cliffs of Kalaupapa Peninsula. Even in this new era of Kalaupapa, its community is still now "home for many surviving Hansen's disease patients, whose memories and experiences are cherished values" ("Kalaupapa" n.pag.). Yamanaka challenges this long-neglected and graduallyrecognized history and untold personal stories embedded in the landscape of Molokai as one of Hawaii's most beautiful yet most tragic spaces.

Hawai'i as the violated landscape connotes the environmental, historical, and personal meanings and messages that Yamanaka explores by her creative force and deep insight. Hawai'i is the significant background for Yamanaka to examine, revive, illustrate, and debate, and the onceviolated landscape encounters the healings and cures in Yamanaka's aquiring her voice of sexual colonianism.

III. The Absence of Mother as the Fortress

In Yamanaka's novels, the absence of mother as the frequently employed scheme embodies the most crucial lack of love, care, and protection that children desperately need both inside and outside the home as the fortress. The absence of mother influences the children's lives from infancy to teenage years and leaves the trauma because of the lack of the most important source of love. Mother's death in *Blu's*

Hanging, for example, means the death of home for three children, Maisie Tsuneko, Blu or Presley Vernon, and Ivah Harriet Ogata. Mother's abandonment and neglect of Emi-lou Kaya in *Name Me Nobody* deprives Emi-lou of possessing the healthy mother-daughter relationship and, instead, leads her to a strong relationship with her grandmother and a sisterhood relationship with her half-Portuguese cousin, Yvonne Vierras. The absence of mother also engraves inside the child the ideal image of mother as Billy Harper, a hapa teenager born of a Caucasian father and an Indian mother, in *Heads by Harry*, is obsessed with the beautiful image of his dead mother. In *Father of the Four Passages*, Sonia Kurisu suffers her internal agony by being neglected and abandoned by her mother, Grace Kurisu, after her father, Joseph Kurisu, left home as a rootless traveler. Because of those complicated emotions, actually or symbolically motherless children are confronted with the difficulty of expressing and controlling themselves and are not led to the right path in their important steps of healthy and appropriate growth.

Children's loss or even immaturity of expressing themselves orally or in writing is the most crucial result from the lack of the closest beloved person, the mother. In *Blu's Hanging*, Maisie's loss of speaking ability and its related problem in reading and writing abilities is caused by her shock due to her mother's death. Her late speech acquisition that started at four and a half embodies the first humiliating experience. It is again described in *Father of the Four Passages* that Sonia's learning disability that she

Chapter 5 : Sexual Colonialism in a Postcolonial Era in Lois-Ann Yamaraka's Novels

did not talk until she was four and a half was "a psychological scar" because of Joseph's freequent absences (41). Maisie's complete inarticulation after her mother's death results from her innermost struggle as a preschool child who still needs a special care and attention from her mother. Her helpless longing for her mother is transformed into her entire loss of verbal communication ability. Her difficulty in communicating with others also influences her learning ability of writing at school where she is overthrown into the harsh criticism and judgement on her disability and put into a special education class. Emi-lou without mother in *Name Me Nobody* is also confronted with the lack of a communicative and healthy relationship with the others both within and without home. The lack of communication between Emi-lou and her mother, Roxanne Kaya, illuminates the lack of care, respect, and understanding between them. The lack of mother's love and care influences the children's inarticulation as the embodiment of their uncured wound.

In addition to the lack of self-expression, that of self-control deprives the motherless children of having an appropriate life with the right habits because of the lack of the right trainings and knowledge. The inappropriate habits range from eating, passing urine to going through menstruation. Blu's gain of weight by his bad eating habit is caused by the loss of mother's cooking and knowledge of nutrition, and, moreover, by his psychological agony over mother's death: "Poor Blu, eating away all the sadness until he's so full that he feels numb and sleepy. . . . Just so he doesn't feel

Mama gone so far away" (*Blu's Hanging* 105). Blu's unusual eating habits are caused by his unstable emotions because of the absence of his mother who cooks, feeds, and cares for him. Emi-lou's gain of weight, similar to Blu's, symbolizes the lack of self-control, her psychological unstableness, and loneliness as an abandoned illegitimate child of a single mother.

Related with the lack of communication ability, the lack of toilet training as one of the most fundamental trainings is another serious problem for preschool children. Both Masie in *Blu's Hanging* and Sonia in *Father of the Four Passages* share the humiliating and embarassing experiences of lacking toilet training as well as that of communication abilities. Both Masie and Sonia cannot control toilet habits because of the inappropriate domestic environments: one is mother's absence and the other is mother's unstable psychological conditions in the almost single parent household. In a conversation among Ivah, Masie, and Blu, Maisie's silenced self is interpreted and the true story behind the failure of toilet training is revealed and finally understood.

". . . . You not taking off your panty 'cause you hot, hah?"
Nod yes.
"See you, Blu. Go on. You take um off 'cause get dirty?"
Nod yes.
"Dirty from playing outside?"
Nod no.
"Dirty from, dirty from — Maisie, you pissing in your

Chapter 5 : Sexual Colonialism in a Postcolonial Era in Lois-Ann Yamaraka's Novels

panty?"

Nod yes.

"Every day?"

"What you doing with your wet panty? How come you get panty every day?"

She lowers her head.

"You using dirty panty?"

"Cannot be, you stupid Blu. You washing your own panty? No wonder I no see too many of your panty in the wash."

"Why you neva tell us, Maisie? We not going scold you."

Sad, so sad.

I'm not stupid. Blu's not stupid. She cannot talk, so she cannot ask like this haole wants the kindergartners to ask, "Teacher, may I please use the lavatory?" (*Blu's Hanging* 47-48)

Masie's silenced and inarticulate conditions in kindergarten lead to her failure in going to the bathroom, her pissing in panties and staying without underwear at school, and ultimately exposing ignorantly her vagina and buttocks to the boys. Her loneliness, isolation, and anxiety at home is enlarged at school, that is, the most cruel outside society for her.

Children's sexual awareness and their trials from childhood to adulthood such as menstruation cannot be undergone in a healthy and knowledgeable way due to the lack of the beloved. Menstruation is employed quite frequently in Yamanaka's works as the first difficult, scary, anxious, and untold experience.[7] The girls who suddenly have menstruation cannot understand what it means and are only scared by the blood. Their trials as teenagers who are doomed experiencing the passage to adults are also expressed only in their inward voice in their first experience of menstruation. Ivah in *Blu's Hanging* and Sonia in *Father of the Four Passages*, especially, blame themselves and hurt their bodies because they cannot tell the fact to anybody so that they cannot find the right way to deal with the blood. The lack of their knowledge before having menstruation means the absence of the mother who educates and trains their daughters. The precaution is also necessary for the women who have to be careful for their unexpected pregnancy because of the lack of the right knowledge of sex. The absence of mother for a growing daughter signifies the absence of knowledge and information about womanhood: "How alone I feel. / No Mama for me. / Nobody to help me with this blood. / Blood. / Nothing in the house" (*Wild Meat and the Bully Burgers* 93).

As the most subtle consequence, the motherless children's hardships are also observed in their unhealthy and unbalanced families with substitute mothers / fathers. From the irresponsible and loveless mother, Roxanne Kaya, and the constantly critical aunt and Yvonne's mother, Aunty Etsuko, Emi-lou is protected and understood only by her adoptive mother — her supportive and giving grandmother, Leatrice Reiko Kaya — and the sister-like Yvonne, within home. As a more tragic example, the younger children have

Chapter 5 : Sexual Colonialism in a Postcolonial Era in Lois-Ann Yamanaka's Novels

their elder sister as mother. Ivah's inward voice is the most accurate and intense embodiment of struggling with a lost fortress, mother, since Ivah at thirteen has to be another mother for Maisie and Blu, and even for their father, Poppy. Ivah's increased and forced responsibility in housework and care for Masie and Blu both during daytime and nighttime while Poppy leaves home for two jobs becomes a burden as an unsolved strife against herself. Ivah's inward voice to ask her dead mother to tell her how to cook as well as "how to be a Mama too" is deeply buried and never conveyed to anyone, even her favorite supporter and cousin, Big Sis (*Blu's Hanging* 65).

> "You gotta cook all the meals?" she [Big Sis] asks.
> "Yeah." I don't want to go on. I feel it all rising in my throat, what I want to say, I want to say it to Big Sis. It's harder than I can ever explain, holding it all in. No Mama, no Ziplocs. No Mama, no vitamins. No Mama, no Pledge. No Mama, no wonder. (*Blu's Hanging* 82)

In contrast to a compassionate perspective to Ivah as the eldest who is obliged to play a substituted mother role, there is an opposite view against the sister / mother situation from the younger children. Sonia's strong hatred to her sister, Celeste Kurisu, is based on Celeste's overwhelming care, control, and even domination due to her immaturity.

> It was Celeste who walked me to school every day, fed me

canned goods and rice for breakfast, and told me what to say when the CPS social worker came looking for us. She got me on the sampan bus after school, down the icy corridors of the hospital, and into the room where Grace spent the next six nights. Every night, we were deposited at Aunty Effie's. And every night by twelve, Celeste made sure we slept in our own beds.

Sister / Mother, it all sounds so loving.

But she of the iron-fisted mommydom became the Sadist.

And I of the get-the-sit / mind / soul-beaten-out-of-me-or-else became the Mesochist.

So your word, Celeste Kurisu-Infantino, twenty years later, I still fucking hate you, wife of Sicilian not Portagee, Michael Onfantino; mother of Tiffany, fat and full of acne, and Heather who draws cat's claws in God's eyes, keep it for me, my: *Sister / sadist*. (*Father of the Four Passages* 6)

The stories from both sides — the elder sister / mother and the younger sister / baby — embody the tragic consequence of the recontructed family frame by the unharmonized members whose roles are forced to be played and recognized.

The absense of mother that embodies the lack of love, care, and protection results in the children's hardships of establishing self-expression, self-control, and self-confidence in the psychologically stable and well-balanced conditions.

Chapter 5 : Sexual Colonialism in a Postcolonial Era in Lois-Ann Yamanaka's Novels

IV. The Hetero / Homo Sexual Abuse as a Crucial Injury and Trauma

In a colonial scheme of local islands of Hawai'i, the children are confronted with the hetero / homo sexual abuse and neglect that leaves them a crucial psychological injury and trauma. In the low-income local family, the children are laborers, caretakers for the younger children and housekeepers, and often become the victims of domestic violence and sexual abuse. The loss of the beloved's protection, especially, causes the danger of children's becoming the victims of sexual, physical, and psychological abuse. The intolerable and tragic case of abuse is that the reliable friends or close people betray the psychologically immature teenagers, and the familiar yet malicious adults sexually abuse and molest the children without the correct knowledge of sex and embrace of love.

The psychologically immature teenagers and adolescents fall into being victims of sexual harrassment, sexual abuse, and worst of all, of pregnancy and abortion or unwanted birth of babies. In *Name Me Nobody*, Emi-lou's immaturity and misjudgement results in the possible rape incident by a good-looking yet brainless hapa, Kyle Kiyabu, and even in the betrayal by her and her family's favorite and respected boy, Sterling Jardine, as described it is "full of the anguish of adolescence: the fierce face of peer pressure, the need to belong and the confusion of love and blooming sexuality" (Oi, "Nobody" n.pag.). More tragically, Emi-lou was born even not as "an option" to abortion when her mother became pregnant. A set of pregnancy and abortion is the consequence of the immature teenagers' and adolescents' thoughtless and careless behaviors. In *Wild Meat and the Bully Burgers*, Crystal Kawasaki, a local highschool student, has love affairs with her boyfriend, Larry, while babysitting Lovey and Calhoon, becomes pregnant, and is consequently sent to Japan for abortion: "Gunfunnit, thass why, you get girls, you get the prize. Boys, they no take home the prize. Ai, pua ting her. She neva going forget this one in her whole life. Ass all she going have is regrets, regrets, regrets. And plenty shame, no, Hubert?" (*Wild Meat and the Bully Burgers* 208). More intriguingly, Sonia's letters to her three whom she "killed" imply her passage from having irresponsible relationships with men, being addicted to drug and alcohol, going through the physical and psychological hardships in abortion, being hunted by those children named Number One, Number Two, and Jar, and searching for the way to redemption.

As an alternative to abortion, bearing the unwanted babies leaves the single mothers the ground of facing hardships of children's care, being possibly involved in children's abuse, suffering the self-hate, yet it ultimately creates the room to resolve their agony and anxiety after a series of complicated emotions such as regret, joy, anger, and pain. Toni, who suppresses her platonic love to Billy, yet who discovers an ecstasy in her affairs with both Santos brothers goes through a process of those complicated emotions. Sonia's initial regret and hatred to her fourth and born baby Sonny Boy is

Chapter 5 : Sexual Colonialism in a Postcolonial Era in Lois-Ann Yamanaka's Novels

revealed in a form of physical abuse and in an internal voice of apology:

> I am screaming inside:
> *Shut the fuck up. Shut up, fucking rotten little shit. You better shut up right now or I will fucking kill you.*
> My teeth grit, my hands fold into fists, and I hit his face, squeeze his cheeks inside my closing palms. . . .
> *Sorry. I'm sorry, baby. Mommy loves her little boy.*
> (*Father of the Four Passages* 26)

Sonia's failure as a student, a woman, and eventually a mother makes her suffer. Sonia's psychological stability is, however, regained in a process of taking care of Sonny Boy as her agony over the children's unknown fathers is overlapped with her father's search for himself. In an interview, Yamanaka believes that the truth exists in the darkness that is so "tantalizing" and "comforting" that darkness feels "almost as warm as light" and insists that her own motherhood is a healing to herself as it is "an incredible moment of relief and joy" (Garber n.pag.). In her portrayal of the young woman who is generally criticized for irresponsibility, insensibility, and ignorance, Yamanaka attempts to evaluate the woman's growth in her awakening to maternal instincts and love.

The children without the correct knowledge of sex fall into being victims of sexual abuse and molestation. Blu at eight becomes a victim of sexual abuse by male neighbors,

Mr. Iwasaki and Uncle Paulo. Mother's repeated warning before her death never to walk past Mr. Iwasaki's house because he is recognized as a sexual pervert cannot prevent Blu from being involved in Iwasaki's sexual abuse and presumably a prostitution by getting "Violet Crumbles, a $100,000 bar, and a box of Milk Duds. Dollar bills" (*Blu's Hanging* 20). Blu's sexual inclination is strengthened by the sucking game by half-Japanese and half-Filipino Blendaine, one of Reyes' sisters who are constantly sexually abused by their twenty-year-old uncle, Uncle Paulo during his babysitting. Blu's sexual crisis which is repeatedly forewarned reaches the final point when he is sexually molested, physically injured, and psychologically tormented. Billy at sixtyeen in *Heads by Harry* as a sexually awakening teenager is described as a possible victim of molestation. In Billy's case, his six-year-old sister-like beloved Toni is aware of the danger of sexually attracting an inexperienced teenager. Actually attracted by Billy, Toni, however, blames herself for becoming an "Emerald Hiramoto, a pseudo-child-molester sicko" and refrains from having a sexual relationship with Billy (*Heads by Harry* 243). Toni's consistent attentions to Billy, different from Uncle Paulo's and Mr. Iwasaki's cruel and selfish desire for powerless children, prevent her from being inclined to have sex with Billy. The lack of love and attentions alters the children into the attention-seeking personalities whose weakness and powelessness are used in abuse and molestation.

The closely-knitted family and extentive family/community

Chapter 5 : Sexual Colonialism in a Postcolonial Era in Lois-Ann Yamanaka's Novels

tie without the appropriate attention and the correct knowledge of sex endangers the children and young people as the most powerless members in the enclosed domestic and local spheres. The hetero / home sexual abuse and neglect of local children and young people embody the crucial factor to encode the violated land and its people's lives.

V. The Caucasian Educators and American-Oriented Educational Institution as the Foreground of Battlefield

The neglect of and racial discrimination against pidgin-speaking local children is housed within the educational institution whose policies are established, supported, and protected by white-oriented educators. In Yamanaka's novels, white teachers' discrimination against local children and their families is caused by their strong sense of superiority over the locals' racial background, lower economical status, and lower educational background. There is especially a great gap between Hawaii's private schools and public schools whose operations are too hard to do.[8] Their crucial target of discrimination is pidgin English that they are convinced should be reformed into standard English. Since American educational system was introduced in the 1880's, Standard English has been encouraged to learn and use in Hawai'i (Kau A3). Caucasian teachers who despise pidgin English as well as local people's life-styles have no understanding of, no respect to, and no care for local children. Opposed to Caucasian teachers most of whom are from the Mainland, local teachers, especially Japanese local women teachers, intend to save the local children: and at the same time, to receive higher education and have such a profession as a teacher becomes the local children's ideal and most respectable dream.

In *Wild Meat and the Bully Burgers*, the white-oriented and American legislature's educational policy that focuses on the reformation of pidgin English is represented by Mr. Harvey who repeatedly insists on the importance of acquiring standard English.

> "No one will want to give you a job. You sound uneducated. You will be looked down upon. You're speaking a low-class form of good Standard English. Continue, and you'll go nowhere in life. Listen, students, I'm telling you the truth like no one else will. Because they don't know how to say it to you. I do. Speak Standard English. DO NOT speak pidgin. You will only be hurting yourselves." (*Wild Meat and the Bully Burgers* 9)

The Caucasian-centered discrimination against pidgin brings out the local children's loss of sense of pride in and respect of their ethnic and cultural heritage and immigration history including their houses, their foods, their manners, their customs, and ultimately their families.

Education is, however, an important key in the sexual

Chapter 5 : Sexual Colonialism in a Postcolonial Era in Lois-Ann Yamanaka's Novels

colonialism, especially for powerless children and women who suffer their unfortunate domestic and social conditions. In the local education, the minority teachers' influence is intense enough for the local children to have the idealized life and the possible future profession. The minority teachers, especially Japanese local teachers, play a very important role to care and save the powerless local children who struggle with domestic, financial, and social difficulties. Against the Caucasian, called "haole," teachers or Americanized local teachers, the minority-oriented Japanese teachers possess a compassionate attitude toward and profound understanding of the local children because they share the same background in the former plantation community and the same experiences of poverty, racial discrimination, and local values. Miss Sandra Ito, a kindergarten's Special Ed teacher, in *Blu's Hanging* is a savior for the Ogata children whose mother passed away and whose father is too busy to look after his children. Miss Ito raises a brave and challenging rebellion against an insensible haole teacher, Miss Tammy Owens, who is originally from the Midwest, had a dream of coming to Hawai'i as a paradise, yet has already become disillusioned, and hates both "the heat and the children" (*Blu's Hanging* 59). The local teachers' embrace of and affection for their students, as shown to Lovey and Emi-lou as well as the Ogatas, represents an important source of local children's awakening and establishing their own sense of self-esteem and identity.

The local teacher who plays a role model motivates their

students to have a positive attitude to study and pursue a career in the future. Encouraged by Miss Ito, Ivah's anxiety over womanhood and her loneliness are turned into her anxiety over her future and transformed into her will to have a well-established life and to fulfill herself by receiving a higher education in Honolulu. Ivah's struggle with her decision-making is also described in her inward communication with her dead mother, a spirit who is wandering around. Ivah's departure to Honolulu which enables the mother's spirit to "find her way to heaven" (*Wild Meat and the Bully Burgers* 26) is a resolution of the once-lost and unprotected home without mother. The life as the battlefield for Ivah as the eldest child without anyone on whom she can depend becomes the ground for the self-search in a possibly acquired new space that is opened for her. Similar to Ivah, Emi-lou's inferiority complex as a fat girl without baseball skills for the Hilo Astros is contrasted with her superiority as an excellent ninth grader with advanced writing skills enough to become an intern at high school. Seemingly opposed to Ivah and Emi-lou's success at school, Toni and Sonia who are given a chance of receiving college education fail in completing it, yet can be engaged in the vocation succeeded by their fathers / teachers, hunting / taxidermy for Toni and music for Sonia.

Caucasian teachers' lack of understanding and right judgement of local children and American education's institutionalized discrimination against local children that cause the trauma in local children and even parents are rescued and reconstructed by local teachers who share the same experience, social and historical background, and the complicated emotions. Education whose purpose is not only to show the academic achievements but also to lead to finding the professions and establishing self-esteem is evaluated as the essential element for women whose selves and voices have been ignored in a context of sexual colonianism.

VI. Conclusion

Yamanaka's sexual colonianism as the most crucial tragic element in her works is what characters, especially local children and teenagers, have to undergo: some are fallen as victims and the others overcome the wounds and resolve their hardships. The physically and psychologically violated and wounded Hawaii's landscape reminds the readers of the long-neglected and misinterpreted history of Hawai'i. The contemporary local people's hardships, both in domestic and social spheres rooted in the violated landscape of Hawai'i, are delineated under such crucial conditions as the actual and metaphorical absence of mother, the physical / psychological / sexual abuse of children, and the Caucasian teachers' lack of understanding of and respect to the local people's poverty, life-styles, values, and pidgin English.

Notes

For putting my idea in this paper, I would like to express the deepest gratitude to The American Studies Foundation for the travel grand to attend the 22nd Annual American Studies Forum by the Center for Asia-Pacific Exchange, in summer, 2002, to all the participants of the Forum, especially President of CAPE Jai-Ho Yoo for his support, and its keynote speaker, Professor Dana D. Nelson, for a long friendship since our graduate school days. I also would like to thank Juliet S. Kono, Joy Kobayashi-Cintron, Joan Hori, Gayle Sato, Harry Wong, and John Watt for their support and assistance. Last of all, I thank Lois-Ann Yamanaka and her son John who shared with me a production of *Heads by Harry* at Kumu Kahua Theatre on March 23, 2003 during my research stay in Hawai'i. My research on Hawaii's local literature was supported by the 1997-2000 Grant-in-Aid for Scientific Research (C)(2) on Hawaii's local literature in a postcolonial view and the 2002-2005 Grant-in-Aid for Scientific Research (C)(2) on Hawaii's local theatres and plays, by Japan Society for the Promotion of Science. This paper wasoriginally published in *Doshisha Literature* 47 (2004): 27-51.

* I preserved all the original spellings of Pidgin English without marking [sic].

1. As for the detailed chronology of the controversy of Yamanaka's portrayal of Filipino by Association for Asian American Studies, see Pisares.
2. See Fujikane ("Book's" B4), Cordero, et al. (A-6), and Fujikane ("Reimagining" 48).
3. See James. As for younger scholars who published their papers more than ten years after a controversy over *Blu's Hanging*, see Seri Luangphinith, Erin Suzuki, Elda E. Tsou, and Cynthia Wu.
4. See Wilson and Dissanayake 1-18.

Chapter 5 : Sexual Colonialism in a Postcolonial Era
in Lois-Ann Yamanaka's Novels

5. According to Law, the "most widely accepted theory is that leprosy was introduced by Chinese immigrants who were brought to Hawai'i to work as indentured laborers. The disease came to be known by two names, *ma'i pake* (the Chinese sickness) and *ma'i ali'i* (the royal sickness), the latter term indicating its incidence among and association with the Hawaiian royalty (n.pag.).

6. According to Law and Wisniewski, Kahili "evolved from a receiving station where patients were simply 'stored' until they could be 'shipped' to Kalaupapa into a hospital where people were medically treated. An act passed in 1909 that a person could not be sent to the settlement until he had been treated for six months, unless at least three licensed physicians stated that he could not be materially benefited by further treatment. By 1910, four new buildings, capable of accomodating up to 96 patients, had been completed at Kalihi" (59-60).

7. In Yamanaka's *Wild Meat and the Bully Burgers*, there is a chapter entitled "Rags" where Lovey's embarrassment and inarticulation of menstruation is vividly and closely described (118-24).

8. Even in 1990's, "about one-third of Hawaii's preschool children are already headed for failure because of poverty, sickness, and other handicapping conditions, coupled with a lack of adult protection and nurturance" (McPhee 29).

Works Cited

Cordero, David, Mary L. Cordero, Alfred Evengelista, Candace Fujikane, Linda Revilla, and Darlene Rodrigues. "Locals Must Listen to Locals." *The Hawaii Herald* 21 Apr. 1999: A-6.

Crawford, David Livingston. *Paradox in Hawaii: An Examination of Industry and Education and the Paradox They Present*. Boston: Stratford, 1933.

Fujikane, Candace. "Book's Stereotypes of Filipinos are Simplistic, Sad and

Hurtful." *The Honolulu Advertiser* 5 July 1998: B1-B4.

——. "'Blu's Hanging': The Responsibilities Faced by Local Readers and Writers." *The Hawaii Herald* 16 Jan. 1998: A-9-A-11.

——. "Reimagining Development and the Local in Lois-Ann Yamanaka's *Saturday Night at the Pahala Theatre*." *Women in Hawai'i: Sites, Identities, and Voices*. Ed. Jongue, Chinon N, Kathleen O. Kane, and Ida M. Yoshinaga. Honolulu: UH Sociology Department and U of Hawai'i P, 1997. 42-61.

Garber, Jon. "Lois-Ann Yamanaka." Rev. of *Father of the Four Passages* by Lois-Ann Yamanaka. *Central Booking* 2001. 11 Sep. 2002 <http://www.cenbtralbooking.com/inconversationwith_current.shtml?interview=28>.

James, Jamie. "This Hawaii Is Not for Tourists." *The Atlantic Monthly* Feb. 1999. 1 Jan. 2000 <http://www.theatlantic.com/issues/99feb/hawaii.htm>.

Judd Jr., M.D., Charles S. "Leprosy in Hawaii, 1889-1976." *Hawaii Medical Journal* 43.9 (Sep. 1984): 328-34.

"Kalaupapa National Historical Park." *National Park Service* 12 Feb. 2001. 31 July 2002 <http://www.nps.gov/kala/>.

Kam, Nadine. "So Many Stories to Tell." *The Honolulu Star-Bulletin* 8 Apr. 1997. 13 Sep. 2002 <http://starbulletin.com/97/04/08/features/storyl.html>.

——. "Writer's Blu's." *The Honolulu Star Bulletin* 6 July 1998. 17 Feb. 2001 <http://starbulletin.com/98/07/06/features/story2.html>.

Kau, Crystal. "UH Group: Respect Ridgin in Schools." *The Honolulu Star-Bulletin* 20 Nov. 1999: A3.

Law, Anwei Skinsnes. *Kalaupapa: A Portrait*. Wayne Levin. Honolulu: Arizona Memorial Museum Association and Bishop Museum, 1989.

Law, Anwei V. Skinsnes, and Richard A. Wisniewski. *Kalaupapa and the Legacy of Father Damien*. Honolulu: Pacific Basin, 1988.

Lauangphinith, Seri. "Homeward Bound: Settler Aesthetics in Hawai'i's Literature." *Texas Studies in Literature and Language* 48.1 (Spring

2006): 54-78.

McPhee, Roderick F. "Public Schools." Roth 29-38.

Monson, Valerie. "The '42 Gang." *Hawaii News, Tourist and Vacation Information*. 29 July 2002 <http://www.maui.net/~mauinews/ainews Oc.htm>.

Oi, Cynthia. "Novelist Captures Essence of Hawaii." *The Honolulu StarBulletin* 5 Oct. 1999. 21 May 2001 <http://starbulletin.com/1999/10/05/news/story9.html>.

——. "Nobody's Somebody." Rev. of *Name Me Nobody* by Lois-Ann Yamanaka. *The Honolulu Star-Bulletin* 25 June 1999. 11 Sep. 2002 <http://starbulletin.com/1999/06/25/features/storyl.html>.

Okihiro, Gary Y. *Cane Fires: the Anti-Japanese Movement in Hawaii, 1865-1945*. Philadelphia: Temple UP, 1991.

——. *Common Ground: Reimagining American History*. Princeton: Princeton UP, 2001.

Pennybacker, Mindy. "What Boddah You?: The Authenticity Debate." *The Nation* 1 Mar. 1999. 13 July 2000 <http://www.thenation.com/issue/990301/0301Pennybacker.shtml>.

Pisares, Elizabeth H. "Passing for Asian: Filipino Americans and Filipino American Studies within Asian American Studies." 1999. 13 Sep. 2002 <http://www.alohatouch.com/asian204/passing-for-asian.html>.

Roth, Randall W., ed. *The Price of Paradise Vol. II*. Honolulu: Mutual Publishing, 1993.

Smith, Kirk R. "Environment." Roth 259-64.

Suzuki, Erin. "Haunted Homelands: Negotiating Locality in *Father of The Four Passages*." *Modern Fiction Studies* 56.1 (Spring 2010): 160-82.

Takaki, Ronald. *Pau Hana: Plantation Life and Labor in Hawai'i, 1835-1920*. Honolulu: U of Hawai'i P, 1985.

Tanner, Mika. "The Real-Life Sequel to 'Blu's Hanging.'" *Asia Week* 6-12 Aug. 1998. 13 Sep. 2002 <http://humwww.ucsc.edu/history/history186/syllabus.htm>.

Tsou Elda E. "Catachresis: *Blu's Hanging* and the Epistemology of the

Given." *JAAS* 14.2 (June 2011): 283-303.

Wilson, Rob, and Wimal Dissnayake. Introduction: Tracking the Global / Local. *Global / Local: Cultural Production and the Transnational Imaginary*. Ed. Rob Wilson and Wimal Dissanayake. Durham: Duke UP, 1996. 1-18.

Wu, Cynthia. "Revising *Blu's Hanging*: A Critique of Queer Transgression in the Lois-Ann Yamanaka Controversy." *Meridians* 10.1 (2010): 32-53.

Yamanaka, Lois-Ann. *Blu's Hanging*. New York: Farrar, 1997.

——. *Father of the Four Passages*. New York: Farrar, 2001.

——. *Heads by Harry*. New York: Farrar, 1999.

——. *Name Me Nobody*. New York: Hyperion, 1999.

——. *Wild Meat and the Bully Burgers*. New York: Harvest, 1997.

Chapter 6

Holding Trauma in Lois-Ann Yamanaka's *Behold the Many*

I. Introduction

Set in colonial Hawai'i between 1913 and 1939, Lois-Ann Yamanaka's latest novel, *Behold the Many* (2006), embraces the long-concealed trauma as the consequence of colonialism. Yamanaka creates her unique narrative style and constructs the layered voices of three Japanese-Portuguese daughters who are infected by tuberculosis and confined to St. Joseph's, a Catholic orphanage in Hawaii's Kalihi Valley. This orphanage — which is geographically, socially, and also psychologically isolated from their parents and the other 'healthy' people — symbolizes the invisible yet deeply-rooted prejudice against patients suffering from tuberculosis, a diagnosis that was much abused during the colonial era. Yamanaka's novel brings into focus conflicts that extended over three generations conflicts that involved essential issues of death and survival.

Linked with her controversial novel, *Blu's Hanging*, *Behold the Many* is Yamanaka's courageous experiment in discovering the long-hidden and untold stories behind the modern history of Hawai'i. *Blu's Hanging* shows how victims of Hansen's disease were oppressed socially, economically, and legally, as sufferers were confined in the remote colony at Kalaupapa in Molokai, Hawai'i, during the colonial and postcolonial eras. *Blu's Hanging* deals with the multi-racial postcolonial sphere, especially pointing out the controversial issue of the local Japanese and the local Filipinos in the postwar era and the invading force of Americanization. Furthermore, *Behold the Many* underscores tuberculosis or consumption, and in addition, deepens the more crucial racial and sexual conflicts between the local Japanese and the local Portuguese in the prewar era. Both Hansen's disease and tuberculosis were diseases of the Empire, insofar as sufferers, together with the diseases themselves, were relegated to a colonized sphere, and insofar as the colonized were seen as infected by social, economic, cultural, and pathogenic germs. *Behold the Many*, therefore, develops the subject of physical and psychological isolation, neglect, and oppression as traumatic experience of tuberculosis in colonial Hawai'i.

In her second experiment in treating "illness" as a theme (in *Behold the Many*), Yamanaka more directly challenges what Susan Sontag calls "Illness as Metaphor," and she does so in the context of the multiethnic community of immigrants

Chapter 6 : Holding Trauma in Lois-Ann Yamanaka's *Behold the Many*

that lived on sugarcane plantations and rural ranches in early twentieth-century Hawai'i. Haunted by the dead, the eldest daughter and the main character, Anah (Susanah Medeiors) — as survivor of both prison and hospital — encodes illness as a metaphor of a "diseased" plantation camp-life, and, furthermore, of the racially and sexually violated colonial life. Through Anah's life and through the lives of those who surround her, Yamanaka deploys her central metaphor in enclosed, disclosed, and integrated narratives, and ultimately continues looking for the lost spiritual space of home for the surviving people.

As witnessed in her other novels, *Behold the Many* consists of Yamanaka's innovative narrative style in which the integrated voices of the living, the dead, and the survivor are enclosed within themselves yet disclosed in the confined and shadowed space of colonialism and imperialism. The double hardships of minority status and mortal disease threaten, and almost destroy, primarily wholesome physical and psychological conditions. As a local writer, Yamanaka is blessed with a highly-cultivated ability to manipulate Pidgin English as a first language. As a contemporary American writer, Yamanaka invents and builds a unique style that blends spoken voices with written texts. In *Living in the Shadow of Death*, interestingly, Sheila M. Rothman points out that the "narrative of illness is very different from the case record" since "each has [its] particular structure, perspective, tone and plot" even as both of them "report the origins, symptoms, and progress of the disease" (1).

The narrative of illness formulates its own literature, and Yamanaka challenges us by constructing a personal yet credible, emotional yet impressive, and intimate yet detailed narrative in her novel. As for the cultural and social significance of tuberculosis in literature: Mark Caldwell makes an interesting comment that American literature "avoided the subject" between 1890 and 1950 when tuberculosis was an everyday word and subject, whereas European literature, exclusively represented by *The Magic Mountain,* "virtually battened on it" (217). In narrating tuberculosis in *Behold the Many*, Yamanaka places illness in imperialism and colonialism, and recreates as metaphor, history, and also landscape.

II. Illness in Imperialism and Colonialism

As evidences of imperialism and colonialism, Yamanaka deliberately and subtly mentions historical figures who influenced colonial Hawai'i which had been religiously, economically, politically, and culturally invaded and therefore colonized by England, and then America, and which at the same time had been associated with Japan. Hawaii's geographical location in the middle of the Pacific Ocean determines her fate with imperialism and colonialism.

In a 1919 section, Hawaii's political crisis is noted and it is echoed in voices of lamenting for the dead of tuberculosis in Kalihi Valley as well as for Queen Lili'uokalani, which

Chapter 6 : Holding Trauma in Lois-Ann Yamanaka's
Behold the Many

is shown in Anah's crying, "Our Queen Lili'u is dead" in a 1917 section (94).

> It was the morning of December 24. In this season of glad tidings, Prince Jonah Kahio Kalanianaole and Governor Charles J. McCarthy had been unsuccessful in their bid for Congress to consider Hawai'i for statehood. In their season of glad tidings, Prohibition was law. But it was Christmas at St. Joseph's. (133)

Historically, Hawai'i was confronted with the crisis of maintaining the Kingdom of Hawai'i after Hawai'i became Christianized, and then economically controlled by Anglo-European capitalists and investors. Hawaii's political decline became definite after Queen Lili'uokalani was forced to be overthrown in 1893. After this monarchy overthrown, she was confined until she died in 1917. In 1898, the Republic of Hawai'i approved a joint resolution of annexation creating the U.S. Territory of Hawai'i, yet this political struggle continued till 1959 when Hawai'i became the U.S. state. Anah's sorrow over her illness and her loneliness without any family visit to the orphanage in Christmas is connected with the Queen's sorrow to end her life in a confinement. Kalihi Valley represents the confinement of Hawai'i which suffered Anglo-European imperialism and colonialism, and prisoners in Kalihi Valley can be compassionate to the tragic queen who lost her power and dignity.

As for Hawaii's association with Japan, on the other

hand, both Emperor Taisho and Prince Komatsu are mentioned as those who supported the possible tie between the Kingdom of Hawai'i and Imperial Japan. Emperor Taisho (1912-1926), enthroned after Emperor Meiji (1868-1912), is a contemporary figure in *Behold the Many*, so that he is portrayed as a honorable and respectable hero. His contributions to social welfare to Japanese immigrants in Hawai'i are, ironically, associated with illness.

> Even those who left for lung operation at the Japanese Charity Hospital on Kuakini Street, endowed by the divine Emperor Taisho and his empress for the many Japanese immigrants laboring on the inhumane sugar plantation in Hawai'i, never recovered or never returned. (159)

Since Emperor Meiji united the treaty with King Kalakaua in 1881, Japan and the Kingdom of Hawai'i maintained cordial relations and promoted the treaty of amity. Japan-Hawai'i friendship and goodwill is proven in the fact that King Kalakaua urged Princess Kaiulani to get married to one of the Imperial family. In Hawai'i, moreover Japanese immigrants kept their respect and admiration for the Japanese Emperor and royal families since the Emperor was believed God before the Second World War.

Japanese immigrants' devotion to the Emperor and royal families is proven in their great esteem for them and also for themselves. Anah's absorb in her fairy tale with the Japanese royal family in Kalihi Valley in 1916 embodies the military and political empowerment of the Japanese Empire which won the wars including the First World War between 1914 and 1918.

> On these nights, Anah told Aki fondly remembered stories of their brother Charles and stories told to her by their okaasan of Japan's brave young Prince Komatsu, who visited Hawaii aboard a mighty warship. She told Aki stories of Okaasan's mother and her mother before her and her mother before her, stories of a lineage of influential women shamans with magical powers who ruled alongside kings. (69)

Japanese royal families are illustrated in the fairy tale or traditional ritual which is created and narrated with a strong sense of admiration for their own ancestors. Imperialism which crucially influenced Japanese immigrants in Hawai'i is not counted as the cause of victimization since Japanese immigrants were not directly involved in it. At home, Japan had already established the imperialistic regime and the Imperial Army began to gain its totalitarian power during the years including the Sino-Japanese War between 1894 and 1895 and the Russo-Japanese Was between 1904 and 1905. The Japanese Imperial Army sacrificed themselves to the First World War (1914-1918). To this Japan's transformation to the imperial state, same as Anglo-European imperialism, Japanese immigrants are blind so that they do not associate their hardship with the consequence of damaged and dethroned Hawai'i.

In *Behold the Many*, imperialism and colonialism affect Japanese immigrants in two conflicting and ironical spheres, inside the Kingdom (later Republic) of Hawaiʻi which declined rapidly and outside the Japanese Empire which increased in power. In order to bring this crossed spheres of imperialism, Yamanaka manipulates illness as the basis for her novel.

III. Illness as Metaphor

Both physically and psychologically sickened, the Medeiors family symbolizes the unstable, unhealthy, and unprotected human conditions in the early settlement era of multi-racial immigrants. Their conflicts were interwoven both inside their racially-mixed communities and in the outside colonial sphere, which was controlled, influenced, and established — and yet also misguided and molested — by Euro-American Caucasian settlers, merchants, sailors, outlaws, and even Christian missionaries. In order to depict this layering of colonial brutality over the will to survive, Yamanaka effectively employs illness as a metaphor of implanted and diseased values; more specifically still, tuberculosis, an infectious disease caused by the tubercle bacillus, underlines the social, economic, and racial oppression of patients and families. Yamanaka's intention to manipulate metaphorical meanings of illness can be examined in her silent revolt against romanticism, in her

Chapter 6 : Holding Trauma in Lois-Ann Yamanaka's *Behold the Many*

reconstruction of a place of treatment in an orphanage (as against the idealized sanatorium), in her effort to rewrite the cultural history of illness, and in her earnest investigation of sexual conflicts in colonial Hawai'i.

Although tuberculosis was quite frequently romanticized in nineteenth-century literature both in Europe and Japan, it had been a dreadful and deadly disease, especially for the poor. Nineteenth-century literature is, according to Sontag, "stocked with descriptions of almost symptomless, unfrightened, featific deaths from TB, particularly of young people" (20), and also with "the image of. a 'diseased' love" and of "passion that 'consume'" (25). Given that the late-nineteenth and early twentieth-centuries witnessed a group of talented writers, poets, artists, and pianists who were infected with tuberculosis and accomplished outstanding things, it was easily and wrongly believed that tuberculosis lay at the root of creative achievements (Fukuda 166-67). Especially in Japan, we find is what's called a "literature of tuberculosis." In *The Modern Epidemic: A History of Tuberculosis in Japan*, William Johnston remarks that the number of works dealing with tuberculosis is so large in nineteenth and early twentieth-century literature that "an entire volume on the literature of tuberculosis" could be completed" (124). This entire volume of literature of romanticized and misconceived tuberculosis which is deeply rooted both in Europe and in Japan is what Yamanaka challenges in reviving the muted voices and neglected selves in the colonial context of America.

Since Yamanaka is a *sansei*, she must be rather concerned about tuberculosis as a serious issue for the Japanese. Tragic death caused by tuberculosis was first romanticized and then virtually rationalized in European and Japanese literature; the pain and agony which the disease brings to patients and their families was omitted or else dramatized as a tragedy. Economic and social status determined the treatment of tuberculosis patients and also the fate of their lives after they were discharged and returned to life outside the hospitals and sanatoriums. As social outsiders, discharged patients were confronted with prejudice and could not readily return to their families and communities. Against the nineteenth-century mythology of tuberculosis, Yamanaka attempts to reveal the long-rejected and inarticulate self of the patient, she encodes this romanticized image of tuberculosis, and she dares to retell what lay behind the disease in early twentieth-century Hawai'i. Yamanaka recreates the symbolical meaning of tuberculosis in her trial to establish a literature of her own.

The most striking symbol of tuberculosis is represented by sanatoriums which provide a clean environment, rich nutrition, and special nursing, and yet isolate patients from families and friends, depriving them of essential human contact, and ultimately marking them as prisoners. Traveling to a better climate and cleaner environment first became prevalent in the early nineteenth-century; tuberculosis became "a new reason for exile" and tuberculosis patients were eager to travel to Italy as Keats did, to islands in the Mediterranean as Chopin did, or to islands in the South

Chapter 6 : Holding Trauma in Lois-Ann Yamanaka's *Behold the Many*

Pacific as Robert Louis Stevenson did (Sontag 37). After sanatoriums began to be established and popularly accepted as necessary institutions in Europe, America, and Japan, tuberculosis again gained more attention in literature. As seen in Thomas Mann's *The Magic Mountain* (1913-24) and in Japanese novels by such writers as Hori Tatsuo, Nakahara Chuya, Miyazawa Kenji, and Dazai Osamu, the tuberculosis / sanatorium theme resigned supreme since victims — whether the writers themselves or simply characters in their works — were highly sympathetic. It is important to notice that *The Magic Mountain* began to be published in 1913, when the story begins in Yamanaka's *Behold the Many*. *The Magic Mountain* critically describes a group of wealthy tuberculosis patients who received treatment in a well-organized and aristocratic sanatorium built in the fresh-airy mountains in Switzerland. Sanatorium as the sanctuary of wealthy patients is registered as an ironical space where the superficial and idealized aspects are too enlarged and exaggerated to be properly recognized and investigated.

In *Behold the Many*, therefore, Yamanaka constructs another scene of treatment in an orphanage, which implies the terminal destination for infant patients, insofar as most of these are literally abandoned by their own parents. Set in the same year as *The Magic Mountain*, *Behold the Many* places helpless children of poor families in an orphanage / sanitarium in the deep valley of Kalihi, "a desolate, hot, and inconspicuous area west of Honolulu, far from the roving eyes of tourists and the disapproving gaze of townsfolk" (Hanley and Bushnell 275). In contrast to the sanatorium for the leisured classes featured in *The Magic Mountain*, *Behold the Many* criticizes the socially-constructed "invalidism" (Sontag 37) of the Romantics. In 1888, due to a decision of the Board of Health, Kalihi was primarily established, by Mother Marianne of the Sacred Heart, as "a receiving and shipping station in Honolulu" for patients of Hansen's disease (Hanley and Bushnell 275). The difference between the conditions of tuberculosis patients is enlarged not only in a global sphere but also in a socio-economic sphere as Dai exclaims to his second daughter, Aki, "You go St. Joseph tomorrow," since they "had mo'money for the sanatoria. Let the holy sisters take care you" (23). In remote mountains in the South Pacific Island, Yamanaka formulates the tuberculosis / orphanage theme as one that involves, at its core, the deprivation of love, the destruction of the healthy body and soul, the damaging of all wholesome human conditions, and the dislocation of the self. The weakest children became the victims of worst living conditions, bereft of parental love and social contact, both of which are needed to develop their psychological growth. Yamanaka's recreation of illness as a metaphor in the post-colonial era embodies her challenge to create a new metaphor of illness in her literature.

Chapter 6 : Holding Trauma in Lois-Ann Yamanaka's
Behold the Many

IV. Illness as History

In the nineteenth and twentieth centuries, a succession of dreadful epidemics was visited upon the isolated Hawaiian islands, which had never been infected by them before. Not only tuberculosis but also most of the other dreadful epidemics threatened and all but decimated Native Hawaiians, as outsiders such as Euro-American sailors, merchants, and Asian immigrants brought the pathogens to Hawai'i. In Yamanaka's *Behold the Many*, a history of epidemics in Hawai'i is recorded in the family history of the Medeiors. This early immigrant family history is remembered when the last record of tuberculosis is added by Dai Medeior, as his youngest daughter Leah is infected.

> Dai nodded, utterly afraid of years of the leprosy that took a second cousin, then an older sister, then an aunt to the dreaded peninsula of no return, Kalaupapa, where a leper colony was established on Molokai's rugged north shore in 1886 by royal order of King Kamehameha V. Afraid of the bubonic plague that swept through an overcrowded and filthy Chinatown in 1900, the Board of Health forgoing quarantine and disinfection in favor of a purging by fire, leaving thirty-eight acres of slum in rubble and ash. Afraid of the epidemic of cholera, the worst outbreak since the ma'i 'Oku'u that swept the Sandwich Islands in 1804, this time taking a paternal grandmother who shared living quarters with the Medeiors family soon after her arrival from the Azores in early 1889. Afraid of the

influenza, typhus, whooping cough, the polio that crippled his younger brother, the smallpox that killed the newborn and the elderly. And now very ashamed of the stigma of the consumption that threatened his entire extended family living in Portuguese Camp Four. And off because of his infected youngest daughter. (12)

It is ironical to note that Leah was sent to Kalihi in 1913, that Aki was sent in 1914, and, finally, that Leah and Dai died of tuberculosis in the same year, 1916. Dai's sexual abuse of Ana also suggests that Anah is "infected" by Dai. Dai's cruelty to Anah, Leah, and Aki — who were never allowed to return home during Christmas and to have family members' visits — leads to his own death of tuberculosis, which is also recorded in the family history of illness and in the history of illness in the Empire in colonial and postcolonial Hawai'i. The record of family illness regarding tuberculosis in colonial Hawai'i, which symbolizes the record of history of illness in modern Hawai'i, conveys to us the inevitable path for the immigrants and their offspring, people whose lives were always influenced and controlled by the colonizers with their invisible force.

The family / local community history of illness was produced and reproduced in racial and sexual colonialism in Hawai'i. The early twentieth century was a transitional period in which first-generation immigrants began to settle and have families in colonial Hawai'i. Next to Hansen's disease, tuberculosis was recognized as a fatal disease that could be communicated through sexual contact. Tuberculosis was believed to be connected with sexual desire and this connotation was frequently adopted in nineteenth-century literature. No matter what inferences we might draw from this sexual connotation in literature, tuberculosis was definitely related to racial and sexual oppression caused by imperialism and colonialism in Hawai'i. Hawai'i suffered a series of epidemics and newly-introduced diseases from the West and also from the East. Native Hawaiians who had never been infected by exotic viruses became easily and quickly victimized, and the population of Native Hawaiians dropped rapidly due to these widespread epidemics. In addition, newly-arrived and settled immigrants, whose camp and ranch lives were not completely sanitary, also became victims of epidemics and newly-introduced diseases. Illness embodies the path through which Hawai'i has gone from the early modern colonial era to the post-colonial era, at least insofar as illness was, inevitably, an invader transplanted to Hawai'i, and insofar as illness determined the racial hierarchy as a transitional ground to the establishment of modern Hawai'i.

V. Illness as Landscape

As illness is crucially employed as metaphor and history, it is also delineated in landscape in Yamanaka's novels. Hawaii's landscape connotes female sexuality and the depth of the rainforest portrays woman's body. Yamanaka always examines sexual colonialism in her works, and *Behold the Many* also dares to depict the sexual oppression of women and children who are easily victimized by male family members, especially husbands and fathers, by molesters, harassers, and even killers. Hawai'i is employed as a symbol of this victimization and its landscape has witnessed the victims. In addition to examining racial oppression, *Behold the Many* examines also the sexual oppression involved in imperialism and colonialism in the feminized and violated sphere of Hawai'i. In this transformed landscape, women and children suffer from domestic, community, and social violence. Just as the racial ratio between Anglo-Europeans and non-Anglo-Europeans — which includes Native Hawaiians, Portuguese, and Asians — is unbalanced, the sex ratio within those non-Anglo-European laborers is quite unbalanced. Male laborers in plantation camps and ranches were oppressed under the white Anglo-European planters and rulers. The laborers' hard workload, lack of economic and social stability, loss of human dignity, and even lack of self-respect lead them to alcoholism, gambling, and domestic violence. Consequently, women and children become the target of domestic violence which is hidden and marginalized in the landscape of Hawai'i.

In *Behold the Many*, the real illness in domestic and community spheres is defined as male violence to women and children and the landscape swallows this illness by way of wide-spread tuberculosis in one family. Tuberculosis in

Chapter 6 : Holding Trauma in Lois-Ann Yamanaka's *Behold the Many*

Behold the Many formulates this landscape, which forces the indigenous people and all livings to change their lives, challenges the transplantation of introduced species and colonists, and eventually threatens the endangered species. This landscape transformation is not only witnessed in natural environments, but also in human conditions. Both physical and psychological crises of human conditions reflect the engendered malady of the landscape of Hawai'i.

In *Behold the Many*, womanhood — which is represented in the landscape of the valley — ultimately becomes the surviving force after it "behold[s] the many" dead. This feminized and suffering landscape conveys to us a cry from the deep valley. Both Okaasan (Sumi Medeiors) and her daughter Anah were wrongly criticized by nasty Portuguese female relatives because she became pregnant soon after she bore a baby, and then had to go through pregnancies, miscarriage, and deliveries. Okaasan is regarded as a sexual object, and sold out as a picture bride to a violent and cruel Portuguese man, Dai. Only her sexuality is evaluated in the immigrant community which suffered a shortage of women.

> Okaasan trudged on ahead of them, crying, wiping her face with both hands. She had no one, no family to turn to, disowned from Nihon to Hawaii to Amerika to Kanada to Buraziru. She had disgraced the aggressive village matchmaker from Yanai City and her own desperate father by running away from her marriage contract, running from the docks of Honolulu Harbor with the filthy, hairy Porutogaru-go. (17)

Sumi's story of a picture bride who was disappointed by her newly-wed husband as soon as she arrived in Hawai'i and run away with another man illustrates the tragic fate of the picture bride. Sumi's fate to become a physical and psychological orphan and homeless is determined by her life influenced and controlled by patriarchal power in the transnational colonial period. Sumi's confinement in the violent domestic sphere is an inescapable condition since her orphanage and isolation in a foreign Hawai'i determines her status, role, and also life.

Sumi's agony in her double confinement with a domestic sphere in the colonial sphere results in her mental depressive illness which has never been understood and treated appropriately. Her mental breakdown is caused by her oppression and silenced self who has been repeatedly abused by her husband, who has never been respected by anyone, and who has only been evaluated properly.

> Okaasan picked white ginger for Dai's table and played the koto she had brought over the ocean with her, the beautiful zither given to her by the blind priestess at the temple. She combed her long, black hair with scented oils, her fragile spirit terribly broken.
>
> With Dai's house in order and his wife earnest in her carnal penance, he indulged her madness. Her melancholia would come to pass soon enough, he said to himself. But past the midnight hour while Dai drank and gambled at the stables, Okaasan, ghostlike, drifted from room to room, humming,

Chapter 6 : Holding Trauma in Lois-Ann Yamanaka's *Behold the Many*

staring, sighing, weeping without sound or tears. (38)

Sumi's artistic and elegant taste and skills to play a Japanese traditional instrument, koto, is entirely opposed to Dai's wild and violent taste and behaviors. Sumi's muted self represents the total victimization of the male violence which is formulated and supported by colonialism. Sumi's transplantation in the wrong ground and her everlasting internal agony affects women of three generations who eventually continue to suffer tuberculosis and its consequences.

Especially, Anah — whose "sin" is being a discharged patient of tuberculosis — becomes a target of harassment by her in-laws. Worse still, of Anah's six children, two are born handicapped and two more (the twins) die. As if to punish her "sin" all the more, Anah's two surviving daughters are destined to become victims of violence. Elizabeth — retarded yet with "the purity of her simple heart" (241) — was found raped by sailors while she wandered outside, looking for her missing sister, Hosona. The cruelest consequence of Anah's survival is the murder case in which another surviving daughter, Hosana — who is grown as "a hearty and bawdy one-eyed cowboy" at age fourteen — elopes, is abandoned, and then is brutally killed. Anah's life as a survivor — which is filled with death and misfortune — outlines the inescapable victimization suffered by former patients of tuberculosis.

In examining the metaphorical significance and the narrative of tuberculosis, the landscape is the truly important space, where double meanings emerge. *Behold the Many* examines the double hardships of women, that is, racial and sexual distress; moreover, their hardships are intensified by the fatal disease which was believed to be communicated within the family and inherited by the next generation. Consequently, the separation from the family, the forced confinement in a remote area, the inhuman treatment and appalling living conditions, and the strong prejudice were all formulated into a set of unjust values and deployed in the colonial policy in Hawai'i.

In this colonial construction, the Medeiors women are violated by prolonged cruel and unjust treatment and exercise of authority, and three lives are interwoven and portrayed in the symbolical landscape and environment of Hawaii's deep valley and rain forest. Yamanaka presents to us landscape as the woman's body which is transported, transplanted, and eventually wounded, humiliated, disgraced, and violated.

> The valley is a woman lying on her back, legs spread wide, her geography wet by a constant rain. Waterfalls wash the days and nights of winter storms into the river that empties into the froth of the sea.
>
> The valley is a woman with the features of a face, a woman whose eyes watch the procession of the celestial sphere; a woman with woodland arms outstretched and vulnerable, a woman with shadowy breasts of 'a'ali'I and hapu'u, lobelias and lichens; a woman, a womb, impregnated earth. O body.
>
> When they find her, she is shiny, she is naked, she is bound, but for her legs, spread open and wet with blood and semen.

Chapter 6 : Holding Trauma in Lois-Ann Yamanaka's *Behold the Many*

> Tears in her eyes, or is it rain? Breath in her mouth, or is it wind? Her thicket of hair drips into her mouth, sliced open from ear to ear. She is pale green, the silvery underside of kukui leaves; her eyes and lips are gray, the ashen hinahina; her fingers and feet are white, the winter rain in this valley.
> O body.
> O beloved Honona. (3-4)

This very beginning of the novel which presents to us the last victim, Hosona, among women of the Medeiors turns to be the conclusion of the narration whose voice echoes and vibrates throughout the novel.

Both two dead victims and one survivor suffer and conflict with one another; however, they reflect a number of nameless victims and ultimately are incorporated into one life which overcomes the institutionalized discrimination and prejudice against women as victims of racial, sexual, and social oppression caused by colonialism. The landscape reflects and buries those women victims after the landscape is infected, endangered, and violated by the newly-introduced force of imperialism and colonialism.

VI. Illness as Narrator

Already and repeatedly mentioned in this paper, illness can bear, nourish, and establish its own narrative. In reviving the voices of physically-weakened, psychologically-wounded, and socially- disgraced patients, Yamanaka transcends the narrative of illness and recreates illness as narrator. Along with her strategy to employ pidgin English as the spoken language common among Hawaii's inhabitants, Yamanaka challenges the revamped voices of infant patients who are transfigured, weakened, and eventually diminished and reconstructs them in a form of letter, and in the living people's possession by the spirit of the dead.

In order to impress the lost and neglected voices of abandoned infant patients, Yamanaka employs a letter form. Those voices are expressed in handwritten letters by the infant patients who disparately seek affection and attention from the families, relatives, and close friends. The first letter was written by each infant patient such as Aki, Anah, and Leah (52-53) and it was sent to their home without any preferable answer to their expectations. A better-organized Christmas letter by Anah was also sent to their parents (54-55), which ironically connotes their total abandonment and neglect. Their friend Shizu's will (130-32) embodies the voice of the dead who realizes that she has already lost their own voice, yet who needs to leave her last words which were never paid attention to. Shizu's will is written with a purpose to leave her last glorified words to her intimate friend, Anah.

> Please do not die, Anna. I was thinking that the Holy Virgin and St. Joseph are like a mommy and daddy to me since mine had bring me here to get cure when I got the consumption. They can ask Jesus to ask his daddy cure you like He cure me.

Chapter 6 : Holding Trauma in Lois-Ann Yamanaka's *Behold the Many*

> Remember how I use to pray real loud when we feed the pigs and water the donkey and goat and you tell me hush up Shizu but in a nice way? (130)

The most crucial example of letters are love letters exchanged between Anah and Ezroh, a Portuguese attractive boy from the nearby ranch (170-72) since their romance and eventually love affairs are prohibited because of Anah's illness and because the strict control over tuberculosis patients by Sisters of the Sacred Heart. Those love letters which are intruded by the scolding voice of the Sister ironically lead them to forbidden love and eventually their marriage after Anah's discharge from the orphanage. The patients of tuberculosis in the orphanage whose physical and psychological activities are limited and controlled discover their freedom to express their inner selves.

As well as in a letter form, the possibility to liberate the confined people from the physical and psychological limitations can be revealed in the living people's possession by the spirits of the dead. Anah, the only survivor who was discharged from her eight-year confinement, has a role to listen to the dead who envies and attempts to follow Anah in vain, as witnessed in dead Shizu (Seth)'s "Farewell" to Anah, which is quite different from her compassionate and merciful will to her dearest Anah.

> Curse your life for leaving me. Your home is here, turn around, come back.

> Curse my love for you. How I loved you those many years, passing myself sister to dying sister.
> Hate you. Heart.
> Hate you. Broken. (130)

This voice implies the dead people's lament for their short lives with leaving what they wanted to do undone. The dead people's spirits convey to us their sorrow and anger over their incomplete lives. Illness can revive the muted voices of the dying and the dead in letters and spiritual whispers, and create a literature of their own.

VII. Conclusion

Victimization of tuberculosis is a compelling metaphor of the compellingly implanted and wrongly transplanted values which infected the multi-racial settlers and their newly established families. In *Behold the Many,* Yamanaka challenges us, reconstructing illness as metaphor in her own work and presenting it in a screen of contemporary America. Her challenge is, furthermore, proven in her trial to reveal and retell history in Hawaii's revolt against imperialism and racial / sexual colonialism. More deliberately, Yamanaka constructs her narrative voice to be echoed in the landscape which was transformed, endangered, and yet survived. In Yamanaka's narrative, Hawaiʻi as the remote and marginalized sphere of the United States of America has been under medical treatment of social and moral disintegration caused by imperialism and colonialism. Tuberculosis as putrefactive bacteria in Hawai'i is adapted as the most crucial factor to be examined and interpreted correctly in order to discover after "beholding the many."

Notes

This is based on a presentation paper at "In the Shadows of Empires": The 2nd International Conference on Asian American and Asian British Literatures on Nov.20, 2008, at Academia Sinica in Taiwan.

Works Cited

Caldwell, Mark. *The Last Crusade: The War on Consumption 1862-1954*. New York: Atheneum, 1988.

Hanley, Sister Laurence Hanley O.S.F., and O.A. Bushnell. *A Song of Pilgrimage and Exile: The Life and Spirit of Mother Marianne of Molokai*. Chicago: Franciscan Herald P, 1980.

Johnston, William. *The Modern Epidemic: A History of Tuberculosis in Japan*. Cambridge: Harvard UP, 1995.

Rothman, Sheila M. *Living in the Shadow of Death: Tuberculosis and the Social Experience of Illness in American History*. Baltimore: The John Hopkins UP, 1994.

Sontag, Susan. *Illness as Metaphor*. 1977. Harmondsworth: Penguin, 1983.

Yamanaka, Lois-Ann. *Behold the Many*. New York: Picador, 2006.

Chapter 7

Sexual Colonialism in Korea / Japan / America Spheres in Nora Okja Keller's *Comfort Woman* and *Fox Girl*

I. Introduction

Nora Okja Keller's novels, *Comfort Woman* (1997) and *Fox Girl* (2002), represent sexual colonialism in the transitional period from colonial to postcolonial eras. The crucially and brutally crossed experiences of Korea, Japan, and America in World War II and the Korean War are reconstructed in Keller's intriguing narrative and mythological implication in order to discover, recover, and reveal the long-neglected and long-lost selves of women and children in sexual, physical, and psychological abuse and imprisonment.

Women's sexual colonialism, on which in my personal interview Keller agreed with me, is what she intends to examine and explore in her art (Keller, Personal Interview n.pag.). The factual history consists of the official records while the mythological story is concealed and frequently lost behind the history. Both Korean sexual slaves (called "comfort women" during World War II) and Korean prostitutes for American GIs after the Korean War are victims not only of racism and colonialism in the historical / national context, but also of sexism in the transnational context. The transition of experiences from Akiko, who was deprived of her own Korean name and forced to become a sexual slave in the Japanese Army's Recreation Camp, to her American daughter Beccah in contemporary Hawai'i in *Comfort Woman* is shifted to three abandoned and neglected children, Hyun Jin, Sookie, and Lobetto, in "America Town" during the post-Korean War era in *Fox Girl*. Comfort Women most definitely embody victims of sexual crimes caused by men's wars throughout the human history in the global scale. America Town also represents "the global lawlessness" beyond "the cyclone fence of any U.S. military facility protecting Pax Americana west of Astoria" including U.S. Army's "outposts in Hawaii, Guam, Okinawa, Japan, Korea, formerly in the Philippines" (Polo n.pag.).

In connecting the issue of comfort women and camptown women with feminism, it is possible to employ Thoma's definition that "[t]ransnational feminisms are recognizable by their coalitional, antinationalist, antiexplitative politics rather than by their association with a particular group of feminists defined by class, race, ethnicity, nationality, or some other monolithic category" (103). Within this definition, sexual colonialism is transmitted from Korea

Chapter 7 : Sexual Colonialism in Korea / Japan / America Spheres in Nora Okja Keller's *Comfort Woman* and *Fox Girl*

during Imperial Japan's invasion and occupation to Hawai'i in the postwar period, and again back to postwar Korea, and eventually binds women of different generations and of different backgrounds who suffer yet survive in search for selves.

Keller's poetic space molds women's vulnerability, empowerment, and emancipation from imprisonment. Her strength exists in her strategy to translate sexual colonialism in multilayered experiences of the oppressed in the transnational scale. Even though Keller was once named as the outsider by a Korean reporter, she gained her readers internationally (Keller, Interview with Birnbaum n.pag.). In order to encode Keller's borderless literature mixed by ideology and mythology, it is essential to examine how the women's voice is silenced, retrieved, and eventually reconstructed in the marginalized sphere where ideology as the factual background of male-centered incidents is confronted with mythology as the inward foreground of women's selves.

II. Women's Voice Silenced under the Male-Centered Ideology

Both in *Comfort Woman* and *Fox Girl*, women's voice is silenced under the dual male-centered ideology; the outside force such as Japanese imperialism / militarism and American militarism / economics, and the inside force of Korean patriarchy. Along with Korean patriarchy as the initial male-power to Korean women, colonialism as the much crueler male-power oppresses women as the most powerless. Behind the men's wars, women's lives are entirely marginalized and their voice is silenced. Both *Comfort Women* and *Fox Girl* examine ideology's wrong values that determine women's lives. Furthermore, there is a transition from *Comfort Woman* to *Fox Girl* in the hidden ideology as Keller insists that:

> I feel the women in *Fox Girl* are the descendants of the comfort women. It's a natural place to go — the "America Towns." So many of the women who came back from Japan after World War II did not, could not, return to their families because they felt so ashamed and ostracized. They had no other choice but to continue to be prostitutes. And the children, especially the daughters, remained trapped in that cycle." (Hong n.pag.) [1]

It is, therefore, significant to examine how *Comfort Woman* and *Fox Girl* represent the consequence of ideology as a multilayered embodiment of violating and victimizing women. As Virginia Woolf insists in *A Room of One Own*, silenced women's voice represents the lost *herstory* embedded in ideology, that is, the officially recorded and formally established history of men's own.

Comfort Woman embodies the most crucial example of the once-lost history of sexual slaves during World War II. It was when a former comfort woman, Hwang Keum Ja, gave a striking lecture in 1993 at the University of Hawai'i that

Chapter 7 : Sexual Colonialism in Korea / Japan / America Spheres in Nora Okja Keller's <u>Comfort Woman</u> and <u>Fox Girl</u>

Keller first knew about comfort women (Gardiner n.pag.: Keller, Interview with Lieu n.pag.; Noguera n.pag.). Keller encounters one of estimated an 100,000 or 200,000 comfort women, 80 percent of whom were Koreans (Oh 9) and most of whom are already killed or dead, too old or sick to appear in public, or too depressed to reveal their life stories.

In her knowledge construction process, Keller makes a further research on Korean comfort women as victims of sexual crimes in a colonial context. As for Keller's encounter with the issue of comfort women, it was after the early researches and publications on comfort woman were achieved both in Japanese and English that the issue of the comfort women became public with efforts of women's organizations in Korea in late 1980's and the first former comfort woman, Kim Hak Sun, testified in public in August 1991.[2] Significantly, Lee remarks that it is the Korean Council for the Women Drafted for Military Sexual Slavery by Japan (established in 1990) that supported Hwang Ja's 1993 lecture in Hawai'i in which Keller participated (164), and furthermore, insists that Keller "offers a revision of the international archive by (re)inserting into our collective memory the complicated and haunting legacy of the Japanese conscription of Korean women as Military Comfort Women" (169). Moreover, in 1992, the Washington Coalition for "Comfort Woman" Issues was organized in Washington, D.C.(Oh 13).

Keller's knowledge construction is grounded upon the transnational layered political activities by women both in Korea and America and their common recognition that comfort women as the wartime sexual victims of militalism and imperialism embody the most defmite example of sexual colonialism. Colonialism is the aftermath to men's wars that result from political, legal, economical, social, and cultural conflicts between nations and races. Under those seemingly important issues, sexual victims are shadowed and consequently become invisible. Comfort women as the sexual victims of colonialism demonstrate the most oppressed example of sexual colonialism.

In *Fox Girl*, Keller sets up another and more contemporary Korean women's *herstory* and challenges the prolonged story of women in the male-centered socio-economic and military context.[3] Keller's awareness of the neglected prostitutes and Amerasian children as the insignificant outcasts of society is molded in her reconstruction of the hidden issue of the "America Town" shadowed in the 1960's in post Korean War and the Cold War eras. In completing *Fox Girl*, Keller, among a number of references and films on Korea / US. relationships, Korean-American bases, and Korean women near the base, received a great impact from Katharine Moon's *Sex Among Allies: Military Prostitution in U.S.-Korea Relations* published in 1997 (Keller, Interview with Lieu n.pag.). As comfort women are systematized sexual slaves, *kijicho'on* (military camptown) prostitutes are also the outcome of "a corporation" on R & R (rest and recreation) system between the American and Korean governments (Moon 18 & 27). The social, economic, and

Chapter 7 : Sexual Colonialism in Korea / Japan / America Spheres in Nora Okja Keller's <u>Comfort Woman</u> and <u>Fox Girl</u>

educational background of comfort women and *kijicho'on* prostitutes are so low that they have to leave their home villages and migrate to cities and even to foreign lands.[4] Both comfort women and *kijicho'on* prostitutes, moreover, function to prevent "the prostitution and rape of 'respectable'" — women by Japanese and U.S. soldiers respectively (Moon 39).[5] After World War II was over, the issue of comfort women was ignored by the U.S. Psychological Warfare Teams and never dealt with by the war-crime trials since those women were racially and sexually discriminated against and therefore neglected in the U.S. military policy that ironically and eventually leads to the establishment of both bases and official brothels to accommodate camptown women to comfort their men stationed in Japan (Tanaka 84-166) and then in Korea.

Along with those similarity and connection between comfort women and *kijicho'on* prostitutes as victims of sexual colonialism, a more crucial bridge between them delineates the meaning of ideology. Differing from the forced sexual slavery in comfort women, *kijicho'on* prostitutes choose to work as registered and paid prostitutes for American GIs. In spite of this difference, *Fox Girl* resonates the political, legal, economical, cultural, and social outcome of Korean War that eventually changes women's lives. America Town is a microcosm of the postwar Korean society where the power struggle between Korea and the U.S. forms economical colonialism. American militarism that is strictly related with American economics largely influences

Korea, and America Town near the base represents a market place of American economics. As a result, the conflicting elements, that is, the economic benefit and the cultural and social collapse as its consequence, coexist in America Town. *Kijicho'on* prostitutes display the most remarkable example of selling sex and corrupting not only body but also self, identity, and pride. Amerasian children born of *kijicho'on* prostitutes and American GIs represent the unwanted and unwelcome offspring of economic and sexual colonialism caused by the Korean War.

Along with the outside ideological force upon comfort women and *kijicho'on* prostitutes, the inside force of Korean patriarchy silence them. Keller is moved by the fact that the former comfort woman was forced to be silenced not only because it was painful to reveal her past experience but also because it was shameful for her family (Keller, Interview with Lieu n.pag.; Ng n.pag.). By listening to the former comfort woman's confession that her silence could be ultimately broken only when all her family had passed away, Keller becomes confident of the vulnerability of comfort women in Korean patriarchy. In the Confucian-based patriarchy of Korea, chastity is the essential virtue both for women and their families, and women were not even allowed to be seen and contacted by men except family males.[6] The former comfort women's silence is led not only by their private sense of shame but also the public consciousness that determines their shame. Similarly, Korean women who serve as bar girls and prostitutes to American GIs are excluded from the

Chapter 7 : Sexual Colonialism in Korea / Japan / America Spheres in Nora Okja Keller's *Comfort Woman* and *Fox Girl*

society as it is the shame of the family and the society. Even though those women emerged due to Korean economic and social instability during and after the two wars and some of them sacrificed themselves to their families,[7] Korean patriarchy does not consider them the outcome and victims of wars and as a result silences them. Korean patriarchy that has been deeply rooted in their mother land torment the wartime sexual victims with invisible, consistent, and endless prejudice and discrimination against them.

Korean women's challenge to colonialism is, interestingly, associated with that to Korean patriarchy in *Comfort Woman* and *Fox Girl*. Both World War II and Korean War motivated women's movements in Korea: the women's emancipation to resist against the loss of Korean identity and advocate Korean independence from Imperial Japan, and the women's empowerment against Korean patriarchy endangered after the Korean War.[8] In Soon Hyo's narrative in *Comfort Women*, her mother was one of the women activists including students of Ewha Womans University who joined the rally for the Korean Declaration of Independence on March 1, 1919. Soon Hyo's mother's spiritual death when she was separated from her activist boyfriend and the activist movement and forced to marry an unknown man by her mother results from both colonial and Korean patriarchal oppression. The women's movement beginning in the 1960's feminist movement was still conservative in the sense that well-educated women were merely encouraged to join social activities and women's organizations (I 188-89).

Consequently they excluded the nameless and powerless victims of sexual abuse and violence such as former comfort women and their contemporary *kijicho'on* prostitutes and had to wait till 1980's when they were awakened to themselves in comfort women's issue. In Keller's retelling women's stories which was, directly or indirectly, informed and influenced by her contemporary feminists and activists and their activities across the Pacific Ocean, however, the solid background of women's movement in Korea is proven in the early stage of Korean women's political activities against imperialism and colonialism.

As long as unknown women are primarily placed at the bottom of Korean patriarchy, they cannot be rescued because they are the most insignificant and powerless subjects in the colonial and national context. When Korean women's bodies were invaded by foreign men, Korean patriarchy labeled those women not victims of wartime sexual crimes but betrayers to their men, race, family, and nation. Keller's encounter with the prolonged male-dominant Korean society where Korean patriarchy is grounded upon by Confucianism creates the double oppression for women in distress under racial, sexual, and economical colonialism. Keller was born in Seoul in the 1960's and immigrated to the U.S. with her Korean mother and her American father at age three. In the 1990's, she, for the first time, strongly recognized herself as a Korean and challenged the ideology.[9] Keller's knowledge construction process is exactly that of encountering and discovering her motherland and the long-lost women's stories in no man's land. In search for sexual colonialism, Keller strengthens the historical and social context of Korea / Japan / and U.S. relationships associated with World War II and the Korean War and attempts to complete her mission to present the most oppressed and silenced women in history.

III. Women's Voice Retrieved in the Mythology

Women's voice once silenced and seemingly lost in men's wars can be retrieved in the mythological sphere where reality as the most cruel and horrifying experience is transmitted to truth in the surreal scheme. Korean legends and folk tales possess a strong force to reveal women's suffering and oppression. The Korean shaman *mudan* in *Comfort Woman* and the legend of fox girl in *Fox Girl* play important roles to encode and reveal women's suffering and agony. Mythology provides the transcendent force to overcome ideology and enables women to encounter their inward selves. Both Shamanism and the folktale of the fox girl originate from Korean legends that have been handed down primarily orally from generation to generation, and have the force to retrieve women's silenced and ignored voice in Keller's story telling.[10]

Shamanism in *Comfort Woman* forms Akiko's explosion of agony.

> When the spirits called to her, my mother would leave me and slip inside herself, to somewhere I could not and did not want to follow. It was as if the mother I knew turned off, checked out, and someone else came to rent the space. (Keller, *Comfort Woman* 4)

Akiko's eccentric behavior of dancing and saying the spells illustrates that of a shaman, and connotes her spiritual journey to the transcendent space.[11] It may be connected with the interpretation of Akiko as being already a Korean (Sato 28). Akiko plays a role as a *mudang* who sings *muga*, communicates with a god, and "solves all the worries and troubles of human beings" (Suh 117). Shamanism consists of the universal methods of the soul-escape from the body and the medical therapy (Hoppál 11) and, more importantly, situated against ideology filled with the industrial, material, self-centered society and culture; shamanism can provide another means of living and self-therapy (Hoppál 47). Shamanism is, moreover, significant as the ground of literature, the initial form of oral story creation, as the song / story is retelling the god's and ghosts' words and spelling / literature possesses the transcendent force (Okabe et al 228).

Keller links shamanism with the woman's tradition and literature against ideology. She remarks that Korean tradition of shamanism is "a very woman centered tradition" that ironically exists "outside the cultural norms for women in Korea" (Keller, Interview with Lieu n.pag.). Akiko, who physically and mentally collapses, is in search for a

Chapter 7 : Sexual Colonialism in Korea / Japan / America Spheres in Nora Okja Keller's *Comfort Woman* and *Fox Girl*

spiritually recovered world where she can communicate with dead people and where she can overcome any physical harm. Akiko experiences a space journey in a sacred narrative as it is "a return trip by the free soul" to either the underworld or the heavens, receiving messages, wisdom and powers from the highest god and returning back to the shaman's body" (Yol-kyu Kim 112). Keller places shamanism in her literature as Akiko's renaissance of self-consciousness by expressing her stories that cannot be expressed in the regular form of communication against the male force.

Most importantly, shaman mythology depicting the origin of Korea is situated against the Japanese mythology of the nation's origin that Koreans were forced to learn and believe during Imperial Japan's colonization. In "*Tan gun* Myth," *Hwan in* (Heavenly God)'s son, *Hwan-ung* marries a bear woman and bears *Tan gun* as the ancestor and king of Old Korea (Yorugi Kim, Kankoku no 21-22; Yorugi Kim, *Kankokushinwa* 32-33: Zong 24-29). It is pointed out that *Tan gun* Myth became enormous energy when Koreans attempted to rescue Korea from their crisis (Yang Ki Kim 40). During World War II, Imperial Japan manipulated the Japanese divine emperor cult for the political / military purpose to colonize the other Asian nations, especially Korea, and control them by their fascist armed and police forces. Especially, though *Kara* (Korea) recorded in ancient Japanese documents and mythology means the country where Japanese gods had gone through and lived as their homeland (Yorugi Kim, *Kankoku* 15), Korea was oppressed under the strict control and assimilation / Japanization by Japan's Emperor as God so that Koreans were required to abandon their language, names, and even religion. Koreans were compelled to believe in the Japanese Goddess *Amaterasu* as the founder of Japan and also of Korea (Yonwa Han 557-78). It is remarked that during World War II Japanese historians had to reject and change the era of *Tan gun* Myth, which is 1,700 years older than enthronement of Japan's first emperor, Kanmu Emperor, in 660 B.C. (Yang Ki Kim 45-46). Korean children and women approximately ranging from the early teens to the early twenties were recruited as comfort women as "chosen to serve the emperor by providing 'comfort' to soldiers fighting for the emperor in the holy war" (Oh 10).

In order to understand the significance of Sharmanism in Keller's literature, it is necessary to compare Shamanism and Christianity, which is another devine force and influence connected with nationalism against imperialism. Christianity as another opposing religious force against Japan's divine emperor cult became the center of Korea's independence movement.[12] Korean Christianity was rapidly developed with nationalism and Shamanism by seeing Christian trinitarianism (God, Jesus, and the Holy Ghost) as "counterparts of *Hwan in*, *Hwan ung*, and *Tan gun*" of *Tan gun* Myth (Palmer 14-15: Ryu 2-3) and Mary as "the prototype of the female bear" (Palmer 15). Christianity with its notions of one supreme god, equal human rights, and humanism is entirely opposed to Imperial Japan's ideology of colonization. Connecting Christianity with Shamanism,

Chapter 7 : Sexual Colonialism in Korea / Japan / America Spheres
in Nora Okja Keller's <u>Comfort Woman</u> and <u>Fox Girl</u>

on the contrary, Koreans gained the spiritual power to resist colonization. By 1910, Christians became the leaders of nationalism: majority of participants in the March First 1919 Independence Movements were Christians (Clark 8), and importantly, Korean churches, both Catholic and Protestant, supported women who were also culturally and spiritually destroyed by Imperial Japan's implantation of immoral habits and customs under the name of cultural assimilation (Sokki Han 239-40). Against Imperial Japan's strict banning of Christianity between 1936 and 1945 and their forced integration with Shinto, their underground force was strong enough to become active after Korea's liberation from Japan at the end of World War II.[13]

In spite of its leading role in nationalism, Christianity is not evaluated as essentially as Sharmanism in Keller's literature. In *Comfort Woman,* Keller focuses on Christianity as an opposing force against Sharmanism since Christianity is grounded upon male-centered values, and especially Korean Christianity was founded and guided by American male-centered activities. Christianity that rescues Akiko at the end of the war and accommodates her in the Heaven and Earth Mentholatum and Matches Company building in Pyongyang as the American missionary's hidden shelter from the Japanese army is grounded in another male force.[14] The only way for Akiko to escape from the unstable Korean society and her past life is to accept an American minister's sexual desire and ultimately his proposal. Her American husband / minister forces both sex and his patriarchy on

Akiko and he asks her, "to protect our daughter, with your silence, from that shame" (*CW* 196). Whether during the hidden life in Pyongyang mission just after the war, their escape from Pyongyang to the Severance Hospital Mission in Seoul, or her travel with her husband from church to church in Mainland of America, Akiko is never cured and recovered from the loss of identity and self. Thus, Shamanism in which Akiko, deprived of her language, name, religion, identity, and self, is indulged in the representation of Akiko's wish to be entirely freed from Imperial Japan's force and even male-centered Christianity upon her body, her soul, self, and identity. Though both Sharmanism and Christianity are essentially associated with nationalism and Koreans' awareness of identity, Keller evaluates Sharmanism as an important source of women's tradition and culture which eventually leads to the liberation of women's selves and the revelation of women's stories.

Like Shamanism in *Comfort Woman*, another Korean legend of transformation frames the novel, *Fox Girl*.[15] The Korean legends and folktales that are orally transferred from parents to children in the novel have a common core even among different versions and interpretations of the story(ies) of the fox.[16] A fox girl can be named "a Korean vampire" because she uses "a dead girl's skin to turn herself into a beautiful woman that no man can resist" (Freely n.pag.). The fox disguised as a beautiful young woman is generally a symbol of seduction and destruction, and represents a wrong and even evil moral code that young girls and women should

Chapter 7 : Sexual Colonialism in Korea / Japan / America Spheres in Nora Okja Keller's <u>Comfort Woman</u> and <u>Fox Girl</u>

not follow.

The story(ies) of the fox in *Fox Girl*, however, conveys dual messages through different story tellers. Transformation is an important key in interpreting the story. Hyun Jin's father's stories to his daughter, which are always "stories of transformation, of ugliness turning into beauty" (*FG* 9), connote the father's lesson to his young daughter with a patriarchal view. Hyun Jin's father's version that ends with the boy's escape from the fox girl with nine tales connotes the father's moral judgment and his warning to the daughter not to become evil as the fox girl.[17] Sookie's mother's interpretation is, on the contrary, different; "Somehow, in real life, we have to become like the fox girl" (*FG* 25). Judged from the Korean patriarchal view and from the Korean fox story, Sookie's mother, who makes a living by working at the bar and serving American GIs as a prostitute, is considered an evil woman. This evilness is, however, what women at the bottom of the society have to bear in order to survive. Those women's transformation into the evil foxes results from the social, economical, and cultural chaos after men's wars whose victims are the powerless and penniless survivors in the homeland.

The dual interpretations of the fox girl determines the destiny of two girls, Hyun Jin and Sookie who are abandoned by their parents and have to live like the fox girls as they are "confronted with one of the starkest lessons of life" (Honré n.pag.). Hyun Jin, whose biological mother turns out to be Sookie's mother and who is rejected even by her father and his patriarchal view, corresponds with Sookie born of a Korean prostitute and an African American GI and neglected and abandoned by her parents. Hyun Jin became a street prostitute with Lobetto, an Amerasian boy of a Korean prostitute and an African American GI, as a pimp and then became a registered prostitute at the bar; Sookie was first sold at age eight by her mother, served sexually for her mother's former GI partners, and bore a Lobetto's baby in her teens. After Hyun Jin learns her biological background, Hyun Jin's stepmother condemns her and says to her husband, "She's no better than the fox girl in those worthless stories you forever told her. Eating up her own family" (*FG* 122). Hyun Jin, with the blood of the prostitute, is compared to the fox sister that eats up her brothers and parents in order to survive. In Hyun Jin's perspective, she recognizes her real face of the fox girl reflected in a mirror as her father once told her: "A fox demon disguised as a beautiful girl could be recognized by forcing it to look into a mirror, which would bare its real face" (*FG* 87). The backbone of fox story(ies) illustrates the lies, betrayals, lack of affection, neglect, verbal and physical abuse, and self-hatred with which Hyun Jin and Sookie have to be confronted in the stage from childhood to adulthood.

 Lessons from legends do not affect the possibility of or wish for women's ideal lives in the transitional process to modern society because in the 1960's the rapid Westernized / Americanized industrialization and urbanization in addition to the traditional patriarchy forced Korean women of lower class into an institutionalized sex business (Marion Kennedy

Chapter 7 : Sexual Colonialism in Korea / Japan / America Spheres in Nora Okja Keller's <u>Comfort Woman</u> and <u>Fox Girl</u>

Kim 49-55). America Town represents Koreans' defeat to America's materialistic superiority and military power by selling whatever they have. *Kijich'on* prostitutes, as Moon says, have "served the Korean government's economic as well as security goals" (44). It implies, as Kay remarks, that "everything in America Town is for sale: friendship, lives, and innocence" (44). The women and their children need to change their lives as disguised foxes because they have to survive in the dual oppression. Korean society's destiny in the global scale is delineated in "Club Foxa" whose context of Korean women's selling sex to Western men is based on the borderless activities proven in Sookie's and Hyun Jin's unchanged lives in "Club Foxa" in America Town and another "Club Foxa" in real America, Hawai'i.

The dual interpretations of the story of the fox girl, however, represents the two possible lives of the Korean / half Korean immigrant women in the new world. Sookie and Hyun Jin, at the end of their journey to American "Club Foxa," interpret the endings of the two fox stories in different ways as their lives in America are conflicting. When Sookie abandons both her half-sister, Hyun Jin, and her own daughter, Myu Myu, Sookie finalizes the story by saying to Hyun Jin, "You're the fox, Hyun Jin. Making yourself what you're not to get more than you need. In the end, you'll destroy yourself and everyone around you" (*FG* 278). In spite of making the ending for Hyun Jin, Sookie's ultimate transformation into a greedy, jealous, material-seeking, dependent fox girl, which is reminiscent of that of "The

Fox Sister and Three Brothers," depicts her strong will to be separated from the past and entirely lost in the new world.

On the other hand, Hyun Jin, who insists that the fox has to eat animals and humans because she has a family to feed on, attempts to discover a jewel of knowledge in the new world and wishes another transformation of the fox girl based on "The Fox with Nine Tales and the Magic Jewel." The novel ends with a mapping game to find the locations of places, and ultimately the roots of identity.

> Her [Myu Myu's] face is a map — an inheritance marked by all who were once most important in my life. I have caught familiar but fractured reflections of Lobetto and Sookie, Duk Hee and even my father. They have traversed time and distance, blood and habit, to reside within the landscape of this child's body. (*FG* 289)

To pursue a new life in America is not to escape from the past but to appreciate and respect the complicated yet rich backgrounds. The survival in the new land is grounded upon their search for a new identity as Myu Myu "possesses the gift of transformation" like "the fox spirit — the hunter and guardian of knowledge" (289) and to possess a new identity is a creation of the new self and life in the new world.

The Korean legends of transformation correspond with women's lives disguised / transformed, and multilayeredly interpreted in the transcendental space that is sprung from the reality. As it is discussed that the legends, whether shamanism or old folk tales, represent the oral story as the ground of literature and the journey to the unconscious world in search for the self (Kim Harvey 230), Keller's employment of shamanism and Korean legends leads to the empowerment or survival power that women can undergo in the supernatural and transcendental space.

IV. Reconstructed Women's Lives in Daughter's Language

Keller intriguingly employs the daughter's language as the inevitable tool to reconstruct women's lives in the transnational sphere. In both *Comfort Woman* and *Fox Girl*, Keller manipulates the layered narratives of mother and daughter as she remarks that *Comfort Woman* is "a mother-daughter novel" (Keller, Interview with Birnbaum n.pag) and *Fox Girl* is also framed within the mother-daughter relationships. The original short story of *Comfort Woman* entitled "Mother Tongue" ultimately became the second chapter of the novel and is considered the core of Keller's fiction. The daughter is the inevitable respondent to and interpreter of the story hidden in the mother tongue and corresponded with her own life. The women's lives changed and determined by the male-centered power are conveyed to their daughters through or in the mother tongue, and consequently reconstructed and retold by their daughters.

The daughter as the closest respondent to the mother's

story is illustrated as the first witness of how the mother has been related with others through her relationship with her daughter. The childhood narrative represents the daughter's innocence, ignorance, yet straightforward and intuitive perception of the mother figure who exposes even her negative emotions to her child in the enclosed space of the household. Even if Beccah in *Comfort Woman* confesses; "When I was a child, it did not occur to me that my mother had a life before me" (26), Beccah's close observation and vague awareness remains so that she can reconstruct the mother's story in adulthood. Through a series of deconstructed narratives, both Akiko and Beccah might deal with their "own set of demons" and seek to "recover or discover their true selves" (Zuege n.pag.). As *Comfort Woman* is "fundamentally the story of a mother and daughter struggling to connect" (Gardiner n.pag.),[18] Beccah encodes her mother's long-concealed story by retrieving mother's voice from the tape, her "mother's last message, last gift" to her (*CW* 191) and remembering "the true voice, the pure tongue" to confess her past as a comfort woman not by Akiko but her true self, Soo Hyo, to which Beccha would often listen in her childhood days (*CW* 195).

In *Fox Girl*, the children's keen perception of and trapped relationship with their mothers endanger yet determine their children's lives. Duk Hee's storytelling to Sookie and Hyun Jin is especially significant as it represents the most powerless woman / mother's unconscious intention to leave her hidden and secret life stories to the daughter.

Chapter 7 : Sexual Colonialism in Korea / Japan / America Spheres in Nora Okja Keller's *Comfort Woman* and *Fox Girl*

Though Duk Hee's lesson to her daughters to be transformed into fox girls expresses the powerless yet survived woman's voice, Duk Hee's past story connotes the most profound and unforgettable memory that has haunted and traumatized her. Duk Hee's past suicide wish due to her pregnancy of Sookie is conveyed with Duk Hee's dream vision related with the *Tan gun* Myth. Her suicidal attempt in her dream to jump into *Chonji*, the Lake of Heaven at *Paekdu* Mountain where *Hwan* in meets and mates the bear woman (*FG* 19), embodies her agony over her half African-American baby, unwanted and excluded in Korea. In the real and trapped world, however, Duk Hee has to tell both daughters the original story of "the Fox with Nine Tails and the Magic Jewel" with her made-up ending in order to teach them how to survive in search for the "lost jewelry" of knowledge / chastity in the disguised form of fox / prostitute. In formulating the mother / daughter narrative, the native language or mother tongue largely contributes to the reconstruction of communication. The reconstructed communication between a Korean mother and her Korean American daughter possesses possibilities of transcending the boundary of community, nation, and relocated / transplanted land. According to Keller, Korean language or the mother's language is a key to open and regain the lost past and to unlock "a small treasure chest of memories" (Keller, Kwon, Namkung, Pak, and Song 18). With an appreciation of the mother tongue, the invisible yet psychological connection is reconstructed between Akiko and Beccah, between Duk Hee and Sookie or Ho Sook, and

Hyun Jin and Myu Myu.

The Korean names definitely embody the significance of the Korean language as the core of Korean identity. The Korean last name is a dominant factor of Korean patriarchy where only the children succeed the father's family name, while their mother is excluded from it and maintains her maiden name. As for the first name, Keller's short story entitled "The Brilliance of Diamonds," Keller makes a Korean single mother narrate the importance of naming: "A name can determine your life, who you will be. Each letter had a certain power, each person a special name, told in the stars. If you can find the secret of your name, you can unlock the universe" ("BD" 132). Naming the newly-born baby, however, has to follow the Korean patriarchal tradition where the baby's grandfather on his or her father's side has to name the baby. The loss or absence of the father or the last name embodies the loss of family or belongings, that is, the political, economical, social, legal, cultural location and stability. The first name that is also determined by the legal presence of the father predicts the future of the child. The fatherless child who has neither his or her father's last name nor the most appropriate first name given by his or her godfather not only to name but also to protect and care him or her symbolizes the most insignificant member of the Korean society.

Reconstructing the namelessness, therefore, symbolizes regaining the lost identity in both colonial and postcolonial eras. In *Comfort Woman*, Akiko is, in this sense, deprived

Chapter 7 : Sexual Colonialism in Korea / Japan / America Spheres in Nora Okja Keller's *Comfort Woman* and *Fox Girl*

of both first and family names as soon as she is forced to become a comfort woman by the Japanese Imperial Army and as a result she is excluded from the Korean society. After her parents' death, Soon Hyo as the youngest daughter is excluded from the protection of the Korean family and has no other way to agree with her elder sister on going to "Japanese recreation centers." At the recreation center or the Japanese Army's official brothel, Soon Hyo is named Akiko as she is deprived of her Korean identity as well as of her Korean woman's chastity. Transplanted in America, again, Akiko has her American husband family name so that she is entirely lost in a foreign land as another persona. The procedure that Beccah has to follow in reconstructing the story of her mother as Soon Hyo is a long way to regain her lost names, her lost mother language and land, and her identity.

Reconstructing the namelessness in a colonial context corresponds to reconstructing the nameless and fatherless Amerasian children in a postcolonial context. In *Fox Girl*, Sookie's illegitimate girl baby whose father is another Amerasian boy Lobetto is ironically named Myu Myu, which means "little no name." In "The Brilliance of Diamonds," Keller inputs her auto / transcendental biography of an Amerasian daughter of no man's land, who was born as a fatherless and nameless baby called Moo Myun whose meaning is "Baby No Name." The cynical first name illustrates the Koreans' keen insight into and ultimate recognition of illegitimate Amerasian children's trapped lives and destinies.

To have American names, therefore, means to have the idealized American life with the future possibilities in a new land. In *Comfort Woman*, Akiko's wish that her daughter would be assimilated into America is represented by the daughter's American first name, Beccah. The Amerasian child's struggle is based on her / his sense of alienation that is crucially described in Myung Ja's desperate finding the most ideal American last name after she emigrated to the U.S. at age of four with her Korean mother. Both American first and last names symbolize the realization of Amerasian children's relocation in and assimilation into America as their new world.

However hard they pursue their future possibilities and the new names in America as the father's land, Amerasians recognize that the Korean first names connote their deep roots in their mother land, Korea. In *Fox Girl*, the fact that Sookie's true name, Ho Sook, means Clear Water, connotes the mother's contradictory yet cordial wish for her newly-born baby-girl to become pure and clear like the Lake of Heaven in Korean. After a two-month namelessness or "a rootlessness of a body and soul," Moo Myun is finally named Myung Ja, "playing on the words for 'name' and 'sparkling'" ("BD" 132). Korean daughters' first names given by the mother in Keller's works, therefore, symbolize the importance of women's identity and self. Keller recognizes that Korean fast names are important to make sure of Korean identity:

Chapter 7 : Sexual Colonialism in Korea / Japan / America Spheres in Nora Okja Keller's *Comfort Woman* and *Fox Girl*

> The older I get, the more I feel a sense of loss at not knowing my mother's language, the language of my birth country. When each of my children was born, I asked my mother to help me choose Korean first names for them, so that an integral part of how they identify themselves would be Korean. (Keller, Kwon, Namlumg, Pak, and Song 18)

The conflict between the Korean name and the American name signifies their unavoidable and everlasting struggle for survival. The Korean first name given by the mother to her Amerasian daughter is, especially, significant as a token of Korean woman's identity and self-respect in reconstructing the women's stories.

The reconstruction of women's stories in the daughter's language embodies the emancipation from physical and psychological imprisonment with which women have to be confronted. The daughter plays a role of linguistic and cultural translator between the native language- and culture- operated mother's tongue and life and the English-operated American audience. As for *Comfort Woman*, Keller repeatedly had to remark that the novel is "not autobiographical" (Gardiner n.pag). Keller as a writer constructs what Thoma calls "a cultural autobiography" (103) by presenting the mother tongue in the daughter's language and creating a transpersonal biography of women's lives in the transcendental time scheme and space.

V. Conclusion

Keller's literature implies both her growing consciousness of identity as a person of Korean descent and her transnational standpoint as a woman who needs to write women's stories in her own style. Keller's writings have been driven by her own struggle in search for self because she has been frequently called "hapa" born of her Korean mother and her American father and also because, as she says, outmarriage is "politically suspect by people who denounce the dilution of blood, of culture, of community" ("Circling 'Hapa'" 19). As an outsider and woman herself, Keller ventures to unveil the intentionally avoided and neglected subject of the oppressed women victimized by a series of unrecorded prejudice, abuse, and violence caused by the male-centered political, economical, and cultural colonialism in a transnational sphere. Keller's search for her identity results in her endless search for the lost dignity and identity of women. Keller's personal history, background, and experience, therefore, widens her perspective and deepens her insight into the conflicting and compromising relationship among Korea, Japan, and America in the colonial and postcolonial contexts.

Keller's strong commitment to the issue of sexual colonialism is presented in her unique style and voice that is blended with and represented by mythology. Keller's sexual colonialism embedded in her novels is the most controversial yet unavoidable theme in this transnational era

Chapter 7 : Sexual Colonialism in Korea / Japan / America Spheres in Nora Okja Keller's *Comfort Woman* and *Fox Girl*

and both *Comfort Woman* and *Fox Girl* are established upon Keller's belief in the survival of women's stories. In order to accomplish writing women's stories, Keller manipulates the backbone and implication of mythology. By displaying mythology, Keller can challenge the profound and concealed facets of ideology so that she can create the subtly-layered and closely-knitted 'women's stories of own.' In addition, Keller's creation of 'women's stories of own' is ultimately achieved by the establishment of communication between the mother as a cultural narrator and the daughter as a cultural interpreter.

Keller's presentation of sexual colonialism in Korea / Japan / America spheres in *Comfort Woman* and *Fox Girl* is grounded upon an urgent need to reconstruct literature as well as history. In this respect, Keller's brave and consistent attitude toward sexual colonialism opens the new era not only in American literature scene but also in the transnational literature scene.

Notes

I deeply appreciate Nora Okja Keller for her support and consideration to answer to my questions in an interview in Hawai'i and also by e-mail. As for my research on local literature, I thank Juliet S. Kono, Joan Hori, and Joy Kobayashi-Cintron for their support, encouragement, and friendship. I thank Professor So-Hee Lee for her kindness to send me a copy of her article on Keller. I also thank Ms. Hejin Kim, an exchange student to Doshisha University from Yonsei University from

2002 to 2003, for her patience to correct my Korean language. Lastly, I would like to express my deepest gratitude to the American Studies Association of Korea for their assistance, generosity, and hospitality to have enabled me to present an abridged paper of this article at the 38th Annual Conference in October / November, 2003, in Chuncheon, Korea. This paper was originally published in *Journal of American Studies of Korea* 36.1 (Spring 2004): 254-83.

1. Moon points out that comfort women of the Japanese military "serve as the historical prototype of U.S.-oriented prostitution in Korea" and "some of former comfort women also worked as GI prostitutes among the fast generation of *kijich'on* sex workers" (46). Moon also introduces the family with a former *kijich'on* prostitute who worked for African Americans during the 1950's and 1960's, her two daughters of different African American G.I. fathers who also worked in the camptown bars, and one of them have four children of different men and remarks that "their marginalization from Korean society was most severe" because of "their black skin and racial features" (6). See also Grace M. Cho who applies "yongongju" as the name of Korean camptown women.

2. Though such English-based critics as Grice remarks that written documents and materials on comfort women have begun to be published recently (11), Japanese writers and scholars wrote books and articles on the subject in Japanese and publish them only in Japan earlier: for example, Kazuko Hirota's *Shougen Kiroku Jyugun Ianfu Kangofu* (Tokyo: Shin-Jinbutsuoraisha, 1975), Ichiben Kin's *Nihonjosei Aishi* (Tokyo: Gendaishishuppan, 1980) and *Tenouno Guntaito Chosenjin Ianfu* (Tokyo: Sanichi Shobo, 1976), Motonori Mabuchi et al's *Teikoku Guntai Jugunki* (Kyoto: Choubunsha, 1975), Kakou Senda's *Jyugun Ianfuhishi* (Tokyo: Elm, 1976) and *Oanatachino Doukoku* (Tokyo: Choubunsha, 1981), and Seiji Yoshida's *Chousenjin Ianfuto Nihonjin* (Tokyo: Shin-Jinbutsuoraisha, 1977).

* I preserve the old type of Japanese pronunciations of some Korean

Chapter 7 : Sexual Colonialism in Korea / Japan / America Spheres in Nora Okja Keller's <u>Comfort Woman</u> and <u>Fox Girl</u>

names in books or journals published in Japan.

3. As represented in America Town in Keller's *Fox Girl*, the American economic power overwhelms Korean economy. Moon remarks that the "economic power that U. S. servicemen represented and wielded in the camptowns easily translated into social and sexual clout over Korean *kijich'on* residents. South Korea in the 1960's became the 'G.I. Heaven'" and gives an example that "over 20,000 registered prostitutes were available to 'service' approximately 62,000 U.S. soldiers by the late 1960's. For $ 2 or less per hour ('short time') or $ 5 to $ 10 for an 'overnight,' a soldier could revel in sexual activities with prostitutes. Servicemen purchased not only sex mates but maids, houseboys, shoeshine boys, errand boys, and other locals with ease" (29-30).

4. In the case of comfort women, they were first in the early to mid-1930's recruited to work as nurses' aids in military hospitals and factory workers because they "volunteered to earn a good salary to help their poor parents and to send brothers to school" with "the enticements of traveling abroad, of high-paying jobs, and even of educational opportunities" (Oh 11). After the Korean War, there was "a migration flow from the countryside to the cities in the 1960's," yet 60% of women ranging from eighteen to forty who were living in Seoul in 1965 were unemployed so that it was easy for them to be engaged in service business because they suffered poverty, low-class status, lack of education, lack of respect as women in a large rural family (Moon 22-23).

5. It is now generally known that there was a rapid increase of comfort stations after the 'Rape of Nanjing' or 'Nanjing Massacre' in order to prevent sexual crimes by Japanese soldiers (Tanaka 12-19).

6. As for the origin and basic characteristics of Korean women under Confucianism, see Kim Harvey's Appendix B: *Women and Family in Traditional Korea* (253-71). Regarding chastity, "Having been victims of sexual violence, a taboo in Confucian cultures where women's chastity is upheld as more important than life, many of these

women have blamed themselves and kept their sufferings even from family members and from the community, fearing the tainting of the family name and ostracism from society (Oh 20). Korean women's involvement in labors outside the household due to Imperial Japan's colonization was a humiliating experience because traditionally women were not allowed to go outside during the daytime as they had to follow the house-based obligations and duties (I 67-68).

7. Imperial Japan's invasion and occupation of Korea forced Korean women to be engaged in labors of low payments in factories, and ultimately sold, deceived, and recruited as comfort women (I 65-70) and the Korean War brought a number of widows and orphans and because of the lack of public support for them, widows had to become prostitutes, especially for American GIs (I 186-87).

8. As for Korean women's movement in modern and contemporary eras, see I and Chu.

9. Keller's rejection and strong sense of shame of everything Korean symbolized by *kimchee* in her teens and her wish of becoming an American, turns into Keller's compassion to and awareness of her motherland (Keller, "A Bite of Kimchee" 198). In another interview, Keller was expected by her mother to be different from her mother and become "the other," and experienced "through a period of feeling really embarrassed and alienated from things that were Korean" and now as a writer, she returns "to that Korean perspective" and tries "to reclaim" what she denied for a long time (Farley n.pag.).

10. Keller says that she got to know about Korean legends orally from her mother and also in books (E-mail Interview). See also Sung-Ae Lee.

11. Keller insists that shamanism "is a very powerful tradition to draw on and so I tried to parallel her [Akiko's] movements, even her sickness, and the experiences she has with the spirits to the studies I did on shamanism" and also "illustrates post traumatic stress syndrome" (Keller, Interview with Lieu n.pag.). See also Young-Oak Lee's interview.

Chapter 7 : Sexual Colonialism in Korea / Japan / America Spheres in Nora Okja Keller's *Comfort Woman* and *Fox Girl*

12. Korean churches abroad, especially those in Hawai'i, very actively supported their native land's independence movement. As for Korean churches abroad and their wartime activities, see Sokki Han (105-06). It is also reported that "the anti-Japanese movement among the Koreans in Hawai'i began in 1905" (Patterson101).

13. As the ideological token, *Chosen Jingu* (Korean Shinto Shrine) was founded in Seoul and by 1925, 42 Shinto shrines and 108 Shinto offices were built in Korea and Koreans were forced to worship at them.

14. As described in *Comfort Woman*, American missionaries not only showed the model life-style and "advanced" American culture, but also "imported commercial goods and supplied them to markets in Korea and put much effort into advertising them" (Gil Soo Han 60). See an article by Jamie S. Scott who makes an overview of an ironical description of Christian missionaries in fiction.

15. In oriental tales, the long-lived creatures such as tortoise, deer, crane, and fox take on "various metamorphoses" and appear "on earth in various forms" as "the special states of spiritual refinement" (Bang and Ryuk 26).

16. In "the Story of the Fox," the minister's son, Yi Kwai, who stayed and studied at the public hall with the boys and met a young beautiful woman, was attracted by her, but soon realized that she is not a real woman but a goblin or a fox, so that he cried for help yet the fox bit him at the nape of the neck and disappeared (Bang and Ryuk 26-28). In another well-known Korean legend of the fox, the youngest daughter of the rich family who was a disguised fox killed cows, then her parents and brother, and was finally destroyed by the surviving brothers who had left home and learned how to destroy the disguised fox ("The Disguised Fox," Yoda and Nakanishi 215-19: "The Fox Sister and Three Brothers," Choi, *Kankolat no* 9-34). At the end of "The Disguised Fox," there is a statement that the seemingly gentle woman who is actually malicious and deceives the others can be called the disguised fox (Yoda and Nakanishi 219).

17. In "The Fox with Nine Tales and the Magic Jewel," (1) a boy student on his way to school meets a beautiful woman and they fall in love with each other. Though the woman is unwilling to kiss him, he realizes that she is a fox" and (2) as the fox keeps the jewel of knowledge in her mouth and student threatens to leave her if she does not allow him to kiss her, she allows a kiss so that he can get the jewel from her mouth, yet he only sees the ground and as a result only knows things on the earth, not seeing the heavenly sky and knowing the heaven, and (3) in a different version, a fox is disguised as a woman and kills ninety students by kissing them in order to go to heaven by killing and kissing one hundred boys, yet could not kill the last boy, who was left alive (Choi, *Kankoku Mukashibanashino* 250).
18. Keller explains how she wrote six Akiko stories and another six Beccha stories, "pieced them together like a puzzle" (Keller, Interview with Lieu n.pag.), and replaced them not in a chronological order but by collage and in a stream of consciousness. Keller's friend and writer, Louis Ann Yamanaka, names Keller's narrative as "a fluid lyricism" and "a kind of elevation of the story into poetry" (Noguera n.pag.). As for the implications of the female body in *Comfort Woman*, see Silvia Schltermandi.

Works Cited

Bang, Im, and Yi Ryuk. *Korean Folk Tales: Imps, Ghosts, and Fairies*. Trans. James Gale. Rutland, VT and Tokyo: Tuttle, 1962.

Cho, Grace M. "Diaspora of Camptown: The Forgotten War's Monstrous Family."*WSQ: Women's Studies Quarterly* 34.1 & 2 (Spring / Summer 2006): 309-331.

Choi, In Hak. *Kankoku Mukashibanashi no Kenkyu* [*A Study on Korean Falktales and Type Index*]. Tokyo: Kobundo, 1976.

——. *Kankoku no Mukashibanashi* [*Korean Old Falk Tales*]. Tokyo:

Chapter 7 : Sexual Colonialism in Korea / Japan / America Spheres in Nora Okja Keller's *Comfort Woman* and *Fox Girl*

Miyai-shoten, 1980.

Clark, Donald N. *Christianity in Modern Korea*. Lanham: UP of America, 1986.

Chu, Wajun et al. *Bundankokufuku to Kankoku Josei Kaihoundo* [*Overcoming the Divided Era and Korean Women's Emacipation Movement*]. Trans. and ed Sune I. Tokyo: Ochanomizu, 1989.

Farley, Christopher John. "No Man's Land." Rev. of *Comfort Women*, by Nora Okja Keller, *Monkey King*, by Patricia Chao, and *The Necessary Hunger*, by Nina Revoyr. *Time* 149. 18 (5 May 1997): 101+. 1 Sep. 2003 <http://proquest.urni.com/pqdweb?index=12&did=000000011575036&SrchMode=l&>.

Freely, Maureen. "Cold Comfort." *The Guardian* 17 May 2003. 1 Sep. 2003 <http:// books.guardian.co.uk/review/story/0,12084,956914,00.html>.

Gardiner, Beth. "Nora Okja Keller Writes Powerful Debut in 'Comfort Woman.'" Southcoasttoday.com. 1997. 14 Apr. 2003 <http://www.s-t.com/07-97/07-01-97/b06ae068.htm>.

Grice, Helena. *Negotiating Identities: An Introduction to Asian American Women's Writing*. Manchester and New York: Manchester UP, 2002.

Han, Gil Soo. *Social Sources of Church Growth: Korean Churches in the Homeland and Overseas*. Lanham: UP of America, 1994.

Han, Sokki. *Kankoku Kirisutokyo no Junan to Teiko* [*Difficulties and Resistance of Christianity in Korea*]. Trans. Masahiko Kurata. Tokyo: Shinkyo, 1995.

Han, Yonwa. *Kankoku Shakai no Rekishi* [*History of Korean Society*]. 1997. Trans.Mitsuo Yoshida. Tokyo: Akashi, 2003.

Hong, Terry. "The Dual Lives of Nora Okja Keller." *The Asian Week* 4-10 Apr. 2002. 24 Apr. 2003 <http://www.asianweek.com/2002_04_05/arts_keller.html>.

Honoré, Finn. "Fine Novel Details Tattered Innocence of 3 Korean Kids." *Honolulu Star-Bulletin* 7 Apr. 2002. 1 Sep. 2003 <http://starbulletin.com/2002/04/07/ features/story2.html>.

Hoppál, Mihály. *Shamanen and Shamanismus*. Trans. Sho Murai. 1994.

Tokyo: Seido-sha, 1998.

I, Hyoje. *Bundanjidai no Kankoku Josei Undo* [*Korean Women's Movement in Divided Era*]. Trans. Sune I et al. Tokyo: Ochanomizu, 1987.

The International Culture Foundation, ed. *Culture of Korean Shamanism*. Kyunggido, Korea: Kimpo College P, 1999. Vol. 2 of *Korean Culture Series II*. Shin-yong Chun, gen. ed

Keller, Nora Okja. "A Bite of Kirnchee. " *Growing Up Local: An Anthology of Poetry and Prose from Hawai'i*. Honolulu: Bamboo Ridge, 1998. 295-99.

———. "The Brilliance of Diamonds." *The Best of Honolulu Fiction: Stories from the Honolulu Magazine Fiction Contest*. Ed. Eric Chock and Darrell Lum. Honolulu: Bamboo Ridge, 1999. 132-39.

———. "Circling 'Hapa.'" *Intersecting Circles: The Voices of Napa Women in Poetry and Prose*. Ed. Marie Ham and Nora Okja Keller. Honolulu: Bamboo Ridge, 1999. 17-24.

———. *Comfort Woman*. 1997. Harmondsworth: Penguin, 1998.

———. *Fox Girl*. New York: Viking, 2002.

———. Interview with Robert Birnbaum. "The Narrative Thread." *IdentityTheory. com*. 2002. 24 Apr. 2003 <http://www.identitytheory.comipeople/birnbaum43. html>.

———. Interview with Jocelyn Lieu. "Releasing the Story to the World." *Coloredgirls. com*. 2002. 24 Apr. 2003 <http://www.coloredgirls.com/Otherviews/nok_interview.html>

———. E-mail Interview with Masami Usui. 17 Aug. 2003.

———. Personal interview with Masami Usui. 23 Mar. 2003.

Keller, Nora Okja, Brenda Kwon, Sun Namkung, Gary Pak, and Cathy Song, eds. Introduction. *Yobo: Korean American Writing in Hawai'i*. Honolulu: Bamboo Ridge, 2003. 15-19.

Kim, Marion Kennedy, ed. *"Once I Had a Dream . . . ": Stories Told by Korean Women Minjung*. 1992. Trans. Wako Kurata and Masahiko Kurata. Tokyo: Nihon Kirisuto Kyodan, 1995.

Kim, Yang Ki. *Kankoku Shinwa* [*Korean Myth*]. Tokyo: Seidosha, 1995.

Kim, Yol-kyu. "Korean Mythology and Musok (Shamanism in Korea)." *The International Culture Foundation* 91-116.

Kim, Yorugi. *Kankoku no Shinwa, Minwa, Mindan* [*Korean Legends, Folk Tales, and Folktore*]. Tokyo: Seikou-shobo, 1984.

——. *Kankokushinwa no Kenkyu* [*Studies on Korean Mythology*]. Trans. Katsumi Tomari. Tokyo: Gakuseisha, 1977.

Kim Harvey, Youngsook. *Six Korean Women: The Socializaion of Shamans*. St. Paul: West Publishing, 1979.

Lee, So-Hee. "A Study of First-Person Narrative in *Comfort Woman*: From a Perspective of Women's Speaking and Writing." *Feminist Studies in English Literature* 10.2 (Winter 2002): 163-88.

Lee, Sung-Ae. "Revisioning Gendered Folktales in Novels by Mia Yun and Nora Okja Keller." *Asian Ethnology* 68.1 (2009): 131-50.

Lee, Young-Oak. "Nora Okja Keller and the Silenced Woman: An Interview." *MELUS* 28.4 (Winter 2003): 145-65.

Moon, Katharine H.S. *Sex Among Allies: Military Prostitution in U.S.-Korea Relations*. New York: Columbia UP, 1997.

Ng, Dana. Rev. of *Fox Girl*, by Nora Keller. *Colorgirls.com*. 2002. 24 Apr. 2003 <http://www.coloredgirls.com/Reviews/review.html?articla_id =24>.

Noguera, Laura. "Sudden Comfort." *Daily Bruin* 10 Mar. 1998. 24 Apr. 2003 <http://www.dailybruin.ucla.edu/DB/issues/98/03.10/ae.keller.html>.

Oh, Bonnie B.C. "The Japanese Imperial System and the Korean 'Comfort Woman' of World War II." Stetz and Oh 3-25.

Okabe, Takashi, Hideki Saito, Hiroyuki Tsuda, and Hirro Takeda.. *Shamanism no Bunkagaku* [*Cultural Studies on Shamanism*]. Tokyo: Shinwa-sha, 2001.

Palmer, Spencer J. *Korea and Christianity: The Problem of Identification with Tradition.* Seoul: Hollym Corperation, 1967.

Patterson, Wayne. *The Ilse: First Generation Korean Immigrants in Hawaii, 1903-1973.* Honolulu: U of Hawai'i P and Center for Korean Studies,

U of H, 2000.

Polo. "Our Second Unspeakable." Rev. of *Fox Girl*, by Nora Okja Keller. *The Asian Reporter* 12.17 (23-29 Apr. 2003): 12. 1 Sep. 2003 <http://www.Asianreporter.com/reviews/17-02foxgirl.html>.

Ryu, Tongshik. *Kankoku no Kirisutokyo* [*Christianity in Korea*]. Tokyo: Tokyo UP 1987.

Sato, Gayle K. "Nora Okja Keller's *Comfort Woman* and Chang-rae Lee's *A Gesture Life:* Gendered Narratives of the Home Front." *AALA Journal* 7 2001: 22-33.

Schultermandl, Silvia. "Writing Rape, Trauma, and Transnationality onto The Female Body: Matrilineal Em-body-ment in Nora Okja Keller's *Comfort Woman*." *Meridians: Feminism, Race, Transnationalism* 7.2 (2007): 71-100.

Scott, Jamie. "Missions in Fiction." *International Bulletin of Missionary Research* 32.3 (July 2008): 121-28.

Stetz, Margaret, and Bonnie B. C. Oh, eds. *Legacies of the Comfort Women of World War II*. Armonk, NY: Sharpe, 2001.

Suh, Dae-suk. "Korean Shamatic Song." The International Culture Foundation 117-168.

Tanaka, Yuki. *Japan's Comfort Women: Sexual Slavery and Prostitution during World War II and the U.S. Occupation*. London: Routledge, 2002.

Thoma, Pamela. "'Such an Unthinkable Thing': Asian American Transnational Feminism and the '"Comfort Women' of World War II" Conference." Stetz and Oh 101-27.

Yoda, Chihoko, and Masaki Nakanishi, ed and trans. *Kin Tokujun Mukashibahashi Shu* [*A Collection of Old Falk Tales Narrated by Kin Tokujun*]. Tokyo: Miyai-shoten, 1994.

Zuege, Unsie. Rev. of *Comfort Woman* by Nora Okja Keller. *Korean Quarterly* Fall 1998. 24 Apr. 2003 <http://www.koreanquarterly.org/Fall1998/revwoman.asp>.

Zong, Insob. *Ondoru Yawa: Krikolat Minwa Shu* [*Ondru Night Tales: Folk Tales from Korea*]. Tokyo: Miyai Shoten, 1983.

About the Author

Masami Usui,
Professor of English, Faculty of Letters,
Doshisha Unviersity, Kyoto, Japan

Short Biography

Masami Usui received her BA and MA from Kobe College, Japan, and her second MA and Ph.D. from Michigan State University in 1989. After teaching at Hiroshima University, she is currently Professor of English at Doshisha University, Kyoto, Japan. Her book, *A Passage to Self in Virginia Woolf's Works and Life* was pubished in 2017. Her recent work is a trilogy, *Asian / Pacific American Literature I: Fiction*, *II: Poetry*, and *III: Drama*, published in 2018.

She has been doing her research and writings on Virginia Woolf and women writers, Asian American literature and culture, and world literature and culture. She published papers in Japan, England, Korea, USA, Germany, etc., and contributed to *Virginia Woolf and War* (1991), *Asian American Playwrights* (2002), *Literature in English: New*

Ethnical, Cultural, and Transnational Perspective (2013), *Virginia Woolf and December 1910* (2014), etc.

Along with MLA, International Virginia Woolf Conference, International Popular Culture Conference, American Studies Association Conference, she has presented her papers in English at Academia Senica in Taiwan, ASAK and KAFSEL in Korea, MESEA in Hungary, CISLE in Canada, International Conference on Asian American Expressive Culture in Beijing, China, International Conference: The Cultural Translation and East Asia, Bangor, England, The 20th Annual Conference of EALA in Taiwan, and International PC/ACS Conference in Poland, and the 2014 International Symposium on Cross-Cultural Studies, Taiwan, International Conference: English Studies as Archive and as Prospecting the 80th Anniversary Conference, University of Zagreb, Zagreb, Croatia, The 3rd International Conference on Linguistics, Literature and Culture 2014, Penang, Malaysia, Expanding the Parameters of Asian American Literature: An International Conference, Xiamen University, Xiamen, Fujian, China, The CISLE 2015, Gottingen University, Germany, the MLA International Symposium in Dusseldorf, Germany, Oxford Symposium on Religious Studies, Oxford Symposium on Women's Leadership, Oxford, UK, etc.

Her hobbies are *Ikebana* (Ikenobo, Professor 1st Grade), *Chado* (Urasenke), and Japanese Calligraphy (Selected by Yomiuri Calligraphy Exhibition in 2014, 2015, 2016, and 2017), etc.